THE TALE OF THE ELM TREES

S. WYATT YOUNG

THE TALE OF THE ELM TREES

Eleora Publishing
www.eleora.com

Published in the United States of America.

Eleora Publishing is a division of Eleora Media LLC. The name and logo of Eleora Publishing, and the imprint of Eleora Books, are trademarks protected under U.S. and international law.

S. Wyatt Young is available for speaking engagements. For more information, please visit his website, www.swyattyoung.com.

Eleora Publishing is not responsible for any websites that it does not own, or for the content thereof.

ISBN: 0996947541
ISBN-13: 978-0-9969475-4-1

Foreword

Ten years. That's how long it's been since I first published *The Tale of the Elm Trees*. Since then, I've gotten married, started a career as an attorney, had a daughter, bought a house, and learned a lot about life along the way. Part of that journey included an effort on my part to translate *The Tale of the Elm Trees* into a screenplay so even more people could enjoy the story. However, as I made my way through the original manuscript in light of my new life experiences, I realized there were certain things that needed changing. The original story included cuss words that were unnecessary, and as a new father, I wanted to ensure *The Tale of the Elm Trees* in all its forms would be a story I was comfortable with my daughter reading one day, and sooner than later.

In this republished version of *The Tale of the Elm Trees*, I have made a few minor changes. I have removed unnecessary cuss words, polished up some dialogue in some places, and changed some names of supporting characters. But the story itself remains essentially the same. I suspect many of you who read the original will agree with me. For those who are reading it for the first time, I don't expect you will notice much of anything, for if nothing else, the story has improved, even if only slightly, and still moves me to tears in much the same way it did its original readers.

So, wherever you are on the journey—whether returning to

this story from the original, or picking it up for the first time—I hope this revised version moves you in the same way that it first moved me and so many others: toward a more hopeful future filled with Light from the One of Wonder. Savor the journey.

—S.

Acknowledgements

The Tale of the Elm Trees is a project five years in the making, not because it took me five years to actually write this book, but because of the journey, both emotional and spiritual, on which I had to embark before I *could* write this book. It is that journey that is captured in this story, and it would not have been possible without my God and King. Though my journey with him has resulted in more tears than I ever thought I could shed, I would not trade it for the world. It has led to an unspeakable chorus of laughter in my soul, a blaze of joy that cannot be extinguished, and for that, I am eternally grateful.

But that journey has not just affected me. To many onlookers, my life only seemed to get worse after I surrendered myself in trusting obedience to the One of wonder. I gave up a lucrative business, tossed aside my plans for grad school, dropped out of seminary after just one semester, took a job selling women's shoes only to quit less than three months in—all in all, I seemed to be falling apart.

Slowly, but surely, though, the Light shimmering in my darkness grew brighter, and guided by its luminance, my life seemed to slowly come together again. I took the LSAT and applied for law school, and later the MBA program; I was accepted to both. I began leading a small group; then a ministry. And just this last summer, I began anew my journey through seminary, and finally wrote this book.

Those who have stood by me along the way deserve the highest of commendations. First and foremost, I must thank my best friend, Matthew Lloyd Cain. At every step along the way, I have remained in awe that we've stayed in sync with one another, growing in similar ways and at similar times. I would not trade our friendship for the world or anything in it.

I also need to thank my dad and sister, Scott and Sadie Young. From the outside looking in, it looked to them like the path of their son and brother was only getting darker, but hard though it was at times, they stuck by me, supporting me and cheering me on. For that, I am most grateful.

I would not be where I am today without the investment of certain individuals. David and Gretchen Figge were my mentors in college, and they have continued to pour into me in the many years since. They are like parents to me, having given me a family and place to call home when my own family and home were quickly falling apart. It was David who first spoke the words that invited me to dream big dreams with a God of wonder, and Gretchen who gave me hope that I might one day find a woman who, though she has thoughts and opinions about the world in which she lives, holds them with humility and grace.

I know that as the road on which I was traveling seemed to take me to dark and dangerous places, David and Gretchen got a little squeamish, perhaps wondering if their investment was in vain. But through it all, they stuck by me, and I will never be able to thank them enough for that.

I must also thank Ken Bohney and the family I have at Capital Church for their continued investment in me, as a person and as a leader; Bryan Bonner, for teaching me the power of story; Jeff Baird, my seventh grade English teacher, for instilling in me a deep sense of creative variation in my descriptions, through countless cumbersome rewrites of my stories; Linda Simpson, my high school English teacher, for packing me full of a verbose vocabulary; and Wayne Hentschel, for giving me an understanding of biology and evolution that has proven invaluable throughout my journey since high school.

I would also like to thank the many friends with whom I have the distinct pleasure of journeying: Ian Ramsrud, Sean and Ashley Rush, Bre Cain, Jackie Wilson, Mike Davis, Emily Harp, Becky Palmer, Jillian Winn, Jamie Allen, Cameron Stark, Lisa Buffmire, and so many more. Thank you all for your continued inspiration, friendship, and loyalty.

Finally, no set of acknowledgements would be complete without words of gratitude to those who have helped to make this book what it is. To Jamie Calloway-Hanauer, who volunteered to edit this book without knowing what she was getting into, *thank you*. This book would not be what it is without your help and insight. Lastly, to Carlie Hellberg and Leif Oines, who provided helpful insights to both the story and the publication process, thank you both so very much.

To all of you, *thank you*: thank you for your friendship, for your investment, and for all of the ways in which you've helped to make this book what it is. I hope it was worth the wait.

This book is dedicated to Eleanor the Joyful,
without whose impact, love, and encouragement, I
would not be where I am today.

1

Charlie

———— ✦ ————

In the heart of Virginia, nestled snugly in the foothills of the Blue Ridge Mountains, lies a small college town called Charlottesville. A mix of eloquence and simplicity, Charlottesville holds in her bosom all the sophistication of an early American colonial town with all the down-to-earth pragmatism of a placid mountain retreat. Tucked away in the midst of towering elm trees and stoic pines, she is a pleasant, albeit unusual surprise to those who are lucky enough to find her.

By the numbers, she doesn't amount to much: just over ten miles square and home to about forty thousand people. Yet travelers depart from the seclusion of her company to find a small part of them missing. She has, in fact, stolen a piece of their heart. Perhaps it's because of her "buy local first" attitude, or the many idols she has birthed and sheltered—Thomas Jefferson, Dave Matthews, and Edgar Allan Poe, to name a few. Or perhaps it's her world-class university, on which some twenty thousand students descend every fall for another year of academic endeavor.

Whatever the case, many thousands of hearts now live captive to her beauty and intrigue. For centuries, people of all races and creeds have walked her streets, bringing with them acts of love and of hate, of violence and of peace. The only living things to have seen them all are the trees, ancient and deeply rooted as they are, both in and around this small, unimposing town. Like stalwart guardians, the trees have stood watch over Charlottesville for many ages.

I'm told by some of the locals that if you stand still enough in her streets, you can almost hear the voices of the trees in every subtle breeze. Gently, quietly, they whisper stories of times past—of Jefferson scaling her hills on horseback in flight from the British troops, of battle-worn soldiers camped on the Lawn during the Civil War, of the Rotunda ablaze in hues of red and amber, of concerts and laughter, families and friendships, joy and sorrow.

The tree families each have their own treasured stories. For the oak trees, it's the story of the Monacan tribe settling in the land that is now Charlottesville because of an oracle delivered by an enemy nation in the Northwest. For the ash trees, it's the story of young Julia Magruder, her life torn by the American Civil War, desperately wishing that the two sides would better understand each other.

They say that the elm trees of Charlottesville are partial to one story in particular, a tale that began a few years back involving a young man by the name of Charlie Shaw.

At a mere ten years old, Charlie became one of Charlottesville's unsuspecting captives on a vacation to the town with his parents and sister. They stayed in a local bed and breakfast owned by an elderly couple, and Charlie had never before experienced anyone quite like them. Like treasured antiquities, this couple had about them a quality and a substance that leaves modern couples wanting. The product of fifty years of commitment and compromise, Herb and Eleanor had become quite the pair. Herb was a former pilot in the United States Air Force and a retired chemist. He was quiet, reserved, conciliatory, and shamelessly polite. He walked with a spring in his step, his torso bent forward and to the right, especially when he walked with haste. He also liked to nap a lot.

If opposites attract, this couple was case and point. Far from being quiet or reserved, Eleanor loved opera, and had a laugh that sung with the birds. She reserved the highest levels of excitement and curiosity for nothing, freely giving it to everything and everyone, especially to her new friends. Always with a plate of fresh fruit on the table and a deck of cards in hand, Eleanor readily anticipated her next adventure, be it an exciting game of Crazy Eights or a most serious and important snail hunt.

One night during their stay at the B&B, the Shaws' plans to attend a concert were foiled by an unexpected rainstorm. Charlie's parents, whose afternoon nap became an inadvertent slumber, awoke to alarm at 3am when their kids weren't in their room. With hearts racing and chests tight, they made their way downstairs to find a light on in the dining room and laughter bellowing out into the sitting area.

As they peered around the corner, they saw Charlie and his sister sitting at a table with Eleanor, indulging in a late-night game of Scrabble. Herb was snoring in the armchair. Stepping lightly,

Charlie's parents returned to their room and slept soundly until morning's light. They knew their kids were in good hands.

When Charlie was fifteen, he was suddenly and violently uprooted from his home and sent to live with his grandparents, in a small town just north of Birmingham, Alabama. Far from walking with a spring in his step, Charlie's grandfather was uptight and stiff. He, too, was the product of military service, but while Herb's heart remained soft and tender in the wake of his duty, the heart of Charlie's grandfather was cold and hard. When Charlie and his sister arrived at their grandparents' house, they were almost immediately subsumed into a routine of church services, youth group, and Bible study—things that in the eyes of Charlie's grandparents, especially of his grandfather, were more the product of duty than desire.

Charlie's grandmother fared no better. Her face was fixed into a permanent frown, her eyes starved for adventure. Although she seldom laughed, when she did, her laughter did not sing with the birds, but seemed a struggle for her soul, burdened as it was by the weight of religious obligation.

Far from unique in their Southern context, Charlie's grandparents fit right in with their culture, for church is a way of life in the Deep South, as vital for sustenance as breath itself. Forced by his grandparents to attend service each Sunday and youth group every Wednesday, rain or shine, Charlie quickly found that the air of Southern people was to him a toxic gas, compounding his hurt with churchy clichés and pious I'll-pray-for-you's, offered with concern that was no deeper than a puddle on a rainy day. Charlie came to hate all things God, and found subtle ways to rebel against the air that had smothered him.

Alabama was the place of a lot of firsts for Charlie: his first car, his first arrest, and his first girlfriend. Her name was Stacy Stevenson. She was a cheerleader at Charlie's high school, and had an unwavering affinity for bad boys. So when word got around that Charlie had been arrested for egging the house that belonged to his grandparents' pastor, Stacy took notice. Three weeks later, the two were an item.

Stacy was just fifteen at the time, which made the fact that Charlie could drive all the more attractive. He was, for her, freedom from the rules and restrictions imposed by her parents. She felt free when she was with him—and rebellious.

One night, in the fall of Charlie's junior year, he and Stacy sat on the hood of his old, beat-up Chevy pickup, parked in a wooded area looking out over the city lights of Birmingham, their lips pressed together, tongues teasing, as hands wandered to forbidden places.

Breaking the bond that held them together, Stacy grinned as she stared down at Charlie's bare chest, then whispered softly in his ear that she wanted to give herself to him. Though lustful passion pumped through his veins, Charlie was nervous. He had never gone that far before. Neither had she. But to them, in that moment, it felt right.

Half-naked, Charlie retrieved a blanket from the bed of his truck and spread it out in the seclusion of some nearby trees. Quickly, passionately, clothes were removed as tongues continued to tease, intensity building; and within minutes, the two were giving in to their heart's desire, bodies interlocked and united in ardent ecstasy under the cool night sky.

Charlie dumped her a week later.

In the fall of Charlie's senior year, he felt the powerful tug of Destiny in his heart, calling him to return to the town that had so captivated him in his youth. So shortly after the dawn of adulthood, Charlie submitted his application to the University of Virginia. Four months later, he received word: he had been admitted. He was going back to Charlottesville.

That spring, excited and anxious to leave the Deep South and breathe a fresher air, Charlie packed his truck full of belongings and headed to the town beckoning in his heart, without so much as a goodbye from his grandparents.

Almost nine grueling hours later, Charlie pulled off the sixty-four onto Monticello Avenue as the sun was setting, only to realize he had no place to stay the night. No sooner had he realized this than his answer came. He pulled into the first gas station he saw and after paying the cashier, asked if he might use the station's phonebook. He looked up the address, asked the cashier for directions, and hurried back to his car.

About seven minutes later, Charlie parked his car outside Herb and Eleanor's B&B. Charlie's car door squealed and clonked as he opened it. He nervously made his way up the walk, rehearsing speeches and stories in his mind. It had been almost a decade since he'd last seen Herb and Eleanor. Would they remember him?

Would they have room for him to stay the night?

Quelling his fears, Charlie gave the door a gentle knock. To his surprise, a young woman answered. She looked to be in her early twenties, with light brown hair and chocolate brown eyes.

"Hi," she said. "Can I help you?"

"Uh," said Charlie, recovering from the jolt of unmet expectations as he peered inside the door, "are Herb and Ellie here?"

Her face clouded over. "You don't know, do you?" Charlie was silent. He knew.

"Herb and Ellie passed away about three years ago," she said softly.

Charlie looked away, fighting back the well of tears building up in his soul.

"Did you know them?" asked the woman gently.

"Yeah," said Charlie with a quake in his voice. "Thanks," he lied, turning hastily and walking back to his truck.

He didn't make it. Collapsing on the curb, Charlie began to sob. Gasping for breath as each heave tore his heart all over again, Charlie's grief was interrupted by a gentle hand on his shoulder.

"I'm sorry," said the woman. Charlie only sniffled. "Do you need a place to stay the night?" she asked.

"No," said Charlie as he stood up. "I'll find somewhere else."

Without looking back at the woman, without even a glance toward the bed and breakfast where his old friends once resided, Charlie climbed in his truck and drove off. To where, or to whom, he did not know.

The only people he knew in Charlottesville, the only people who still knew *him*, were gone. He was alone—or so it seemed.

2

Katie

———— ✦ ————

THE FAMILIAR RING OF THE old brass bell echoed through the silence of Crossroads Bookstore as Charlie opened the store's aged wooden door, letting a zephyr of summer with a hint of autumn rush in to mingle with the musty air of the store's many old books.

"See ye later, Charlie!" came an old Scottish voice from the back of the store.

"See you tomorrow, Ben," Charlie hollered back, letting the door close behind him.

The burning scent of autumn leaves was in the air, carried in the subtlety of every small breeze blowing through the streets of Charlottesville from the mountains that enveloped her. Charlie paused outside the store, staring through its French bay window like a child dreaming outside a toy store, his face caught up in the wonder of the many antique books on display. Books had become the only friends that Charlie knew, offering him a welcomed escape to the days of his youth, before Charlie had lost everyone that he knew and loved.

The window was painted Christmas red, but the colored coat was cracked, exposing the wood beneath its veneer and giving passersby a peak at the store's age. Charlie had worked at Crossroads for just over three years—a small fraction of its life in the town—yet every moment he spent at the store was just as wonderful and captivating as the first.

Two weeks after arriving in Charlottesville, young Charlie had set out to find a job that would get him through college. He started with the Corner, a twelve-block span of eateries and businesses located across the street from the university. It was a spot frequented by students and faculty alike, and Charlie figured it would be a good place to begin his quest for work, not only for its proximity to campus, but for the sheer number of encounters he would have with the town's notoriously beautiful college women. Dating—or whatever it was that Charlie did at that time—was merely a numbers game: if you asked out enough beautiful women, one of them would be foolish enough to say yes.

When Charlie first heard the ring of the old brass bell, Crossroads was more of a distraction than it was a legitimate job pursuit. Tucked away in a small strip of boutiques and art galleries, something about this small bookstore tugged at Charlie's heart, inviting him to put his job search on hold for what he thought would be no more than fifteen minutes. Once inside, he stood in awe of the towering bookshelves and began to walk up and down the aisles they created, running his hands along the rough fabric spines of the store's many antique treasures, tightly packed away on those shelves. Several hours later, Charlie found himself halfway through a tattered copy of *The Lion, the Witch, and the Wardrobe*.

"'At thaur is an autographed farst edition preent," came a voice from behind him, thick with a Scottish accent. Charlie turned to see an older man with nothing but gray stubble left on his head. Clean-shaven but disheveled, with a slender, pointed nose and wrinkled brow, the man had stale blue eyes that stared at young Charlie through a pair of round, black-rimmed spectacles. He stood tall, about six-foot-two, and wore a pair of chocolate brown corduroy pants, a navy blue sweater vest, and a white oxford shirt with a small, red stain on its collar.

"Mah father and Jack were goid friends," said the old man, smiling. "Ah see tha the two uh yoo are, as weoo."

Charlie forced a smile, averting the stranger's gaze. "My mother used to read this to me."

The two were silent for what felt like several minutes as Charlie stared at the old, sea green carpet. It had what looked like a coffee stain not three feet from where Charlie sat.

Charlie turned to see the stranger still smiling at him, just as before, but with a twinge of hurt in his eyes. He felt Charlie's pain.

"Ye can have it," said the man, placing his hand on Charlie's shoulder with a gentle squeeze.

"Are you sure?" asked Charlie, surprised at the man's gesture.

"Def'nitely. Jack woold've wanted ye to have it."

Charlie ran his hand over the cover of the now-closed book, unaware that his face had found the first smile it had shown in years.

"Say, whit brings ye in haur, anawey?" asked the man.

"Oh, I was out looking for a job. I just moved to town for school, and—"

"Yer harred," said the man, interrupting Charlie.

Charlie's gaze turned abruptly to the stranger. He was almost offended. "But…you don't even *know* me!"

"One doos nah need ta knoo the facts aboot a man ta knoo his hart," said the old man, relaxed in his pose as his gaze met Charlie's with a smile, his hands resting comfortably in his pockets. "But, I s'ppose I ooght ta a'leest know yer nam," he said, his smile morphing to a grin.

"Charlie Shaw," said Charlie, extending his hand.

"Benjamin Barr," said the man, his liver-spotted hand grasping Charlie's with a firm handshake, "but folk 'roond here jist cah meh ol' Ben."

"Well, it's nice to meet you, Ben. Uh, when do I start?" asked Charlie, releasing Ben's hand.

"How 'boot tomorruh at 10am? Ah hate wakin' up 'arly."

"You've got yourself a deal," said Charlie, smiling back at this kind stranger as he picked up his bag full of résumés and made his way to the door. Realizing his impropriety, Charlie turned back to ol' Ben, still standing relaxed with his hands in his pockets. "And, uh, thanks," said Charlie, lifting the book he now held upward by the spine against his forearm and forcing an awkward smile.

"Ah'll see ye tomorruh, Charlie," said Ben, his eyes looking on his young new employee with compassion and sympathy. What Ben saw in him, Charlie did not know at the time, but he was glad to have found a job with such a kind stranger.

The autumn air tickled Charlie's nose, carrying with it a whiff of Dried Leaves and a hint of Impending Rain. Turning his gaze skyward, Charlie saw the dark clouds that had been mounting, crowding out the sun as their forces prepared to unleash a devastating blow on this small, helpless town.

Slightly panicked at the threatened onslaught, Charlie hastily unlocked his bike and mounted, securing his bike lock around his waist and raising one of the pedals in preparation to launch. In his bag was a postal package containing a copy of Charlie's portfolio with an application to one of the biggest architecture firms in New York. He had hoped to mail the package that day, but the looming gray clouds now threatened his plans.

Charlie was defiant. This application was his ticket to bigger things, and no amount of rain was going to stop him from mailing it. With the push of his foot, he took off down University Avenue, passing orange V after orange V, painted on this major thoroughfare as a reminder of the school to which the town had pledged its allegiance.

He had just passed the last shop on the Corner when he felt the first raindrop on his cheek. Defiance boiling in his veins, Charlie pressed on, pedaling faster as he passed over the old rail bridge. The raindrops increased in frequency and potency; the attack was beginning.

As raindrops fell harder and faster, so Charlie pedaled, passing the Lewis and Clark memorial. But he was not fast enough.

With the crack of lightning and the thunder of war drums, the merciless gray clouds that had heretofore taunted him with just a few drops now unleashed a torrential downpour. Charlie's vision clouded over as water ran down his face. He glanced up as he pedaled, squinting to keep the water from his eyes, as he looked for somewhere, anywhere, to take refuge.

Off in the distance, he spotted a large, square bay window letting warm light bleed out into the now cold and dark world. From a distance, Charlie couldn't make out the name of his place of refuge, but as he neared the window, he found it to be a coffee shop called Charming Beard, and painted on the window to the left of its name was a black-and-white cartoon sketch of a bearded Irishman wearing an Irish top hat, grinning as he winked at passersby.

To the left of the bay window was a single-pane French door, chocolate brown around the edges with a large bronze bar that ran almost the height of the door and served as its handle.

After locking his bike, Charlie grasped the bar and pulled the door open, flooding his ears with a discorded symphony of voices immersed in lively conversation. His olfactory senses were overwhelmed by the warm and welcoming aroma of coffee beans as Charlie stepped inside. Cold and soaking wet, Charlie stood in line behind three other patrons and began to survey the shop.

Separating the line of patrons from the seating area was a small pony wall with round two-chaired tables on the other side, and on the wall opposite where Charlie stood was a large, open fireplace ablaze with warm, mountainous flames that countered the darkness now reigning in the outside world.

Evenly spaced along the same wall as the fireplace were large four-seater tables. Each of them had two chairs on one side, and on the other, mounted to the wall, was an oak bench with a tufted leather back that ran the length of the wall without interruption, save for the fireplace. All of the tables were occupied.

"Next!" came a voice that sounded from a distant land.

Charlie turned to place his order and was greeted by a woman of average height with large blue eyes and curled brown hair. Her figure was petite, cloaked by a ruffled summer skirt that was adorned with flowers and a white top that clung to her torso. The small placard pinned to her shirt told Charlie that her name was Anna, and she wore a look of irritation on her face as she anxiously awaited his order.

"Sorry," said Charlie as he stepped forward, gazing up at the menu. "Uh, can I do a blueberry muffin and a grande Americano to stay?"

With that, Anna turned to prepare his order. From the way she moved, Charlie could see that she carried the weight of the world on her shoulders. Watching as she stood on her tiptoes and reached into the jar with a pair of tongs, Charlie could not help but follow her legs, smooth and toned with fading hints of a summer tan, up to where they vanished behind the cover of her skirt. He weighed his options for hitting on her as he stared at her backside, longing to see what the skirt now hid.

Charlie's thoughts were interrupted when Anna spun around, holding a plate with his muffin. "Five seventy-two." Her statement was abrupt—she was a no-nonsense kind of girl who was clearly not in the mood to be hit on. If Charlie knew one thing, it was when to abort.

Charlie handed her the cash and received his change, dropping the coins in the tip jar. He took one last gaze at Anna, his eyes following the contours of her figure, then turned to resume his survey of the coffee shop, hoping for a place to sit.

Under the bay window was a large brown leather sofa, faced

by two matching armchairs with a small oaken table in between. There was a group of five young women seated there, probably mothers. Four of them were listening intently to a larger woman with curly black hair and excessive makeup, sipping coffee as they were told a story that seemed worthy of the tabloids.

"Charlie," came a call from behind him. This voice was that of a man, raspy, but not old.

Charlie turned to see a man about his height. He had a straight, well-kept beard, brown in color, and wore a sand-colored flat cap and a pair of black, rounded-square-rim glasses. His army green t-shirt bore no name tag, but from the smile on his face, Charlie saw that this nameless man was happy. Perhaps he was the owner, or just someone who really liked coffee. Maybe both.

"Here's your Americano," said the man as he extended his arms, one hand supporting the plate and the other holding the steaming, white ceramic coffee cup.

Charlie took the plate and cup and resumed his search for an empty seat. His eyes slowly reviewed the parts of the shop he'd already surveyed, looking for something he missed, and ended at the area of the shop to which he had not yet paid much attention.

Between the fireplace and the seating area under the bay window, the tufted bench continued with just enough room for two four-seater tables. On the bench at the table closest to the bay window sat one of Charlie's former professors, a philosophy teacher who had told him that the existence of evil and suffering disproved the very notion that God could exist. It was a welcomed notion for Charlie, who knew both the depths of despair and the noxious gas of religion.

Next to Charlie's old professor sat a brunette, tucked away behind a stack of books. She was reading, highlighter in hand, as her thick, silky brown hair hid her face from view.

Charlie continued to sip his coffee, his eyes fixed on the mysterious brunette seated next to the fireplace, desperately wondering what her face might look like. He had just finished taking a bite of his muffin when he looked up to see the brunette staring at him. She was beautiful, her face slender and petite, with chocolate brown eyes and light freckles adorning her cheeks and nose. She wore almost no makeup.

Their eyes locked, and she smiled at him. It was a small smile, but one that welcomed his advance all the same. Charlie smiled back. She giggled.

Only then did Charlie realize that he still had a fresh bite of muffin in his mouth. He must have looked like an idiot. Breaking their gaze, Charlie hurriedly chewed his muffin and swallowed.

He looked back, hoping he hadn't lost her interest. She was now relaxing against the bench on which she sat, her hands folded as she looked at him. The playful smirk on her face told him she was still amused, while the look in her eyes told Charlie that he had not lost her interest.

Charlie did a mental double-check to ensure that his mouth was empty before returning her smile, and was both surprised and intrigued to see the chair opposite this beautiful woman sliding out from under the table—a not-so-subtle invitation for him to join her.

Still smiling, the brown-haired beauty broke their gaze, raised her brow, and nodded at the chair that now looked silly without an occupant.

Charlie welcomed the invitation, picking up the plates that held his coffee and muffin and moving to the table where she sat.

"Hi," he said as he neared the table, trying to be sexy and recover the ground lost by his muffin-smile.

"Hi," she said, not needing to try. "I'm Katie."

"I'm Charlie," he said in response, now seated and gazing across the table at her.

"Ohhh," she said, "you must be Charlie *Shaw.*"

Charlie's heart tightened as he began to panic, his eyes narrowing as he stared at her. She knew who he was, which meant that she knew about his reputation in this town.

"You really *are* as attractive as they say," she said before biting her bottom lip.

Charlie continued to stare at her, pressingly determined to see if she was kidding. When she didn't bust up laughing with the cruelty of sarcasm, Charlie relaxed, suddenly feeling much more confident.

"Except when you smile with a muffin in your mouth," she said as she smirked at him. "Then you just look like a chipmunk."

Charlie chuckled. This girl could play. "So you know me, huh?"

"Correction," she said as she uncrossed her legs under the table and sat up tall, "I know *of* you. There's a big difference between knowing *of* someone and knowing them."

Charlie was somewhat surprised by her statement. This girl was more than met the eye.

"Tell me, Charlie Shaw," she said, "what's your greatest fear?"

Charlie hesitated at the question. This was not normal conversation. He had just met this girl. Shouldn't she be asking him something along the lines of whether he was a student, where he was from, or what he did with his life?

"Well?" she said, leaning forward as she awaited his answer.

"I—I guess I'd have to say failure," said Charlie.

She leaned back against the tufted leather, folding her arms as she smirked at him. "That's a lie," she said.

"Oh, so you only know *of* me, but somehow you know my greatest fear better than I do?"

Katie sat for a moment, smiling at him. "So tell me about you."

For what seemed like ages, Charlie remained engulfed in conversation with Katie. She was a nursing student in the third year of her program, and she talked very little of herself. She was more intrigued by who Charlie was, hanging on his every word and asking probing questions about his hopes and dreams, his motivations and passions—sometimes *too* probing. They spoke of current events, scientific discovery, and the arts. She was not just another pretty face; she had opinions and thoughts about the world in which she lived, yet held them with humility and grace. Charlie was mesmerized.

The glimmer of tangerine hues on the wall above Katie's head broke Charlie from his trance and his gaze darted to the bay window. The shop was now almost empty. Not only had the sun emerged, cleansing the outside world of the gruesomely wet war that had just raged outside, but it was now setting behind the mountains of Charlottesville.

"Wow," said Charlie, "I didn't realize how late it's gotten."

"Yeah," said Katie as she began to pack up her things, "I need to get going."

"Can I walk you out?" asked Charlie, still hoping to land a date with this girl.

"If you dare," she said, playfully. The two then walked out together into a world refreshed and renewed. The sidewalks still showed signs of rainfall, with the fragrance of moisture lingering in the air, but it was clear that the war had stopped; the rain had retreated.

"It was nice to meet you, Charlie," said Katie as she turned to walk away. Charlie wasted no time grabbing her arm, and she paused, turning back around.

"Can I see you again?" Charlie asked as the two stood under the awning outside Charming Beard.

Katie hesitated, averting his gaze as she glanced at the ground.

Was she not interested in him? Had something about their conversation turned her off? Or was she remembering his reputation, which she apparently knew quite well? Charlie was not sure, and his heart began to beat harder as his chest constricted around it, awaiting her yes—or her no.

What *was* this? She was just another girl, just another tail to chase; why had Charlie let himself get so worked up over her? If she said no, there'd be another girl tomorrow, and if he was lucky, he'd have company in his bed by the weekend. And more than all that, *he* was Charlie *Shaw*, for heaven's sake. Why had he gotten so caught up in *this* girl?

"What are you doing tomorrow night?" she asked softly, interrupting his thoughts.

Charlie had reminded himself of his goal. He knew his tactics. It was time to use them. "Spending an evening with you?" Charlie responded, hoping the facade of romance would seduce her into a date with him tomorrow night, and that if that went well, she'd be warming his bed by Saturday.

Katie stood with her hands crossed over a textbook, holding it between her forearms and her hips. She broke her gaze with Charlie and stared behind him. "How about Julienne's at six o'clock?" she asked, nodding in the direction of her gaze.

Charlie turned to confirm where she was staring.

Julienne's was a local pizzeria owned by Antony and Julienne Abello, and was the only place in Charlottesville where you could get genuine, Italian pizza, uncorrupted by American culinary influence.

"It's a date," said Charlie, as their eyes locked once again, his mind imagining what her face might look like on Saturday night, resting with his pillow behind her head as she gave herself to him.

"Great!" said Katie as she turned and began to walk away. "See you then!"

"W-wait!" stuttered Charlie, his mind forgetting his tactics, confused by the lack of convention. "Don't I get your number?"

"Mmm," she said, dawning a smile of mischief as she walked backwards in the same direction, "I'm not sure about you, Charlie Shaw. Maybe some day, though!"

She giggled, then turned back around and walked off. Charlie's eyes remained fixed on her until she was out of sight. This girl had once again knocked Charlie off his horse, his mind and heart captivated by the mystery that enshrouded her.

Charlie unlocked his bike and rode the rest of the way home, thinking of nothing else but her.

3

A Night on the Mall

———— ❧ ————

Charlie's eyes stared at the small digital clock on the bathroom counter. He jerked his gaze back to the mirror as he hastened the speed with which he buttoned his shirt. It was 5:36pm.

"Daaamn, son," said Michael, chuckling as he leaned, cool and composed, against the doorway to the bathroom, watching his roommate get ready. "You must really like this one."

Charlie stared back at him with scorn as he rolled his sleeves. "You know me better than that."

The son of a Baptist preacher, Michael was a six-foot-eight, two-hundred-fifty-pound, African-American lineman recruited by the University of Virginia out of North Atlanta High School in Buckhead, Georgia. He earned his chops in Charlottesville at a frat party in the spring of his freshman year when he hurled a would-be rapist through a wall, breaking a few of his ribs and sending him to the hospital. He was hailed a local hero, with the paper dubbing him "Defender of the Innocent" and "Protector of the Weak."

It was at that same party that Michael and Charlie met. Michael took a liking to Charlie, despite his questionable "dating" practices, and a few months later, the two of them moved in together.

Charlie brushed passed Michael in a flurry. "Hoo!" said Michael, chuckling as he stepped aside in an attempt to dodge his hasty roommate. Charlie walked briskly to his bedroom where he filled his pockets with his usual things, then pulled on his laced-up shoes and made his way to the door.

"See ya later, Mike," said Charlie as he walked out.

"Have fun," said Michael, now reclining in front of the TV. "Oh, and don't you do anything I wouldn't do."

Charlie gave Michael a contemptuous stare as he closed the door. Michael just laughed as he turned on the TV to watch that night's college football game.

A gentle breeze blew outside their apartment as the sun lingered in the evening sky. Racing down the metal stairs, Charlie made his way to the bus stop and waited—one minute, two minutes, three minutes...

The bus finally pulled up (on schedule), and Charlie hastily hopped on and showed the driver his student ID, which he kept on his keychain. The driver nodded, and Charlie took a seat at the back of the bus.

At last, Charlie was able to relax, knowing that he was on his way to the Downtown Mall. Charlie began to notice the people seated around him. To his left, on a row of seats that ran parallel to the bus's direction of travel, sat a middle-aged woman who held a cheap, beige-colored faux-leather bag in her lap. She had very light brown hair that was graying at the roots, and wore a knee-length floral skirt with white sneakers, her feet crossed at the ankles as she stared straight ahead, pressing her lips tightly together. She did not have much money, but she remained stubbornly dignified in her circumstances.

Closer to the front of the bus, seated in a row that faced Charlie, were an older man and his wife. The man wore a gray wool flat cap and carried a cane that looked like it was made of mahogany. He had sapphire-blue eyes and a nose that was bulbous but not overbearing, his face exhausted but nevertheless excited to be with the woman he loved. His wife had blonde hair that was starting to gray, with an elvish face that didn't look a day over thirty-five.

To Charlie's right, opposite the stubbornly dignified woman, was a young blonde girl with very fair skin and brown eyes. She wore a baby blue t-shirt and a white pair of mini shorts, exposing most of her legs. The shirt bore the logo of one of the sororities on campus, followed by the word, "Wannabe." She had not yet been recruited; she was a freshman.

Charlie sat staring at the young blonde for several minutes. When she noticed his gaze, she smiled at him, inviting his advance.

But Charlie averted her gaze, staring instead toward the front of the bus.

What was going *on*? In any other circumstance, whether or not he was on his way to a date, Charlie would have struck up conversation with this girl. Dating was, after all, a game of sheer numbers. The more women that Charlie hit on, the more likely it was that Charlie would find at least *one* who was willing to warm his bed that weekend.

What's more, not only was this girl attractive, but she had the naïvety of a freshman. This girl didn't have a clue about Charlie's reputation, increasing the odds of him sealing the deal. Katie, on the other hand, hadn't even given him her phone number.

Why *wasn't* Charlie pursuing this? It did not make any sense.

The bus squealed to a halt near the east end of the Downtown Mall, and Charlie stepped off, staring at his watch as he did so. It was 5:56pm.

The Downtown Mall was an eight-block mix of art galleries, restaurants, coffee shops, and boutiques, and on Friday nights, it came alive. Local entrepreneurs set up bazaar-like shops to sell their creations, and local painters emerged with colors and brush to publicly craft their beautiful canvases.

Realizing he had only four minutes to walk eight blocks, Charlie increased his speed. Hasty and determined, he kept looking down at his watch, keeping tabs on his pace: 5:57, 5:58, 5:59.

At 6:02pm, Charlie finally stood outside Julienne's, staring at its large, rustic door, natural in color, with two large, dark hinges that spanned most of its width, making it look like something out of the Middle Ages. Charlie was late, and he glanced around, looking to see if Katie was outside. She was nowhere to be seen. Pressing down on the latch as he grasped the dark metal handle, Charlie pulled open the rather heavy door and stepped inside to the sound of voices and laughter.

The atmosphere of Julienne's was dark, yet warm, with vintage brick walls on either side connected by dark cedar four-by-four beams that ran the width of the room. On the walls hung paintings and photographs by Charlottesville's local artists, and from the ceiling hung rustic chandeliers that cast cozy, incandescent hues down on the restaurant's patrons.

Charlie looked around for Katie, seated at a table and waiting for him. His eyes darted from one occupied table to another. Katie was nowhere to be found. Charlie's heart sank.

Charlie turned, grasping the knob of a door that now seemed much heavier than it was before as he pushed it open, each step away from Julienne's more grueling than the last. When Charlie was but two steps outside the door, he heard a familiar voice.

"Hey, stranger!" Charlie's soul brightened a shade as he looked up to see Katie, standing in a pair of red, suede leather heels with her ankles crossed, her hands interlocked, holding her clutch in front of her hips.

"Why the long face?" she asked.

Charlie could not find words fast enough. He knew, but did not want to answer.

"You didn't think I stood you up, did you?"

"Uh, no. No," said Charlie, fumbling for a lie. "I was just comin' out to see if you were here yet."

Katie saw right through him. She took a few steps toward him as her eyes narrowed, gazing into his soul as she searched for the truth.

"Liar," she said as she came closer, grazing his shoulder as she passed.

Charlie's face quickly found a smile as he turned around and hurried ahead of her to open the door. The two stepped inside, and made their way to the line.

"I really *was* just seeing if you were here," Charlie said as the two stared up at the menu.

"Mmmm-*hm!*" Katie said, smirking.

"What can I get for you guys?" came a kind voice from behind the register. He was a shorter man who, though his hair line was receding, didn't look much older than Charlie. He wore round glasses without any noticeable rims, and bore a smile that was happy to help.

Charlie and Katie stepped forward.

"What do you want?" asked Katie.

"Whatever you want," said Charlie.

"Can we do the Carnivore?" Katie asked, turning to the cashier. The Carnivore was a nothing-but-meat pizza, adorned with thick slices of pepperoni, made-in-house Italian sausage, massive slices of cured ham, Tuscan salami, and Julienne's own secret tomato sauce. Far from choosing a light salad with dressing on the side, this girl had chosen the most meat-heavy pizza that Julienne's offered.

"And I don't know about Charlie here, but I'd *love* a pale ale."

"Yeah…" said Charlie, staring at Katie with intrigue, "I'd love one, too, actually."

"Sure, you bet!" said the cashier as he wrote their order down. "That'll be twenty-six thirty-three."

Charlie reached into his back pocket to retrieve his wallet. His chest tightened when his hand grabbed at nothing but air. His wallet was not there.

In a panicked haste, Charlie patted down his pockets, reaching into every one of them in a desperate search for something resembling money. His search bore no fruit.

Embarrassed, Charlie turned his gaze to Katie. The usual snark and sarcasm in her face had faded, but her smile had not. "I'm *so* sorry," said Charlie, "I must've left it in my bag. I meant to grab it."

Still smiling at him, her eyes screaming that she was far more worried about *him* than she was about twenty-six dollars and thirty-three cents, Katie opened her clutch and handed the cashier a card without breaking their gaze. "It's not a problem at all," she said to Charlie.

The two stepped away from the cashier and began to look for a table. "I really am so sorry," said Charlie.

"Don't worry about it," said Katie, smiling at him.

"Well, I mean it," Charlie insisted, as though Katie really didn't believe him.

"Look," said Katie, her mischief returning as she paused their pace and turned to look at him.

"I don't see what *you're* so worried about. You just owe me dinner now, which means *another* date. *Me* on the other hand…"

She nudged him with her elbow as Charlie's face dawned a grin and his eyes watered over ever so slightly. "I think I'm alright with that."

"Oh, don't be so sure there, mister," she said. "You don't even know me yet. For all you know, I could be as needy as they come. I could be all, 'Oh, Charlie…love me love me love me.' You might just be begging me to get out of that second date, but I'm not gonna let ya. Mm-mm. No can do. You *owe* me."

Katie looked at him with a playful smirk. Charlie chuckled. He wasn't worried.

"So, where do you wanna sit?" he asked. Together they found a table near the back of the restaurant. A few minutes later, Katie's name was called and Charlie retrieved their pizza and beers. Katie wasted no time readying a slice for devouring.

"So, Katie," said Charlie, his memory harkening back to a familiar question, "what's *your* greatest fear?"

"Spiders." Katie was quick, with a serious look on her face, a slice of pizza in hand.

"Liar," said Charlie, smirking at her.

"Just giving you as truthful an answer as you gave me," said Katie before taking her first bite.

Charlie grabbed a slice and put it on his plate. The two were silent as Katie chewed. Katie's napkin fell to the floor. She began to retrieve it.

"Abandonment," Charlie said softly, staring at the floor as Katie picked up the napkin. His gaze met hers, permitting her a rare opportunity to look into his soul.

Katie halted her efforts to retrieve the napkin, her face filled with compassion and tenderness. She knew in that moment that Charlie was sharing something he had never shared before, and she cared much more about meeting him in that moment than she did about a clean face.

"My greatest fear is abandonment," Charlie clarified, speaking a little louder and matter-of-factly.

Gently, without breaking their stare, Katie put her hand on his knee and gave it a gentle squeeze. "I know," she said softly.

Charlie's soul was confused. His eyes had clouded over, moved to the brink of tears by this girl who seemed to know so well when to be funny and when to be serious. But at the same time, he was almost offended by her presumption.

Charlie voiced his complaint as he wiped away a tear in his eyes with a chuckle. "How could you *possibly* have known that?"

Katie picked up the napkin and wiped the corners of her mouth. "From the look on your face tonight," she said, matter-of-factly. "You know, when you were 'coming out to see if I was here,'" she said, making air quotes to mock his earlier lie. "Your eyes said it all."

"Yeah, but," Charlie retorted, his mind stumbling for reasons to discredit her. "How do you know my greatest fear wasn't…I dunno…rejection? I mean, you not showing up would be you *basically* rejecting me…"

"Because if your greatest fear were rejection, you never would have been able to ask me out in the first place. You would've been too scared of a no."

Charlie stared at her, narrowing his eyes as he tried to find some reason why she was wrong. Katie sat in cool repose as she took another bite of pizza.

"You better eat some of this before I eat it all," Katie said, smirking with a mouthful of food.

Charlie just continued to stare. Seeing that he still wasn't eating and with a mouthful of food, Katie opened her eyes wide and pointed authoritatively at the slice of pizza, still sitting untouched on Charlie's plate.

Begrudgingly, Charlie took another bite and swallowed. "I'm gonna have to watch myself around you," he said, glancing out of the corner of his eye at the beautiful girl sitting next to him.

The two finished their pizza and beer, exchanging playful glances as they ate. They then stepped out into the cool, crisp air of an early autumn evening. The sun had set over Charlottesville.

"So, where to now?" asked Charlie.

Katie had an answer ready on the tip of her tongue. "How about we walk the mall and see where it takes us?"

"Sounds good to me," said Charlie. The two then began to walk in the direction from which Charlie had so hurriedly come, the slow pop of Katie's heels on the old red brick setting the pace for their movement.

Charlie was surprised when Katie leaned into him as the two of them walked, but it seemed strangely natural for him to put his arm around her, bringing his hand to rest on her outside hip as her hand reached across his lower back and came to rest at his side.

"You wanna see a movie?" asked Katie softly as the two neared the old Paramount Theater.

"I dunno," said Charlie, smirking as he looked down at the top of her head. "You're kinda clingy." She turned her face to meet his gaze as they arrived at the theater.

"Oh, shush," she said, smiling back at him as he opened the door to the theater's box office and guided her through. "I'm a hoot."

The movie that was showing at the theater was an independent film produced by some filmmakers out of New York. It was titled *Survivor*. Charlie and Katie stood in the box office surveying the poster that showcased the film. On it was a young woman dressed in an astronaut's suit and plagued with fear as she looked dreadfully out of the corner of her eye. She was surrounded by the stars and galaxies of outer space, with the International Space Station behind her, and beneath her terrified portrait were the words, "When Two Superpowers Collide," with faded images of the Russian and American flags overlaying the distant planet earth.

"You okay with this?" Katie asked.

"Yeah, it looks good," Charlie replied, standing just behind her.

"Can I get two tickets to the 7:15 showing?" Katie asked, turning to the large lady sitting behind the ticket counter.

"That'll be $25.86," she said, speaking through her nose with a raspy voice.

Katie handed her card to the large lady, who swiped it through her register before handing it back to Katie along with their two tickets. Charlie and Katie then made their way into the theater and found two seats in the middle section near the back.

The movie lasted just over two hours. It was about a group of American astronauts who find themselves aboard the International Space Station with a team of Russian cosmonauts when World War III breaks out, seemingly instigated by the Russian assassination of the American Secretary of State. Lending credence to Russia's foul intentions is the fact that the cosmonauts have brought fully loaded military assault rifles aboard the space station, in violation of international law.

As the two superpowers ready their troops for battle on the ground, the cosmonauts begin stealthily taking out American astronauts, one by one. When just two astronauts remain, the young woman featured on the movie's poster asks her lone companion, the mission's captain, if they're going to die.

Her captain tells her that he thinks it's likely, and with a tear-stained face, she asks him if he believes in God. He nods, and says that without God, he could not see how there might be any real sense of good and evil in the world, that without God, they could no more hate the Russians for their merciless slaughter than they could for the color of their hair.

Shortly after answering her question, the captain is gunned down by the cosmonauts. The lone survivor races up the airshaft and makes her way to the escape pod, pushing off from the space station as the cosmonauts look on. As she returns to what is bound to be a very different world on the ground, the lone survivor cannot help but contemplate the answer given by her captain, and as she gazes out the window at the planet she's returning to, she prays a desperate plea for justice to a God who may or may not exist.

As the lights came back on in the theater, Katie, who had been resting her head on Charlie's shoulder, let out a small yawn as she stretched.

"That was good," she said.

"Yeah," said Charlie, his tone blank as he stared at the credits rolling on the screen.

"You okay?" asked Katie.

"I'm fine," said Charlie, slightly irritated by her question.

Together, the two got up and walked out of the theater, maintaining six inches of space between them.

"Seriously, what's wrong?" asked Katie, turning her head to look at him.

Charlie continued to stare straight ahead, silent as they walked.

"Do you believe in God?" asked Charlie.

Katie turned her gaze forward as the two continued to walk. She understood why he was upset.

"I do," she confessed. "Do you?"

"No," Charlie said bluntly.

"Why not?" asked Katie gently.

"Because of all the horrible things that go on in this world! Either God exists and doesn't give a damn, or he doesn't exist at all. Either way, there's no such thing as a 'good' or 'just' God."

The two continued to walk in silence, save for the slow pop of Katie's heels that paced their movement.

"Sorry," said Charlie as he exhaled his frustration.

"For what?" asked Katie matter-of-factly.

"For making the conversation awkward."

"Who said anything about it being awkward?"

"Well, it's just…you believe in God; I don't. I should have just respected your beliefs and kept my mouth shut about why."

"But I asked you why," Katie said, pointing out the flaw in his logic.

"Sure, but any time you talk about God, or politics, the conversation gets awkward, so it's better for everybody if we all just shut up about it."

Katie was quiet for a moment as the two continued to walk. "The only time conversations about God or politics get heated or awkward is if you're having them with people who care more about comfort than they do about truth."

Katie's response caught Charlie off guard. He turned his head to look at her. "And you're not one of those people?"

Katie turned and smiled at him.

"So, my reason for not believing in God doesn't bother you?" asked Charlie, waiting for an irrational outburst from Katie.

"Nope," said Katie, turning her gaze face-forward as the two continued to walk to the rhythm of Katie's heel-pop.

"Can I ask why not?" Charlie inquired, bracing himself for the irrational outburst that characterized most conversations he'd had about religion and the existence of God.

Katie looked up at Charlie, smiling. After a few more steps, she answered, her tone softening. "When I was a sophomore, I took a trip to Ethiopia with the nursing program, near the border of Sudan, to care for a camp of refugees who had been displaced by the Sudanese civil war.

"When I was there…" Katie paused, choking on her words. "I met a young girl named Lela," she exhaled, clearly reliving the pain of her past. "She was eleven years old and had long, beautiful black hair and a smile that lit up the room." Katie's eyes were now filled with tears, some of them spilling down her cheeks as their pace slowed.

"She had been gang-raped in her own bed by Janjaweed *thugs*. And they didn't just rape her; no, *that* would have been too easy." Katie was now angry. "They'd also raped her mom and her younger sister, all while holding Lela down so that she couldn't fight them off. Her mom was hurt so badly from it that she couldn't even walk, so Lela and her sister had to make the trek to Ethiopia all by themselves.

"And they did!" she said, sniffling as she smiled, thinking about the courage of these young girls. "Only to find out that they both had HIV and were going to *die* because we didn't have the medicine they needed."

Katie paused their walk, sniffling as she wiped away her tears.

Charlie gently put his arm around her. "I'm sorry," he said, as he gave her a gentle squeeze.

"Do you know what she said to me when I told her how sorry I was?" said Katie abruptly, turning her tear-stained face to look up at Charlie.

Charlie looked down to meet her gaze.

"She said, 'Don't be sorry. God knows my pain.'"

Charlie's heart was curious, but his mind remained skeptical. "How could God *possibly* have known her pain?"

Katie gazed up at the night sky, salted with starlight. "You still don't see it, do you?"

"See what?" asked Charlie, gazing instinctively in the direction Katie was looking.

Katie laughed. "No, not up there," she said. "Why was Lela able to believe that God knew her pain?"

"I mean, God can *know* someone's pain, I suppose. But maybe he can't do anything about it."

"But for Lela, God knowing her pain made it so that she could hold onto hope even in the midst of sorrow. If God knows our pain but can't do anything about it—or worse, if he doesn't *want* to do anything about it, how could that make it so that Lela could trust him with her pain like that?"

The two continued to walk. Charlie was silent.

Katie continued. "The only way that God knowing our pain leads to us trusting him with it is if God himself has *experienced* our pain. If God remains aloof to our pain, then we have no basis to trust him with it. But if God stepped into this mess of a world and felt our pain, *that* changes everything. It means that whatever the reason God lets pain and suffering go on, we can trust him with it because he has not exempted himself from the same pain we feel."

"How does that even happen?" asked Charlie. "No religion believes that God himself has experienced pain!"

Katie turned and stared at Charlie with a face that told him he'd missed something. Charlie suddenly felt unsure of himself. "… Do they?" he asked, hesitantly.

Katie smiled, gently pulling Charlie down an alley.

"Wait. Where are we—" Charlie stammered. "Are you dodging my question?"

"What do you know about Christmas, Charlie?" she asked.

"It's Jesus's birthday, I think," Charlie responded, unsure of where she was going with her question.

Katie remained calm and composed as she slowed her pace near a small, white, four-door sedan. "This is me," she said as she stopped by the car. It had a large, pink flower sticker in the back window and an old radio antenna that sprouted from the hood.

"Wait, are you gonna answer my question?" Charlie protested.

Katie smiled at him. "Christmas is not about the when, Charlie," she said gently. "It's about the what."

"Wh—what do you mean?" Charlie asked, intrigued but confused.

"Christmas is when we celebrate the moment God became a man," Katie said, pausing to let that sink in for Charlie. "G'night, Charlie Shaw." Katie opened her car door.

"W—wait, can I see you again?" Charlie asked.

"What are you doing tomorrow morning?" she asked.

"Spending time with you?" Charlie asked. This time, his goal for the weekend was the furthest thing from his mind. He wasn't playing around. He genuinely wanted to spend more time with Katie, not for what he could get from her, but simply for the mystery she carried with her.

"Let's go for a hike," said Katie as she wrapped her arms around him, interlocking her hands behind Charlie, pinching his sides with her arms.

"Okay," he said. "Where do you wanna go?"

"Where do you live?" she asked.

"Uh, Bellside Apartments. Corner of Church Street and Monticello."

"Perfect. I'll pick you up at eight," she said, breaking free from their lover's tangle and getting into her car.

"Eight in the *morning*?" Charlie whined. "You know tomorrow's Saturday, right?"

Katie turned to look back at him, smiling as she climbed back out of her car. Charlie was nervous, unsure what was coming next. She again entered Charlie's personal space, bringing herself close to him as she stood on her tiptoes and gently kissed Charlie on the cheek.

"Be ready," she whispered softly in his ear as her lips parted from his skin.

Charlie's heart skipped a beat. He was speechless as Katie slowly pulled away, turned around, and got back in her car.

His heart and lungs slowly resumed their rhythm, catching up as he watched her drive away while holding one hand to the now-sacred spot on his cheek. He looked foolish, but hardly noticed.

4

Shady Side

———— ❧ ————

THE SUN PEAKING INTO CHARLIE'S room whispered in his ear that morning had come far too soon. Drearily, he rolled over in his bed to stare at his alarm clock, obnoxiously buzzing to wake him up. It was 7:39am. On a Saturday.

"It *was* Saturday," thought Charlie, coming to. This morning's hike would be Charlie's last chance to find a bedmate for the weekend. Encouraged by the thought, Charlie rolled out of bed and made his way to the bathroom to empty his screaming bladder. He then moved groggily to the kitchen for some breakfast before rolling on deodorant and brushing his teeth as he began to get dressed for the day's hike.

At 7:56am, Charlie made his way to the door. Michael was still sound asleep, snoring like a bear. Charlie envied him.

As Charlie made his way down the metal stairs outside his apartment, the crisp morning air invigorated his lungs while the breaking sun, now in full view, warmed his face. His body, though, still complained about how early it was.

When he reached the bottom of the stairs, Katie was already there, leaning against the side of her car with two cups of coffee in hand. "Morning, Sunshine!" she said, smiling as he squinted at her.

"Uh-huhhh," groaned Charlie as he stretched and yawned a lion's roar then accepted the cup of coffee in her outstretched hand. "Where's this from?" he asked.

"Where else?" she said, grinning.

Charlie then took a peak at the collar on the coffee cup. Charming Beard.

When he looked up, Katie was holding the passenger door open for him.

Lazily smacking his mouth, Charlie protested. "I know it's early, but shouldn't this be the other way around?"

"Mmm…too late!" said Katie, grinning ear-to-ear. "Now get in and drink your coffee, sleepy head."

Charlie got in and Katie closed the door behind him. Charlie then watched as she walked around the front of her car to the driver's side. She was wearing a pair of short, hot pink running shorts with a white, long-sleeved, off-white cotton t-shirt that bore a red cross on the front, and on the back, in large, red, block-letter font, had the words, "Nurse in Training."

This was the first time Charlie had seen Katie's bare legs. His eyes fixated on them, remembering his desire for a bed-warmer that night.

Charlie took a sip of his coffee as Katie got in and started to drive. With every sip, he found himself remembering more and more their conversation from the night before as they paced the Downtown Mall.

"So," said Charlie, breaking the silence, "are you gonna tell me what you believe?"

Katie turned her head to look at him, taking her eyes briefly off the road as she smiled at him. Katie then returned her eyes to the road, and Charlie smiled as he took notice of the way she drove. She leaned slightly forward in her seat, her hands barely lower than the ten and two o'clock positions on the steering wheel.

"What would you like to know?" she asked.

"Well, for starters, how old do you believe the earth is? Are you one of those nut jobs who believes the earth is only six thousand years old? Or do you live in the rational world and accept that the earth really *is* billions of years old?"

"Yes," said Katie as she took her eyes off the road again to look at Charlie, this time grinning ear-to-ear.

"Okay, I know it's early," groaned Charlie as he rubbed his eyes, "but I wanna say that's not a valid answer." Katie giggled.

"How do we measure a year?" asked Katie.

Charlie just groaned. "You *do* know how early it is, don't you?"

Katie laughed. "Just answer the question!"

"Well," said Charlie, "a year is 365 days. I guess it could be 366 days, too, if it's a leap year."

"Right," said Katie, "but what makes a year a year? Why not 200 days? Or 400?"

"Well it takes about 365 days for the earth to make its way around the sun," said Charlie, his mind still struggling to wake up as caffeine flooded his veins.

"Exactly," said Katie. "Now, Charlie," she continued, "has it *always* taken the earth about 365 days to rotate around the sun?"

"Uhhh," said Charlie, vocalizing the hum of his brain cells. "I guess we have no way of knowing." This was a thought that had never before occurred to Charlie: that it might have taken more or less time for the earth to make its rounds in times past.

"It gets better," said Katie gleefully. "How do we measure a day?"

"Well, there's twenty—" Charlie caught himself. "That's not the answer you're looking for, is it?"

Katie turned and looked at him again, still grinning.

"A day is how long it takes for the earth to rotate on its axis."

"Yup!" said Katie. "Now tell me, Charlie, has it *always* taken 24 hours for the earth to rotate once on its axis? Or, put another way: even if we've always divided the time it takes from sunrise to sunrise into 24 evenly spaced blocks, can we *really* be sure that those blocks have always held the exact same amount of time in them?"

It was not yet 8:15 on a Saturday morning, and Charlie's head was already beginning to hurt again. But he knew the answer. "We don't know," said Charlie. "We can't know."

"Exactly," said Katie. "Time is in flux. It is nothing but a human construct, and therefore not an objective measurement. So, sure, standing at this point in history, it looks as though the earth is billions of years old, and that's a very true statement…based on how time looks *today*. But standing at some other point in history, where it may have taken more or less time for the earth to do its thing…who knows?

"Either way, because time is a human invention, we *cannot* know the age of the earth with any semblance of objectivity."

The ground underneath Katie's tires began to rumble as she

pulled off the road onto a gravel park strip and brought her car to rest in the shade of some nearby elm trees.

"Fun, huh!" said Katie, turning toward him, her face beaming.

"Fun is one way to describe it," said Charlie. "My head's already hurting."

"Well, you asked the question, mister!" she said, popping the door open and hopping out.

She then opened the door behind the driver's seat and began to gather her things. Charlie leaned forward, peering through the windshield as he read the sign next to the trail that vanished into the trees. "Shady Side."

Charlie set his coffee cup in one of the cup holders, then opened his door and hopped out.

"Hey," called Katie from behind him.

Charlie turned, instantly startled by the object now flying through the air in his direction, shimmering in the morning sunlight. Though he fumbled to catch it, he was successful. It was a bottle of water.

"Thought you might want that," said Katie, squinting in the morning light as she shaded her eyes to look at him.

Charlie's eyes turned from Katie to the bottle in his hand. Perhaps it was the warmth of the morning sun, or the caffeine making its way through his system, but it felt as though a part of Charlie was thawing, a part of him that he had not felt in years.

"What's wrong?" asked Katie, still squinting in his direction.

"I—" said Charlie, fumbling to put words to this new, yet very old, feeling, "I, just haven't had anyone to look out for me in a while," he said. "That's all." It was, for Charlie, perhaps the first honest statement about his heart that he had spoken in almost seven years.

"Well, now you've got me!" said Katie cheerfully as she found the strength to fully open her eyes. The two locked gazes for a moment as they again stared into each other's souls. Katie looked stunning in the morning light, dawning her usual smile with her thick brown hair pulled back in a ponytail. She cared about him, and she had now seen a thawing part of Charlie's heart that had not been seen by anyone in almost a decade.

"You ready to get going?" asked Katie, tilting her head sideways in the direction of the trailhead.

"Yeah," said Charlie, smiling at her, and together the two set off up the trail.

The warmth of the morning sun disappeared as they stepped into the thick foliage that characterized much of the forest around Charlottesville. Katie was walking ahead of Charlie, and on an ordinary day with an ordinary girl, Charlie certainly would have enjoyed the view; but today, he felt different. He felt almost criminal for fixating on this girl. She was more than a tail to chase, more than a heart to conquer and dump. She had thoughts and opinions, unlike many of the girls in Charlie's past; and above all else, she cared very much about him, even when she knew he probably didn't care much about her.

The two were silent for several minutes as the trail began to gently climb.

Charlie piped up. "So, what *do* you believe about our past?"

"You know," said Katie, stepping over a tree that had fallen across the trail, "when I was a freshman, I had this terribly nutty professor. Her name was Cecilia Wong, and she had snow white hair that was always a frizzled mess and looked more like a mop than it did like a head of hair.

"As part of our lab with Cecilia, we had to do an experiment. We each took two petri dishes and grew the same bacteria in each of them. After about a week or so, when there was plenty of bacteria to see, we introduced penicillin to one of the trays but left the other untouched.

"The next week, we took bacteria from each of the trays—the one that had been untouched and the one that had whatever bacteria that managed to survive the penicillin—and we grew them in two *new* petri dishes."

Katie looked back to make sure Charlie was still engaged. He looked up to meet her gaze. "Uh-huh," he said, wanting to hear where she was going with this story.

"When *those* bacteria had grown," she said, returning her gaze to face forward as the trail began to climb more steeply, "we *again* introduced penicillin to the mix, and you know what happened?"

"What?" asked Charlie, entertaining this storyteller.

"The bacteria that had been exposed to the penicillin survived in much greater numbers than the bacteria that hadn't. We had *seen* natural selection in action. And at the same time, this group of nursing students had gotten a glimpse of why resistance to antibiotics is such a *hul*—"

Katie slipped on a moss-covered rock that lay stealthily disguised as part of the steep terrain.

"*Cheese*muffin!" she yelled as she rolled over on her sit bones and pulled her knee into her chest.

Katie's knee had been scraped pretty badly and was starting to bleed. Charlie felt helpless, unable to do anything to alleviate her pain. "Are you okay?" he asked, panicked as he knelt beside her.

"Yeah…" said Katie, rocking back and forth as she held her knee against her chest.

"Do you wanna go back?" asked Charlie.

"No, no…" said Katie, "just gimme a minute."

Charlie looked around to see if there were any other hikers who might have some first aid supplies. The trail, however, was vacant. It was just the two of them alone in the forest.

He turned his gaze back to Katie, who was now peering around her leg to look at her wound. "Cheesemuffin?" he asked with a smirk on his face.

Katie looked up at him. "Yes, cheesemuffin!" she said, matching his smirk. "You *know* you're just jealous of my awesome word."

Charlie chuckled, shaking his head. "You know, it's ironic."

"What's that?" asked Katie, wincing as she extended and contracted her injured leg.

"It's ironic that the one wearing the 'Nurse in Training' shirt is the one who needs the nurse."

Katie playfully glared at him as she bent and extended her leg.

"Okay, smarty pants, I think I'm ready to get going," said Katie, standing and starting up the hill again, this time with a slight limp.

"You sure?" asked Charlie. "We can stay here and rest if you want."

"Yeah, I'm fine," she said, continuing up the trail. "C'mon, slowpoke."

Charlie shot back. "Right behind you, cheesemuffin."

Katie shook her head, and Charlie knew that she was smiling.

After a few steps, Katie's walk had returned to normal. "Okay," she said, "where was I?"

"Well," said Charlie, "I had asked you what you believe about our past, and—"

"Oh, yeahyeahyeah," she said. "If that experiment taught me anything, it's that adaptation is certainly a part of our world today, and probably *has* been a part of our world for a long time."

"But you don't think it's *always* been a part of our world?" asked Charlie, catching the subtlety of her words.

"You remember my trip to Ethiopia?" asked Katie. "I decided to stay there an extra two weeks to be with Lela when the rest of my team went home. Because of the countless diseases that were rampant in the refugee camp, she had gotten sick pretty quickly, and I wanted to be there when it came time to say goodbye.

"We spent *hours* talking about all kinds of things: boys she'd crushed on in her village and the guys I'd dated back here at home, the hopes and dreams she had for her future…. She wanted to go to school and be the first female president of Sudan and finally bring peace to her war-torn country.

"And every time she laughed," said Katie, her voice smiling, "even when it was painful for her, it brought new life to my soul. She still had that childlike chuckle and a face that radiated like the sun.

"I remember thinking, '*How* could this girl be so *happy* when she's been through so much hell?'

"About ten days after my team had left, Lela breathed her last breath," said Katie, choking on her words as she remembered her friend. Katie paused their hike, trying to regain some composure.

"I sobbed so violently in that tent that some other workers who were fifteen tents away heard me and came to see what was the matter. I was so outraged and *so* devastated, all at the same time.

"I mean, she hadn't even kissed a boy!" Katie began to sob, reliving the sorrow of losing her friend. Charlie put his arm around her in silence, and Katie turned, melting into his embrace.

The two stood there for some time, mourning together in the Shenandoah forest over a girl named Lela, whom Charlie did not even know but somehow felt attached to. He knew the depths of suffering, the pain of losing those he loved. Charlie not only knew Katie's pain, but felt what she felt.

After a while, the flow of Katie's tears had stopped, but she remained cocooned in their hug as Charlie rested his head on top of hers, gently rocking back and forth.

"You ready to go, cheesemuffin?" Charlie asked quietly, breaking the silence.

Katie pulled back. "Jerk!" she said, hitting him in the chest.

"It's *your* word," said Charlie, grinning back. Katie simply glared at him in playful romance as the two continued their hike through the Shenandoah forest.

They hiked a good half-mile in silence before Katie resumed the conversation.

"And you know," she said, "as I sat there in Lela's tent, staring at her lifeless body, my soul shredded by agony, I asked myself why I was so upset. I had known from when I first met this girl that she was going to die. I had known when I first met this girl that she'd been through hell with those Janjaweed thugs. So why was I so upset *now*, having known before all of it that this amazing girl who had been through so much hell was going to die far too young?"

Katie's words sank deep into Charlie's heart, as though she was somehow giving voice to questions that his heart had been bellowing but that he had never dared to explore. Everyone dies, many far too young. But even though we know this, we are always surprised, even devastated, when they breathe their last. Something deep within us cries out in unbearable agony. But why?

"Why?" Charlie asked after a moment of silence as his mind processed what his heart was feeling.

"I was so devastated," continued Katie, "because deep in my soul, in the depths of my heart, I *knew*—with as much certainty as I know that these trees, that you, are real—I knew with certainty that death should have never been a part of this world."

That was it, and a small layer of tears coated Charlie's eyes. Katie had both asked and answered the deepest cry of Charlie's heart. But his brain still objected. "So, what are you saying?"

"Look, everyone likes to assume that because things adapt we're just a bunch of glorified apes. But that assumes we are the chicken who hatched from the egg instead of the egg laid by the chicken. It assumes that we are the most complex organisms to have ever existed, instead of more simple, broken organisms that have devolved from something much, much more glorious.

"Charlie," said Katie, stopping abruptly and turning around to stare him in the eye. "If you and I are nothing but the product of chance mutations in DNA over billions of years that left certain creatures to live and others to die—if death is all we've ever known

—then where did we ever get the idea that death should never have been a part of this world?"

"Well," said Charlie, his brain roaring in protest, "we could have just imagined a world in which death was not a part of our existence; we could have imagined it as the place that Evolution might one day take us."

Katie turned, staring at him with a face that called his mind's bluff. She knew that he didn't really believe what he was saying, but she entertained him all the same.

"Talk to any artist, any creative person who uses their imagination on a day-to-day basis, and they will tell you that they do not create in a void. Their creations are the products, not of their mind's supernatural ability to extrapolate some evolutionary process they do not even know, but of their past *experience*.

"The human imagination requires experience to create," said Katie, with all her passion wrapped up in the wonder of human imagination. "Some of the world's best artists have been those who have gone through some of the most painful experiences.

"So sure, the notion of a world without death might be one that persists in our imagination today, but at some point in our past, it must have come from our experience. At some point in our past, we must have not just known, but experienced a world in which there was no such thing as death."

Charlie's heart beat to a new rhythm at the sound of her words. As a child desperately longs for wonder, so Charlie longed for Katie's words to be true, but his brain continued its protest.

"So, what?" he said, his prefrontal cortex mocking her words. "Are you saying that we've actually existed from the beginning?"

"Yes," said Katie, humble yet confident, "I am."

"Well," said Charlie, continuing to fight his thirst for wonder, "don't you think it's awfully childish of us to believe that we came from something greater, to believe that we actually existed from the beginning of time?"

"To believe in creation?" Katie shot back, turning to look at him with a brokenhearted smile. "To believe that we once lived in a world better than this, where Janjaweed thugs don't rape young girls, and powerful dictators don't torture innocent dissidents? Where greedy businessmen don't step mercilessly on the shoulders of their poor employees and families aren't torn apart by senseless wars?

"Tell me Charlie," she said, her tone hinting of passionate anger, "when our hearts cry out that the world we live in was not supposed to have been this way, how is it childish to believe that we once lived in a world that was not this way, that we were created for something far better than this?"

Charlie was silent. He had no answer. To say that it was childish and persist in his argument would be to forsake things he could not forsake: that rape and torture were wrong, that greed and violence should never have been. To say that something is wrong, that it should never have been, is to admit that we have some knowledge of what is right, of what *should* have been—and then we must face the inevitable question of how we ever came to know such things.

Katie's anger subsided as she gently put a hand on Charlie's shoulder, her eyes softening as she gave it a gentle squeeze, giving him, in turn, the courage to look her in the eye.

"Charlie," she said, "if you and I are nothing but the product of *chance*, then there is absolutely no *meaning* in this world. Our feelings, our morality, our very existence; the knowledge in our hearts that death should never have been—all of our love and friendship, even our thoughts themselves—all of it amounts to nothing but the random movement of chemicals in our brain, and it *means* nothing.

"And the problem with that is that science, by its very nature, *needs* our thoughts to mean something. Science needs our world to be more than just an accident because science assumes that there is nothing accidental about the way things in our world behave. If our thoughts mean nothing—if this world is nothing but an acci-dent—then science also means nothing.

"And ironically, if science means nothing, then the claim that we're all just one big accident is made for the empty lie that it is because the claim itself is derived from science.

"Do you see the problem with that?"

Charlie gazed up into her eyes, now glistening with tears of affection. Her words were slowly calming his brain, and his heart beat fiercely with gratitude.

She continued, "If anything in this world, including evolution-ary theory, is to have any meaning, we *must* believe in creation. And if we believe in creation, we *must* accept the possibility that we are not the chicken hatched from the egg, but the egg laid by the chicken; we must accept the possibility that we are fallen from a greater world, even a perfect world, and that death was something that was never meant to be."

Katie paused, letting Charlie's mind wrap itself around the

words she had just spoken. The birds nestled high in the trees above them seemed to huddle around them, chirping a morning symphony almost as though they were excited by the conversation of which they served as witnesses.

"So no," Katie said, gently squeezing his shoulder, "I don't believe it is childish to believe in creation. I actually think it's quite necessary."

Katie then turned to continue their hike. Charlie paused, still processing her words as he watched her take several steps up the trail, then hurried to catch up.

"So," he said, briskly jogging as he caught up to her, "are you saying that science is wrong about our past?"

"Not at all," said Katie. "In fact, I think science pretty much nails it, save for that one fatal assumption."

At this point, the two of them reached the bottom of a rather rocky ascent that climbed some eighty feet. Side-by-side, they began pushing themselves as they heaved their way up the steep incline of this rocky hill, trying to maintain a firm footing as the large rocks slipped underneath their feet.

For what felt like hours they climbed, until at last, the ground leveled out as they stepped once again into the morning sun, now higher in the sky and beaming its glory down on these two budding lovers, bent over and heaving as their hearts and lungs fought to catch up with their limbs.

"And let's face it," said Katie between breaths, still hunched over, resting her hands atop her knees. She stood up with a deep exhale as she readied her final thought. "Are you *really* willing to believe that all *this* is nothing but an accident?" She nodded in the direction she faced.

Charlie, who was apparently in poorer shape than she, was still hunched over catching his breath as he turned to see where she was gazing.

The earth vanished before their eyes, only to reappear some four hundred feet below, spread out in all directions. The gilded rays of the morning sun gave fire to the clouds hovering overhead before pouring down on the trees below, many of which had begun to change color. Wide streams cut through the trees, pouring into a glassy lake in the valley spread out before their eyes, all of it reflecting the glory of creation.

Charlie exhaled a gasp of air when he saw it, as though someone had punched him in the gut. He could not help but laugh. He had climbed that steep ascent only to be robbed of his breath by the view, and he was beaming. The war that had raged between his head and his heart was finally ending. His heart was thawing.

But there remained one last battle to be waged.

After several minutes of panting, the two sat down on three logs that had been placed in such a way that hikers could relax and enjoy the view. Katie sat with her legs stretched out, crossed at the ankles, with hands on either side of her. Her knee had begun to scab over, although it still looked painful to Charlie as he sat catching his breath.

"Okay," Charlie asked, exhaling a deep gust of wind. Katie turned to look at him, her face radiant with morning sunlight. "So what do you do about the fossil record?"

"What about it?" asked Katie.

"Well, for one, humans don't show up in the record until only a few million years ag—"

Katie tilted her head in disappointment as she looked at him. Charlie caught himself.

"Okay, fine, we don't show up in the record until what *looks* like a few million years ago." Katie nodded in affirmation.

He continued, "So, if, standing where we're at, the earth looks not just a few million, but *billions* of years old, then why don't humans show up earlier in the fossil record if, in fact, we've always existed?"

Katie smiled at him, then looked around at the ground behind her. Twisting her torso, she reached around and pulled out a rock that was about the size of a tennis ball. She then bent her legs and held the rock at knee height. She dropped it on the ground in between her feet.

"Suppose I tried to derive a theory of gravity from that," she said. "How accurate do you think that theory would be?"

Charlie was confused, but by now he'd learned that he wasn't going to get a straight answer from this girl, so he happily played along. "Not very accurate."

Katie picked up the rock and dropped it three more times in the same way. "Now suppose I tried to derive a theory of gravity from those observations. How accurate would that theory be?"

Charlie was beginning to catch on. "Well, probably more accurate than the first, but still not great."

"Okay, fine," she said, playfully pretending to be upset by his statement that her theory wasn't great. "Let's say that I got some really fancy measuring equipment that allowed me to measure both the mass of this rock, and how long it takes it to fall to the ground.

Now how accurate would my theory be?"

"Probably the best you've come up with," said Charlie.

"Great!" said Katie. "You ready to get going?" she said as she got up and started down the steep ascent.

Charlie sat bewildered, and he wondered if Katie had gone a little mad. "Wait! Where are you going?" He asked as he hurried to catch up with her.

"Back to the car. Where else?" she said hastily, still walking in front of him.

"But you didn't answer my question," Charlie protested as he finally caught up with her.

"Didn't I?" asked Katie, turning to look at him with a grin on her face as the two walked down the steep, rocky hill side-by-side.

Charlie stared back at her as they walked. What had he missed?

"You know," said Katie, "when I was seventeen years old, my grandmother passed away."

"Did *she* become a fossil?" Charlie asked, his snarky tone a retaliation for Katie's sudden get-up-and-go.

Katie's eyes glared at him, but she was still grinning. "We had her funeral the morning of the following Saturday, with a reception at the house she and my grandpa had lived in.

"Later in the evening, after everyone had left, my family and I found ourselves in the attic going through my grandma's things: old photo albums, her wedding gown, things my dad and his siblings had made for her as part of their school projects.

"One of the things I stumbled across was this old box of Polaroid photographs. Most of them had labels on them. My dad's first birthday party, my aunt's baptism…

"But there was this one photo that had no label, no inscription whatsoever. It was a photo of my grandma in her late twenties, sitting on the lap of a very handsome man, with her arms wrapped affectionately around his shoulders as she kissed him on the cheek. Based on the ring clearly visible on my grandma's finger, she was married to my grandpa at the time."

Katie paused, turning to look at Charlie. "So, Charlie, did my grandma cheat on my grandpa?"

"What?" Charlie asked, staring back at her like she'd lost her mind. "How could I *possibly* know that from a single photograph?"

"Exactly," said Katie, reassuring Charlie that she hadn't gone insane as the two resumed their descent. "Do you know what it takes for something to become fossilized?"

They were finally getting back to his question. This was encouraging. "Not really," said Charlie.

"Well, first of all, the animal needs to basically die and fall into something like a tar pit, some quicksand, or a riverbed where it can be almost immediately covered. Otherwise, it would've just been gobbled up by another creature, bones and all, and we'd have no trace of it."

"Okay…" said Charlie, racking his brain to see if he could figure out where she was going with all this.

"So, Charlie," said Katie, "do you think tar pits and quicksand were like an ancient Starbucks or McDonald's: one on every street corner?"

Charlie smiled at her analogy. "Probably not."

"Right," said Katie. "So what does that say about the probability of an animal being fossilized?"

Now Charlie saw where she was going. "That the chances are pretty slim."

"Exactly," said Katie. "So what does *that* say about the nature of the fossil record?"

Charlie stopped on the trail, staring straight ahead at the abundantly green foliage as he tried to piece it all together.

After giving him almost a minute, Katie softly broke the silence. "It's a photograph," she said.

Now it was all coming together. "Which means we can't really rely on it to tell us about our past because it's not the full story," said Charlie, the energy in his heart now burning.

"Exactly," said Katie, as the two started walking again, "and the quality of the theory depends on the quality of the observations."

They passed the spot where Katie had fallen, careful now to avoid the stealthy rock.

"What did the photo of my grandma *really* tell you?" she asked.

"That your grandma sat in the lap of a good-looking guy and gave him a kiss on the cheek," he said.

"Yup!" said Katie, walking with a spring in her step as they neared the trailhead. "And the fossil record, what does *it* really tell you?"

Charlie stopped again, pausing to think about the fossil record as a photograph. "That things once roamed the earth that aren't around anymore," he said, looking at Katie for confirmation.

"Yup!" she said, beaming at him before resuming their

descent. "That's it. The fossil record doesn't preclude the existence of other creatures in the past. It's just biased toward species with large populations. So the more of a certain creature there is, the more likely it is that the creature would've made it into the fossil record."

The two emerged from the tree cover into a sun that was now high overhead and made their way to Katie's car. Judging by the sun's position in the sky, it was now late morning.

For the first time he could remember, Charlie felt *alive*. The blood in his veins pumped with passion. The warmth of the morning sun felt more invigorating than it had before. The sound of birdsong coming from the surrounding trees gave voice to the chorus in his soul.

The two drove back in silence as Charlie continued to process their conversation.

"You're smiling," said Katie, having taken her eyes off the road to look at him.

Charlie was suddenly aware of himself again. His facial muscles were quite sore. He had been smiling for quite some time.

"I guess I am," he said, not for a second losing the grin stretched across his face. His heart had thawed. His soul was awake.

5

By the Moonlight

———— ❧ ————

It had been almost two weeks since Katie left Charlie at his apartment after their hike through the Shenandoah forest. Though the two had met up several times on campus and in coffee shops for what could hardly be described as dates, Charlie had not had Katie to himself for more than an hour since that Saturday morning, and his soul ached with longing to hear her, to hold her, to be with her, as he rode his bike along University Avenue to the Rotunda, where the two had agreed to meet before they last parted ways.

The dome of the Rotunda came into view as Charlie passed the Corner. His heart's longing to be with Katie only increased with every push of his pedal as he pressed on, climbing the shallow ascent as he passed the Corner and the street leveled out on the north side of the Rotunda.

After waiting for a navy blue Mercedes Benz to pass him in the opposite lane, Charlie turned off the road, pulling into the shadow of the tall dome and dismounting his bike as he rode it one-footed-ly to the bike rack. Desperate to see Katie, Charlie hurriedly locked his bike, growing irritated with himself as he fumbled with the chain, then with the padlock. But when he turned to see his brown-haired beauty standing in the shadow of Thomas Jefferson's statue, the rest of the world and all of Charlie's irritation melted away. She smiled when she saw him, and the two met in the warmth of mutual embrace. Charlie's heart breathed a sigh of anxious relief as he held her in his arms.

"How *are* you?" asked Katie, leaning back from their hug as she tilted her head to look Charlie in the eye.

Charlie smiled back at her. "Much better now," he said as he stared deep into her eyes, his heartache soothed by the radiance of her smile.

"C'mon," she said, pulling him by the hand, "I'm starving."

Charlie resisted her pull, longing to spend just another minute or two in the stillness of her arms. Katie smiled as she continued to pull him, and Charlie's heart eventually gave in to the hunger of Katie's stomach. He jogged a few paces to catch up with her, wrapping his arm around her as the young lovers slowly made their way to the Bluegrass Pub.

When they arrived at the Pub, Charlie opened the door with his free hand and guided Katie through. Once inside, the two of them found each other's hand as they made their way to the hostess stand where, on a large black sign in white serif font, were the words: "Please Wait to Be Seated."

"Be right with you," came the nasally voice of the hostess who looked up only long enough to see them before returning her stare to her stand, where she was scribbling notes on a piece of paper. With a definitive pounding of the pen against her pad to form the final period in her notes, the hostess looked up once again at the young couple waiting for a seat.

She was an overweight curly-haired ginger with a permanent scowl fixed to her face. "Just the two of you?" she asked, forcing a smile.

"Yeah, just the two of us," said Charlie with a smile, still holding Katie's hand.

"Right this way," sighed the hostess as she grabbed two menus and showed them to a booth near the front of the restaurant.

Charlie had been to the Pub many times before with other "dates," but this time was different. Perhaps it was the girl he was with, or maybe just the effect that their conversation the Saturday before had on his soul, but whatever the case, Charlie drank in the Pub's old-fashioned charm with a new sense of admiration.

"Here you are," said the grumpy red-head as she set their menus down on the table and stepped back to allow them to slide in. Katie slid in the seat that faced the back of the restaurant, and Charlie took the seat that faced the front. Through the large glass panes that composed the front of the restaurant, Charlie could see the sunset glowing on the famous dome of the Rotunda as evening settled once again over Charlottesville.

When the two of them sat down, Charlie's attention turned from admiration of his surroundings to an admiration of the woman sitting across from him. Sensing that she was being watched, Katie looked up from her menu and caught his gaze. She smiled at him with a giggle.

"What?" she asked. Charlie just continued to stare at her, smiling from ear to ear.

"Hi there," came the southern twang of their waitress as she came and stood beside them. "My name's Shaantai, and I'll be your server for the evenin'."

Shaantai was a rather short girl with curly black hair and dark brown eyes. In accord with the Pub's dress code, she wore black pants and a black shirt, but the pen with which she scribbled her tables' orders had forest green tape wrapped around it with a large flower at the top. She was a girl who, though choked in the mundanity of a dress code, had found a way to let her inner spunk shine for the world to see.

"How's *your* night going?" asked Katie as she smiled at Shaantai.

"Ah, ya know, it's good, thanks. How 'bout y'all?"

Katie turned and smiled at Charlie. "We're doing *great*."

"That's good," said Shaantai. "Can I get y'all started with some water or somethin'?"

"You want a beer?" asked Charlie.

"Mmm, I think I'm okay," said Katie. "I'm already kinda tired. Just water for me, please," she said, turning to face their waitress.

"You got it, sweetheart," said Shaantai, turning to Charlie.

"Water for me too, then," said Charlie.

"Two waters, comin' right up!" Shaantai spun around toward the back of the restaurant and took off.

"So, I'm curious," said Katie, "why did you choose architecture and not something like philosophy?"

Shaantai arrived back with their drinks and set the two dripping glasses of water on the table. "Ooooh-kay," she said, "do you kids know what you wanna order?"

Charlie nodded in Katie's direction. Katie turned her head to look up at Shaantai as she spoke. "I'll have the bleu bacon cheeseburger with sweet potato fries," she said.

"You got it, sweetheart. And for you?" Shaantai asked, turning her head toward Charlie, her flower pen waiting to scribble down his order on her mint-green pad.

"I'll do the same," said Charlie, without looking up at Shaantai. He was again in awe of Katie's choice of meat over salad.

"You guys are easy," said Shaantai as she finished scribbling down their order and took their menus. "I'll have those burgers right up!"

As Shaantai departed, Katie turned her attention to Charlie. She had not forgotten her earlier question. "So, c'mon!" said Katie as she finished taking a sip of water. "I wanna know why you chose architecture!"

"I mean," said Charlie, stammering as he tried to piece together a cohesive answer. "I guess…when I was five years old, my parents bought me this Lego kit—you know, the ones that you have to piece together?"

Katie nodded, smiling with interest.

"The kit was built for ages nine and up, but I managed to put it together in less than a week."

"That's awesome!" said Katie, beaming.

"Yeah," said Charlie, bashful at her admiration of him. "And then once I'd put it together the way the instructions said, I took it apart and built something new."

Charlie's face dawned a smile as he immersed himself in the

memory of his childhood. "I spent weeks cooped up in my room, building and rebuilding this kit in as many different ways as I could muster. And each time I'd finished another build, I'd run out to my mom's office, grab her hand, and pull her back into my bedroom to see what I'd built.

"She never once told me she was busy, even though I knew she was. She always had time to come and look," he said.

"That's wonderful," said Katie as she reached across the table and wrapped her hand around his.

"Yeah," said Charlie, "I guess I've just always liked to build stuff, so when it came time to choose a major, architecture was the obvious choice."

"So, you're close with your parents?" Katie asked.

Charlie felt a bolt of pain shoot through his heart as his smile quickly faded. Unsure if he winced, Charlie pulled his hand away under the guise of unrolling his napkin and putting it in his lap. Softly, he answered her question, averting her gaze. "They're not really in the picture," he mumbled.

"I'm sorry," she said, her tone soft and sensitive.

The two sat in silence for several minutes until Shaantai returned with two plates in hand, each of them holding mountainous burgers and a truckload of sweet potato fries. "Okay, here you go," she said as she set them down. "Can I get you kids anythin' else?"

"No," said Katie, her voice still soft, "I think we're good. Thanks, Shaantai."

"You bet, darlin'. You just let me know if there's anythin' else you kids need." Shaantai then returned to the back of the restaurant as Katie and Charlie began to eat their food in silence.

They'd both just finished their first bites when a sound that echoed like the thud of a bass drum bellowed through the restaurant, taking the lights down with it. Patrons who'd been watching the football game exhaled loud cries of lament. The only light left in the Pub came from the candles at each of the booths.

Forgetting the awkwardness of before, Katie and Charlie grinned at each other, Katie's eyes filled with excitement at the prospect of another adventure.

Shaantai hurried back to their table. "Uhhh," she said, "I'm not sure what to do, here." She looked around as though searching for a solution. "All the registers are down," she said.

Katie pulled out her wallet to give Shaantai some cash.

"Nope, I got this," said Charlie, hurriedly finishing a bite as he pulled out the wallet he had double- and triple-checked he had with him this time.

"You sure?" asked Katie.

"Yeah. I owe you dinner, remember?" said Charlie, smiling.

Katie of course remembered, but as was the case just two weeks ago in the coziness of Julienne's, Katie had no expectation of repayment. It was clear that she did not believe in tit-for-tat, but radiated generosity.

"Can we get boxes for these?" asked Charlie, handing Shaantai almost double what the food was worth.

"Sure!" she said. "Do you need any change?"

"No, that's alright," said Charlie. "I hope that makes up for any lost tips tonight, with the power being out and all."

"Thank you, thank you very much!" she said, her eyes excited as she turned on her heels.

Charlie smiled at her as she hurried off to retrieve some boxes, then turned his head to see Katie beaming at him. "What?" asked Charlie, smiling.

"You had *great* parents," said Katie.

Charlie smiled. He felt no pain this time, no need to avert his gaze. It was his parents who had taught him to always be kind to those who served him, and it was a lesson that, even in his darkest and most selfish days, Charlie had still carried with him.

Less than two minutes later, Shaantai was back with boxes. "Are you sure ya don't want any change?"

"Yes, I'm quite sure," said Charlie, chuckling at their spunky waitress.

"Well, thank you again," she said. "Y'all have a wonderful night, okay?"

"Thanks Shaantai," said Katie. "You too."

The two of them then packed up their food and carried it out onto University Avenue. The entire street was dark; not a light could be seen, save for the headlights of the occasional car.

"C'mon," said Katie, grabbing Charlie's hand and taking the lead as she pulled him across the street, her voice filled with the thrill of adventure.

"Where are we going?" asked Charlie, gently resisting her pull.

"Just trust me," said Katie as she stepped up onto the other side of University Avenue. By now, Charlie was used to Katie taking charge in their relationship, and he knew that he could trust her to do so.

They made their way through one of the breezeways between the old student dorms that formed the borders of the Academical

Village and emerged onto the Lawn, a sprawling expanse of open grass lined by maple and elm trees with the Rotunda at one end and Old Cabell Hall at the other, and the school's first student dorms on either side. The entire place was dark, lit only by the moonlight.

As Katie pulled Charlie out into the middle of the Lawn, he noticed movement between the old dorms. Students were walking back and forth between their rooms, some of them with flashlights, panicked at the loss of power.

"Sit," she commanded. Charlie turned his head to stare at Katie, now sitting on the lawn, still holding his hand as she looked up at him.

Smiling at her sense of authority, Charlie sat, and the two began to eat. Several minutes later, burgers and fries were nothing but droplets of barbecue sauce and a mix of salt and crumbs.

Pounding gently on her chest as she exhaled her stomach's fullness, Katie inadvertently let out a small belch. She looked at Charlie, her face slightly embarrassed by her slip. Charlie just laughed, relieving her of any embarrassment. She then gathered their boxes and set them off to the side, laying back in the grass. "C'mere," she said.

Charlie's heart pounded in his chest. Was she asking what he thought she was asking? Not to say that he hadn't done it plenty of times before, but this time was different. If he screwed up this kiss, it meant much more than just the loss of a weekend bed-warmer. If he screwed up *this* time, it meant losing a girl he longed to be with for more than just a one-night stand.

Fighting to suppress the tension mounting in his chest, Charlie leaned back in the grass, laying down on his side next to this brown-haired beauty as he stared at the contours of her face, the softness of her skin glowing in the evening moonlight.

"Look!" said Katie, her voice full of excitement as she pointed up at the sky.

Charlie rolled onto his back as he turned his gaze skyward. His lungs and heart lost their rhythm. The sky above them was ablaze with galactic glory. It looked as though a shaker had spilled glowing grains of salt across the deep blue canvas spread out before them, mixed with the watercolors softly radiating from the nebulae of distant galaxies.

"Wow!" said Charlie, caught up in the wonder dancing across the sky before them.

"Isn't it wonderful!" came Katie's voice in a soft whisper.

The two lay with hands behind their heads, staring up at the night sky for what felt like hours. As the initial childlike awe faded, Charlie tilted his head just enough to whisper in Katie's direction.

"To be honest," he said, "when you asked me to lay back with you, I thought you were asking me to make out. But *this*," he said hushly, turning his gaze skyward once again, "wow!"

Charlie turned to look at Katie again when he heard the sound of her shuffling in the grass. She had scooted herself closer to him, nestling her body against his. As she laid her head atop his shoulder, Charlie wrapped his arm around her and the two continued to gaze up at the heavenly artwork splashed across the canvas on display before their eyes.

But as great as the evening splendor in the night sky was, it was nothing compared to the symphony in Charlie's heart when this girl was in his arms. His heart beat with more vigor to a new rhythm, charged with affection for this girl who, with all her emotional depth, would somehow manage to always come out on top in their philosophical discussions. Katie was someone who did not spend her days merely *thinking* about what she believed; she actually experienced and lived it.

"You wanna go somewhere?" Katie whispered softly.

Peering down, Charlie stared into Katie's eyes as her head tilted back on his shoulder and her eyes stared up at him. Charlie answered without hesitation. "I'll go anywhere with you."

"C'mon!" Katie said, whispering with excitement as she stood up and pulled Charlie to his feet.

Still holding his hand, she pulled him up the Lawn, toward the Rotunda. "C'*mon!*" she said as Charlie lagged behind, his heart shining through his face as she led him on yet another adventure.

Charlie just smiled as the two hastily made their way to the steps of the Rotunda. When they reached the top, Katie spun around, gazing again at the night sky as Charlie wrapped his arms around her, no longer concerned with the glory above but saturating himself instead in the glory of the woman he held in his arms.

"Look!" said Katie. "Isn't it beautiful?"

"It sure is," said Charlie, gazing not at the stars, but at the beauty in his arms.

Katie spun around in his arms to face him. "You're not even looking, are you?"

Charlie smiled, gazing into her eyes. "It's prettier down here," he said.

Katie's eyes melted as she wrapped her arms around his neck.

"Charlie Shaw…" she said with an all-too-familiar grin of mischief on her face as she closed her eyes and slowly rose to her tiptoes, welcoming the advance of Charlie's lips.

Hearts pounding and passion burning, their lips met for the first time on the steps of the Rotunda under the spectacle of evening majesty on display above them. Sparks flew and electricity shot through their veins as tongues interlocked and they pressed their lips together, again and again, their hearts full yet longing for more. Charlie had never before felt what he felt that night. In the past, Charlie had seen kissing only as foreplay: an excuse to begin removing clothing as tongues teased for something more.

But this, this was different. For the first time in his life, Charlie did not want something *from* Katie; he simply wanted *her*—all of her, forever, every day. In that moment, Charlie had a taste not of earthly lustful pleasure, but of eternal magnificence, and it brought new breath to the stale air of his soul.

Katie's hands released their grip behind Charlie's neck as she gently slid her right arm down his left, still pressing her lips to his. Their hands met, and she slid a small piece of paper into the palm of Charlie's hand, closing his fingers around it.

"Mm," said Charlie, breaking their bond. "What's this?"

"Open it," said Katie, smiling at him. The two turned to look at the small piece of paper together as Charlie unfolded it in his hand. His eyes then locked with Katie's as the two smiled at each other. There was no need for words; their hearts said it all. Charlie again wrapped his arms around her, pulling her gently into his embrace as the two stood atop the stone steps in a warm hug that only scratched the surface of their mutual affection.

There, by the moonlight on the steps of the Rotunda, Katie had slipped her number into Charlie's hand.

6

Poker Face

———— ❧ ————

THE CHIME OF THE DOORBELL interrupted Charlie's train of thought as he sat hunched over at his desk, holding a pen in his hand. He paused, his pen still pressed to the pages of his journal, bleeding ink into their fibers as he listened for the faintest sound of movement.

"Hey Mike, can you get that?" Charlie called. The apartment was silent, save for the tick, tock, of a small clock that Charlie kept on his desk.

Frustrated by the interruption, Charlie gently slammed his pen down on the book sitting open on his desk and made his way to the door. As he passed Michael's room, Charlie glanced in to find his roommate passed out on his bed. His hands were interlocked, resting atop his sternum, with his head propped up on two pillows, pushing his chin into his chest while his feet, clad with workman's boots, rested atop his footboard.

Charlie smiled and shook his head, continuing his trek to the door. Mike had returned from Boston earlier that afternoon, and he was exhausted. The Cavaliers had lost their game the night before, which meant that they'd be running extra laps at practice. Mike needed the rest, and the more steps Charlie took from the pages of his journal, the more he became okay with Mike's nap.

Glancing through the peephole, Charlie got a very wide-angle view of Louis, staring down at the parking lot and tapping his foot with irritation as he held in front of him with both hands the small nickel-hued metal box that housed his grandfather's poker set.

Louis was a scrawny man with narrow eyes and a short, thin mustache on his upper lip. He had coffee brown hair that was usually covered by something resembling a flat-cap that he (of course) purchased in a store no one had ever heard of. He wore black, square-rimmed glasses and jeans that were too skinny for most men, with a pair of beat up wing-tip oxford shoes and a cardigan that covered most of the t-shirt that probably bore the logo of some obscure band.

With a twist of the deadbolt and a turn of the knob, Charlie opened the door to greet his friend.

"Hey, Lou," he said.

"What took you so long?" said Louis, smacking his gum as he stared back at Charlie with a smirk.

"Uh," Charlie stammered, "I was in the middle of somethin'."

Lou narrowed his eyes, peering at Charlie as he attempted to read the emotional state of his opponent for the evening, his mouth still fixed in a gum-smacking smirk. "Well where the hell's Michael? Poker night starts at seven." Once a month, Charlie and Mike would host poker night at their apartment, and each of the guys in attendance would boast about their exploits with the opposite sex.

Charlie smiled in the doorway as he stared into Lou's eyes, knowing all too well what Louis would do once he learned of Mike's whereabouts. "Mike's in his room. Asleep."

Charlie paused as he watched the mischief glaze over Louis's eyes. "I'm gonna go wrap something up," said Charlie. "I'll be right with you."

Louis came in and laid his poker set atop the kitchen table that was just inside the door. He then surveyed the room, getting himself acclimated to its "aura," while Charlie returned to his bedroom to put the last words to the latest entry in the journal he'd used on and off for almost a decade to hash out what he was feeling.

Entries had been sparse for the last three years. In fact, Charlie had not written in the pages of this small book since he first arrived in Charlottesville to find that Herb and Eleanor, the only two people he had left in the world, were dead and gone.

Sitting down at his desk, Charlie picked up his pen once again and began to read the last few lines he had written to get himself back in his train of thought. He continued where he'd left off:

"I simply cannot describe to you what I felt last night as my lips pressed against hers. It was deeper than a desire for sex. I wanted *her*. But in the midst of all of this, I cannot shake this persistent anxiety deep in my heart, and I don't know why. Every time I wake up and throughout the day, this anxiety presses on my heart, not obnoxiously, but subtly, like a small pin poking a distant corner of my being, and I don't know what it is. This is not my first rodeo with a woman, and I know I can commit because I've done that before. But I didn't feel this anxiety with them, and I don't understand it. Nevertheless, the excitement in my soul overwhelms my anxiety. This girl really is something else, and I can't wait to see where this leads."

Charlie had just pressed the pen to form the final dot in his journal entry when he heard a bellowing shout from the other room: "*Lou-WISS!*" Charlie knew that roar all too well, and leaned sideways in his chair to peer down the hall and watch what was about to ensue.

The hallway had barely come into view when Charlie saw Louis dart from Michael's room, marker in hand, turning to look back at his dreary pursuer. His eyes became wide as golf balls when he saw the angry giant he'd awoken, and he hurried frantically off into the main room to hide behind the kitchen table.

Grinning ear-to-ear, Charlie closed his journal and capped his pen. As he stood up, he stared once again down the hallway just in time to see Michael emerge from his room. Mike looked first in Charlie's direction, his face in a scowl with half a French mustache drawn on his upper lip.

"Where *IS* he!?" Mike roared.

Charlie pointed in the direction of the main room.

"Louis, I'm gonna *KILL* you!" Mike yelled, stepping toward the main room: fee-fi-fo-fum.

"Charlie told me to do it!" came the soft-toned, hasty voice of Louis.

Michael glared back at Charlie, scowling with a half-mustached face as he searched for the truth.

Charlie smiled, fighting laughter. "*I* just told him you were asleep," said Charlie matter-of-factly, putting his hands in his pockets as he leaned against the door jam to his room.

Michael turned his glare back in Louis's direction and continued his march.

Charlie stepped out of his lean against the door jam and hurried after Michael to prevent another man from being hurled through the wall.

By the time Charlie caught up with him, Mike was standing opposite the kitchen table from Louis. Cowering in the shadow of a six-foot-eight, two-hundred-eighty-pound lineman had stripped Lou of his confidence. His cunning grin had vanished, and he looked as though he'd seen a ghost.

Reaching up, Charlie put his hand on Mike's shoulder and gently began to massage it. "Relax, Mike. It's a good look on you." Mike turned sharply, glaring at Charlie, but Charlie knew him too well to be afraid.

"Besides, I'm *sure* Lou would be happy to buy the pizza tonight to make up for it," said Charlie, turning to Louis. "Right, Lou?" Now Charlie was the one smirking.

"Eh, right!" said Lou, smiling nervously and nodding frantically, hoping to spare himself of Michael's retaliation.

"Hmph." Michael snorted, exhaling his anger as he turned back toward the bedrooms. Charlie watched him go.

Once Michael had disappeared into the bathroom, Charlie turned back to Louis. Charlie's face went from smile to grin as laughter bubbled up inside him. Lou's did the same, and together, the two burst out laughing.

"*Shudd-UP!*" came Michael's bellow from the bathroom. That silenced the two of them, especially Louis, though they both still wore grins of mischief on their faces.

The chime of the doorbell quickly reset the mood. Charlie and Lou both made their way to the door and opened it to find Cooper standing cool in the evening breeze with two six-packs in hand and a brown bag under his arm. Cooper was an art history major in his junior year. His clean-shaven head was covered by a black wool beanie, and his face sported a beard that would've made the Vikings jealous. He wore his usual attire: a pair of dark straight-leg jeans, black Fry boots and a poly-cotton t-shirt that, together with Cooper's carefully tailored cocktail of subtle scents, made hugging him quite the enjoyable experience, especially for the many women who made their way through Cooper's life.

"Evening, gentlemen," came his soothing voice as he stepped inside and put the alcohol on the kitchen counter. "Charlie, I got the Belgian white you requested, and then I got Michael's favorite IPA, because we all know we don't wanna piss him off…"

"Yeah, Lou," said Charlie without looking at him.

Ignoring them, Cooper continued. "And for the rest of us…" he said, breaking a bottle out of the brown bag, "a Highland single malt."

Charlie was no longer listening. He had retrieved a bottle opener from the kitchen drawer and was in the process of opening his first beer for the evening when another chime of the doorbell pulled him away. It was the pizza delivery man.

"Lou," said Charlie from the door, "pizza's here."

Louis looked at Charlie as though about to protest the duress of their earlier agreement when Michael reentered the room, his upper lip red from the vigorous scrubbing it had just undergone.

Standing again in Michael's shadow, Lou hurried lightly to the door, breaking out his wallet and handing the pizza delivery man two twenties.

"Thanks, Lou," said Charlie with a satisfied glee, smirking at Lou while he handed over his cash to the delivery man.

Louis glared back at him. "Anytime, Charlie."

Charlie then took the pizza from the delivery man and closed the door. He had barely set them down on the kitchen counter when the doorbell chimed again.

"Can one of you guys get that?" asked Charlie as he pulled down a stack of plates.

Michael made his way to the door and swung it open. It seemed easier for him than it was for Charlie and Louis, almost as though he might rip it from its hinges.

"Hey Mike," came Trent's low and sullen voice as he stepped through the door. "How's it goin'?"

"Ask Lou," growled Mike as he closed the door. Louis's hand found the counter as he tried to remain cool, projecting confidence to his would-be opponents.

Trent was a second-year running back who'd been recruited from out west to play for the Cavaliers with Mike, though he looked like a young boy standing in Mike's shadow (as most men did).

The guys each grabbed several slices of pizza and their desired beverage for the evening, then sat around the table as Louis unpacked the chips and began to shuffle the cards.

"So, Charlie," Louis said as he split the cards, "tell us about your latest conquest."

Charlie could be a master of manipulation when he wanted to, especially when it came to finding women to warm his bed. Sitting around the poker table with these guys was the only time Charlie ever laid his hand out there for anyone to see, and they thoroughly enjoyed hearing of his exploits with the opposite sex.

"Her name's *Katie*," taunted Mike as he took a sip of his IPA.

At the mention of Katie's name, Charlie found himself defensive. Fortunately, his tactics with the opposite sex came in handy for maintaining his composure in the face of his opponents, and Charlie just played along.

"Yup, her name's Katie," he said after swallowing a bite of food.

"Alright boys," said Louis as he finished shuffling the cards. "No limit Texas Hold 'Em, five- and ten-dollar blinds."

Cooper and Trent, who were seated to Lou's left, tossed in their bets, and after arranging the three red chips in a neat little stack, Louis began to deal the cards.

"So, Charlie," said Lou, trying to elicit a reaction from his most formidable opponent, "you shagged this girl yet?"

Anger began to bubble in Charlie's veins, but he remained silent, not making eye contact with Louis as he picked up his cards from the table. He'd been dealt a nine of hearts and an eight of clubs.

Curious at Charlie's lack of response, Louis turned to Mike. "Mike, has Charlie shagged this girl or what?"

Mike looked at Charlie. "Not here," he said. "But I wasn't here last night, so I dunno." Michael knew Charlie better than anyone else around the table, but when it came to poker, Mike could not read him.

"Hmph," said Lou, picking up his cards. "Alright, Charlie, turn falls to you."

"I'll raise," said Charlie, tossing a green chip in the pot.

"Ho-*ho*!" said Michael, stomping his feet as he reeled at Charlie's move. Michael struggled to keep his cool during poker, which made him an easy read for Charlie and everyone else around the table.

When Michael didn't play his turn right away, Lou encouraged him. "Mike?" Mike darted a glare at Louis, and that shut him up.

"Call," said Mike, laying a green chip in the center of the table. He then leaned back in his chair, satisfied with his move as he took a sip of his beer.

The turn fell to Louis, who paused as he peered around at his opponents, seeking both to read and intimidate them with the weight of his stare. "I'll call," said Lou, setting another green chip in the pot and turning to Cooper.

Cooper took a sip of his scotch, swishing it between his teeth before he swallowed in a wince. "Ahhh," he said as he looked at his cards. "So tell me, Charlie: how long have you been seeing this Katie girl?"

Charlie looked back at Cooper with a face that said he knew what Cooper was up to. "Just play your turn, Coop," he said, shaking his head as he took another bite of his pizza.

"Touchy, touchy," said Cooper as he turned to Louis, picking up four red chips in his hand.

Knowing full well that splashing irritated Louis, Cooper tossed his chips into the pot, making a mess of it as he watched Louis squirm. "Call," said Cooper with a look of pleasure on his face. Cooper liked to find people's buttons and push them on occasion, especially when he wanted to elicit a reaction, and he knew that the OCD-plagued Louis could not help but react.

Louis was quick to tidy the chips as the turn fell to Trent. "I fold," said Trent, almost immediately after Cooper tossed his chips into the pot. Like Mike, Trent was an easy read and always folded, unless he held a straight flush or higher. The boys had learned quickly that if Trent raised, they had better fold.

Louis then laid the flop on the table: a seven of diamonds, a three of clubs, and a two of spades.

"Alright boss," said Louis as he turned to Cooper, "your move."

Cooper took another sip of his scotch, swishing it in his mouth and swallowing again with a wince. "Ahhh," he said as he picked up one green chip and two reds. "Thirty-five," he said, tossing them into the pot and making a mess that again made Louis cringe.

"Really though, how long you been seein' this girl?" asked Cooper.

Charlie paid him no mind, and set two red chips and a green chip in the middle of the table. "Call," he said as he sat back in his chair, avoiding Cooper's piercing gaze as he took a sip of his beer.

Mike looked at Charlie, trying to see what was really going on in his roommate's heart.

"I fold," said Mike. Cooper paid him no mind, keeping his stare fixed on Charlie.

"And I," said Louis, "will call." He then laid his chips down in the pot and began to clean it up, stacking the chips according to their color.

"Alright boys," Louis continued. "Two-hundred *fifteen* dollars in the pot," he said as he laid the fourth card down on the table. It was a five of clubs.

Cooper's stare was hot on Charlie. "How *long* have you been seeing this girl?" he asked.

Charlie was silent as his stare moved from his cards to the cards on the table and back again.

"Mike," said Cooper, irritated with Charlie's lack of response, "how long has Charlie been seeing this girl?"

"Uhhh…" said Mike. If there was one thing that Mike did not know, it was when to shut up. "Just over two weeks, I think."

"Two *weeks!?*" said Louis. "And you still haven't sealed the deal?"

Anger now boiled in Charlie's veins at the way Louis talked about Katie. His words were nothing new. Louis had always talked about Charlie's conquests in a grotesque, objectifying manner. But Katie was different, and Charlie knew it. He was just hoping he could hide his sentiment from the rest of the table.

"Oh, my, God!" said Cooper as he chuckled, leaning back in his chair with a smile. "You actually *like* this girl, don't you?"

"Just shut up and play your turn," Charlie snapped, irritated by the gleeful smirk on Cooper's face as he sat back in his chair, his eyes still staring intensely at Charlie.

"Okay, fine," said Cooper as he leaned forward and pulled not one, not two, but three green chips from his pile and tossed them into the pot. (Louis cringed again.) "Seventy-five," he said, staring hotly at Charlie to see what he would do.

Charlie stared at his cards, then up at the pot, then again at his cards. His heart pounded with frustration as he felt his cool facade melting away under the heat of Cooper's continued stare.

He looked up at each of his opponents, all anxiously awaiting Charlie's move. It seemed, though, that they were less concerned with the pot than they were with Katie. Had Charlie slept with her? Was he just keeping her around because the sex was incredible? Or had this woman finally averted Charlie's tactics and found her way beyond the facade of his exploits into the depths of his heart?

"Make your move, already!" said Louis, practically yelling.

Charlie again stared at them. Even Trent's curiosity was piqued by Charlie's lack of response.

"I fold," he said with a defeated face as he laid his cards down on the table.

"Aw, shit," said Michael, laughing as he slapped his hand on Charlie's shoulder.

Charlie just shook his head, glaring at his opponents. Cooper just smiled and laughed. Normally, Charlie walked away from poker nights with more of the pot than anyone else. That night, however, the boys had found the chink in his armor. That night, they had pierced his poker face.

7

Retaliation

CHARLIE MADE HIS WAY HASTILY down the narrow staircase of the Alderman Library, bumping up against its mint green metal walls as he chased after Katie, his footsteps louder with every anxious thud. He rounded the corner in the stairwell and began to skip stairs, fighting to keep up the chase.

"In here!" Katie whispered as Charlie stepped out of the stairwell onto the fourth floor in the basement.

Charlie slowed his pace, listening for another clue as he began to search the aisles between each of the bookcases. "Where!?" he whispered.

"Here," she said from right behind him.

Charlie spun around to see Katie, wearing her usual mischievous grin. He barely caught a glimpse, though, before Katie jumped him, wrapping her arms around his neck and pressing her lips passionately against his as they stumbled together down one of the aisles between the bookcases.

"I missed you," she said as her lips repeatedly captured and released him in small kisses.

The stacks reached almost to the ceiling, and the two finally came to rest hidden in the privacy that these tall bookcases afforded them. Katie's hands found a place on Charlie's hips while he placed one hand on the small of her back and the other against the aged spines of the books that were behind her.

"I missed you, too," he said, closing his eyes and forging a bond between their lips as his hand left the rough fabric of the old books and found the softness of Katie's skin.

He gently caressed the porcelain surface of her cheek, then tenderly brushed her hair behind her ear, all the while holding the bond of passionate intimacy between their lips.

The two paused, touching noses as they looked deeply, longingly into each other's eyes. Their eyelids then closed and they continued to taste each other's lips in ardent ecstasy for what felt like hours as their hands wandered over the thick layers of their clothing. It was early November in Charlottesville, and the cold chill of the outside air meant that autumn was in full swing and winter was on their doorstep.

Breaking their bond, Katie stared up into Charlie's eyes with a soft smile. "Are you hungry?" she asked.

Charlie broke their gaze and stared blankly at an old book about the Persian Empire that sat about a shelf and a half above Katie's head. He *was* hungry, but he hadn't thought much about it.

"Yeah," he said, "are you? We could do the Pub again. Or there's that new place with the subs on the Corner."

"I've got a better idea," said Katie as her eyes lit up with excitement.

"C'mon!" she said, her voice exhilarated at the prospect of another adventure with Charlie.

She pulled him by the hand up the narrow mint green staircase and out of the Alderman Library to her small, white sedan, parked outside on McCormick Road next to the old chapel.

"Are you kidnapping me again?" quipped Charlie as he followed closely behind her, still holding her hand.

"You wish," said Katie, smirking at him.

"I do, actually," Charlie said matter-of-factly as he chuckled.

Katie popped her trunk to reveal a caramel-colored whicker picnic basket and a red-and-white checkered blanket. "Let's have a picnic!" she said, her voice singing with excitement as she lifted the basket out of her car. The basket seemed almost as big as she was, and Charlie was quick to act.

"Here, I'll carry that," said Charlie, taking the basket from her.

The two of them then made their way down McCormick Road, through one of the breezeways between the old student dorms and out onto the grassy expanse where not too long ago they had lay in wonder at the display of heavenly glory in the skies above. Together, they found a spot on the grass about fifty yards from the Rotunda and spread out the checkered blanket on blades of grass that were now dried and yellowing in preparation for the cold ahead.

The elm and maple trees that ran the length of the lawn were in full autumn bloom, and many of their leaves had fallen to the ground as they prepared to enter yet another season of dormancy.

The two then sat down, and Katie opened the picnic basket to retrieve a large bottle of water and two plastic glasses. She poured each of them a drink, then pulled two large peanut butter and honey sandwiches and a small bowl of grapes out of the basket. "I hope you like this," she said, her voice tentative.

"I love it," said Charlie, brushing his hand behind her ear as he stole another kiss before unwrapping his sandwich.

The two began to eat, and as Charlie's mouth filled with the sticky sweetness of his first bite of the sandwich Katie had made him, he remembered a question he had wanted to ask her.

"You know what I don't get?" he said to Katie as he swallowed his first bite. She was in the process of stealing some grapes from the bowl.

"Hmm?" hummed Katie, her mouth full of food.

"Why wasn't Lela angry?" asked Charlie. "I mean, with everything she'd been through, all things God could have stopped if he wanted to. Why wasn't she angry?"

Katie chewed her food in silence as she thought about how best to answer Charlie's question.

"What does God require of us?" asked Katie as she swallowed her grapes.

"Well, there's a bunch of rules, aren't there?" Charlie responded before taking another bite of his sandwich.

"Yes, but only two that matter: Love God, and love others," said Katie. "That's it. Everything else follows naturally."

Her words rushed into Charlie's heart, soothing it like a flood of water in an arid drought-ridden land. For all the religious banter flung around in his grandparents' small, suburban, church-going community, they somehow seemed to have missed what Katie had stated so simply, so perfectly. It was the missing ingredient that made dry, crumbling chocolate chip cookies into rich, savory, melt-in-your-mouth treats.

"Okay," said Charlie, recovering from the sticky peanut butter and honey now making their way to his stomach, "so I get that, but how does that explain why Lela wasn't more angry with God?"

Katie sat quietly, again contemplating how to respond as she took a bite of her sandwich then licked the honey off her fingers.

"Did the Janjaweeds do what God requires?" she asked. "Did they love God and love Lela?"

At the outset of their relationship, Charlie would have been offended by such a question. To him, the answer was obvious. But through their now many discussions, Charlie had learned that Katie's questions held value. They helped him to consider his own assumptions and logical leaps that led to many of his conclusions, and to reconsider them if necessary.

"Of course not," said Charlie, his voice somber as he stared down at the blanket on which he sat.

"Right," said Katie. "Now Charlie, do you think *Lela* loved perfectly? Do you think she *always* loved God and loved others without fault?"

Charlie paused to consider her question. He did not know much about Lela, but he knew a great deal about human beings in general, and from what he saw, humans failed to love all the time. "I guess not," he said. "But that still didn't give the Janjaweeds the right to do what they did."

"I know," said Katie, treading softly. "But Charlie, if Lela herself had failed to love perfectly, how could she point the finger at anyone else for failing to love *her*?"

Charlie looked at Katie, expecting her to be kidding. She wasn't. Charlie's face darkened. "But what they *did!*" said Charlie, raising his voice. "I can't believe this! You're saying that because I or anyone else don't love perfectly, people are justified in doing bad things, *terrible* things, like *rape!*"

"No, Charlie," said Katie softly as he stood up, shaking with rage, "that's not what I'm saying." Her voice, too, was beginning to shake. She didn't know why Charlie was acting this way. (Neither did he.)

"I mean," he continued, "are you telling me that if I believe in Jesus that because I suck at loving others, that every bad thing that ever happened to me was *okay!?* Because that's *seriously* messed up."

Katie stood up, too, joining Charlie, who now had his back to Katie and had started taking several steps away from their blanket.

"*CHARLIE!*" yelled Katie, her voice shaking with a mix of confusion, hurt, and anger.

Charlie stopped, still refusing to turn around and face her as he held half a sandwich in his hand.

Her tone softened.

"What *happened* to them?" she asked, her voice laden with tears.

As the smallest seismic quake can cause the crack that breaks a dam, so Katie's words unleashed a torrent of emotion within Charlie's heart. His eyes watered over and tears began to roll down his cheeks. How did she know? How did she know that *they* were the reason he was so upset? With the skills of a most experienced carpenter, Katie had struck the nail precisely on its head.

Charlie turned to face her, tears now streaming down his face.

When Katie saw him, she ran and lunged herself into him, holding him as the dam burst and water cascaded out. Charlie dropped the sandwich in the grass as his arms found their way around Katie and he began to sob violently, his face contorting to the shape of his soul. She held him tightly in her arms, refusing to let go as emotions he had bottled up for years came tumbling down the mountainside with the force and might of an avalanche. His soul gasped for air, unable to keep its head above the downpour.

But Katie held him there, not letting go—refusing to let go— as he sobbed. There, in the grassy expanse of the Lawn, on a cold autumn afternoon, the walls that had so stalwartly defended Charlie's heart came tumbling down, sinking into their foundations as Charlie found that he was, for the first time, not alone in his grief. He had someone who was not only there as he grieved, but some- one who refused to let go, a woman who insisted on sharing his pain with him. In the midst of his anguish, Charlie knew that his soul had found a friend.

The cold autumn breeze grazed the skin beneath Charlie's eyes, threatening to freeze the salty tears that had just overflowed their banks. There were no tears left to cry, and yet Charlie contin- ued to sob, his soul still gasping for air. Katie's grip around Charlie was tight as ever as she buried her face in his sweater.

After an hour or so, Charlie let his hands fall to the side and Katie pulled her head back to gaze up at his tear-ridden face. She did not lessen her grip around his waist.

"Guh!" said Charlie on an exhale, wiping the streaks from his skin with his woolen sleeve.

Almost instinctively, Katie released her grip on his waist and, with one arm still wrapped around him, began to wipe the tear tracks from Charlie's face, the sleeve stretched over her fingers serving as her handkerchief. "I'm so sorry," she said softly as she tended to the wounds of his soul.

Charlie looked down at her, his eyes still aching. "But you don't even know what happened," he said.

Katie did not answer, but with tender care continued to clean his face. When she'd finished, she again wrapped her arms around him and nestled into his chest. Charlie's arms found their way around Katie, and the two stood there again for several minutes as Katie gently rocked him back and forth.

"Do you wanna know what happened?" asked Charlie softly. It was the first time he had ever invited someone into this corner of his heart, and for the first time, he was not scared. He felt strangely comfortable with Katie, more than he had with anyone before her.

"Only if you want to tell me," said Katie, gazing up at him with a small, soft smile, her eyes wreaking of heartache.

"C'mon," said Charlie, picking up his sandwich and walking with Katie back to the picnic blanket. A few dried up leaves had fallen on the blanket in their absence, almost as though the trees themselves were sharing in Charlie's grief.

Charlie sat with his legs crossed, his torso propped up by the arms that were outstretched behind him, his hands resting on the dry grass.

Katie sat next to Charlie, kneeling on her heels with her knuckles pressing into the blanket on either side of her. She faced him attentively, ready to listen.

"I grew up in Richmond," said Charlie, "though neither of my parents were from there." Charlie sniffled. "My dad was from a small suburb about an hour north of Birmingham, and my mom was from upstate New York. The two met in college, and when my dad got a job with the FBI after graduation, he was stationed in the Richmond field office. My mom joined him a month later, and that fall, the two of them got married.

"We all knew my dad's job was dangerous. When my sister and I were kids, my dad ran our family through drills, teaching us what to do if someone bad was in the house. We all knew where he kept his gun.

"His primary role at the FBI was investigating violent crimes, mostly gangs." Charlie paused, taking a deep breath, and continued on an exhale. "He helped to put away some of the biggest kingpins in the underground smuggling rings throughout Richmond: drugs, human trafficking, the works. But he made a lot of enemies along the way.

"One night in the summer after my freshman year of high school, I went to have a sleepover at my friend Zac's house. I still remember the smell of the perfume my mother wore that day as she drove me to his house. I keep a bottle of that perfume in a small box under my bed, though I've never opened it."

Charlie paused, looking at Katie and anticipating some judgment in her eyes for the treasure he kept. There was none to be found. Her eyes spoke of nothing but sorrowful compassion.

"I remember her face as she dropped me off," Charlie continued, "smiling at me from the car with the window down. As she began to back out, she said, 'I love you Charlie!' I was too cool to say it back." Charlie choked on his words.

"It was the last time I saw her alive."

Katie's eyes were now welling up with tears as she gently placed her hand on Charlie's leg.

"There was this gang in Richmond. They called themselves the Bloodhounds. Dealt mostly in human trafficking. My dad helped to put away some of their biggest players, costing them millions of dollars, and they wanted revenge.

"That night, while I slept in safety, two gang members from the Bloodhounds broke into my house. They tied my parents up and tortured them for hours. And after *that*, they took my sister, who was just seventeen at the time, and brutally raped her, my parents helpless to do anything to stop them."

Charlie paused as a fresh tear rolled down his cheek. Katie was quick to wipe it away.

"I still remember my friend's parents waking me up that night. I walked downstairs with them to find two Richmond policemen standing in their living room with my dad's partner. After sitting me down on the couch, my dad's partner told me that my parents had been—" Charlie paused as the waters of grief he did not have splashed against his eyelids. His soul heaved three more gasps of air before he continued.

"He told me that my parents," he said, swallowing hard, "had been killed as a retaliation by one of the gangs whose operations my dad had helped cripple. It wasn't until later that I found out how they died. He then told me that my sister had survived but was in the hospital being treated for rape."

"Charlie," said Katie, her voice cracking with anguish as tears streamed gently down her face. "I'm *so* sorry."

Charlie simply looked at her and smiled a small, heartbroken smile before continuing with his story. "Two weeks later, my sister and I were sent to live with my grandparents—my dad's parents—in that same small suburb outside of Birmingham.

"Their 'solution' for all that we'd been through was *church*," Charlie said, as dolorous anger began to bubble in his veins. "Every Sunday, every Wednesday, they'd drag my sister and me to church so we could hear the 'good news,' which was usually nothing more than how our country was going to hell and the liberals and gays were to blame.

"My sister told me late one Wednesday night after youth group that she'd finally had the courage to share what happened to her with a small group of girls. The church's youth leader told my sister, in front of the entire group, that she was no longer 'pure' because of what had happened to her, and a month later, my sister hung herself."

Charlie again heaved sobs as the tears he did not have continued to drip onto the blanket.

Katie was quick to wipe them away, her sleeve still stretched over her fingers. As Katie tended to his broken soul, a small elm leaf fell into Charlie's lap, one of the only leaves the tree had left to give as winter neared.

Charlie continued. "My grandparents told me that my sister's death was a sin, and that she probably didn't go to heaven." Anger seethed in his veins as he recounted their role in his grief.

"That's when I decided I was done with religion, and wanted

absolutely nothing to do with God. As soon as I could get out of there, I did. And I'm never going back. I don't ever want to see them again."

"C'mere," said Katie softly as she rose to her feet, extending a hand to help Charlie to his. She wrapped her arms around him and pulled him in close as his arms found their way around her and his eyes gently closed. He stood soaking in the warmth of her embrace as she gently rocked him back and forth.

There, in the shadow of that tall elm tree, sitting on the dry grass of the Lawn barely a football's throw from the Rotunda, Charlie had shared a part of his heart with Katie that no one had ever seen before. It was the part that was packed away when Charlie was sixteen and had never seen the light of day since, but Katie had somehow drawn it out, not to pour salty clichés into his open wounds, but to sit with him in his grief, gently caring for the wounds of his soul as a good nurse tends to those of her patient.

Bending her torso back from their embrace, Katie looked up at Charlie and Charlie looked down at her, his spirit weak and empty. She dawned another brokenhearted smile as she looked up into his eyes through tears of her own.

"*Now* I know you," she said with a definitive sadness in her voice, taking him back to the very first time they met, in that small, warm coffee shop next to a blazing fire. She was glad to finally know him—*all* of him—but was grief-stricken by the intense pain that Charlie had carried alone for so long.

Katie then melted back into his embrace, gently rocking him back and forth, until the sky laid the sun to rest over Charlottesville.

8

Cranberry Sauce

———— 🌿 ————

IT WAS THE MONDAY BEFORE Thanksgiving, and Charlie met up with Katie after work for another one of their passionate rendezvouses between the bookcases of the Alderman Library. Their lips had been longingly interlocked for not more than thirty minutes when another student walked by. They broke their bond and looked at him with stares of confusion as he stood wide-eyed like a deer in the headlights.

"Oh…uh, sorry," said the scrawny, pale-skinned freshman before walking awkwardly away.

He returned moments later, just as the two were about to pick up where they'd left off. "Actually, would you, uh, mind if I, uh, grabbed a book?"

Katie and Charlie looked from each other to him, then back at each other, and reignited the passionate bond between their lips.

"Oh, kay then. I guess I'll come back later," said the freshman's voice from a far off place as the two lovers pressed their lips tightly together, yearning for deeper intimacy.

Katie gently pushed at Charlie's chest. He pulled back as she exhaled a sigh of disappointment, almost as though regretting her move. "Do you think we should've let him get his book?"

"Nah," said Charlie. "Virginia's for lovers, not for studying," he said as he began to kiss Katie's neck.

Katie wasn't falling for it. Her mind had started back up again. "Hey," she said as Charlie continued to kiss her neck, "what're you doing for Thanksgiving?"

Charlie realized that his attempt was in vain and resigned his effort, bringing his gaze to meet hers with a look of affectionate disappointment.

"Nothing," he said softly as he brushed Katie's hair behind her ear. "Why?"

"Well that's silly," said Katie. "You should come to our house!"

Charlie's chest tightened at the thought of meeting her parents. "Um…I mean…it's just that—"

"What, are you scared to meet my parents?" asked Katie with a smile. (She knew him too well.)

"Well, I mean," said Charlie, trying to manufacture a fib, "it's just that I…"

She looked at him with a head-tilt scowl that called him out for his lie.

Charlie sighed, gazing at the spine of an old biology dissertation that sat on a shelf just above her head. "Yeah…" he confessed.

Katie stood up tall and fixed herself up, then began to lead the two of them out from the place where time stood still, back into the "real" world, where lives were run by schedules instead of passion, agendas instead of love.

"Well, don't be," said Katie, looking over her shoulder at Charlie.

"*That* makes it easier," thought Charlie to himself.

"Besides," Katie continued, dragging him by the hand up the old mint green staircase, "they've already heard a lot about you, and they *really* like you." She turned and smiled at him. Her words did nothing to help Charlie's nerves, but only exacerbated the anxiety throbbing in his chest as the two reached the top of the staircase.

"So," she said as they paused, standing opposite each other on the dark linoleum floor, "will you come?"

Charlie looked into her longing eyes, yearning with excitement for him to join her family for Thanksgiving dinner. Gently, with all the tender care that had come to characterize their relationship, Katie wrapped her arms around his waist, pinching his hip bones as she slid her hands into his back pockets. Charlie couldn't help but give in to her demands.

"Yeah, I'll come," he said.

"Yay!" she said with the glee of a child as she nestled herself in his arms and pulled him in close, removing her hands from his pockets and wrapping her arms tightly around him.

Charlie's arms gave in as the rest of him had, and he held her tightly as he thought about what in the world he was going to do, to say—to wear.

Charlie had not met a girl's parents since Stacy Stevenson, and that had only been for two minutes while he waited for Stacy to finish getting ready for their date. Never before had Charlie spent an entire evening with a girl's parents, much less a girl he cared so deeply about. What would he say? What would he do? And most importantly, what would they think of him?

Three days later, Charlie walked down the metal stairs of his apartment with a bottle of Spanish cabernet in hand as the autumn sun lingered in the afternoon sky. There was Katie, waiting at the bottom of the stairs as she leaned casually against her car, wearing a forest green oversized wool sweater and sky blue scarf with a pair of black leggings and some tan zip-up booties. She smiled as their eyes met while he descended.

When he reached the bottom, she ran to embrace him, throwing herself at him with so much energy that he had no choice but to swing his brown-haired beauty around in his arms.

"Hi," she said, staring up at him after stealing a kiss.

"Hi," he said, chuckling as he brushed her hair behind her ear and stole another. Charlie then held up the bottle of wine in his hand as he leaned back from their embrace. Katie still had her arms locked around his waist as she turned to look at the bottle.

"I wasn't sure what to bring," he said. "But I figured everybody likes wine, so…"

Katie turned to look at him, her eyes beaming with admiration. "You didn't *need* to bring anything," she said. "Just yourself." She looked again at the bottle in Charlie's hand. "But yes, we do love wine," she said, giggling as the two of them turned and made their way to the car.

Charlottesville seemed empty on days like today, when many of its students traveled home to spend the weekend with their families. Even Mike had left, leaving Charlie feeling especially alone. As the two wove their way through downtown Charlottesville and into the neighborhoods on the north side of town near the banks of the Rivanna River, Charlie prepared himself to meet her parents by pestering Katie with questions.

"Okay, so what are your parents' names?" asked Charlie.

"David and Angie," she said slowly, allowing their names to sink into his mind. "Most people just call my dad Dave, but it's an invitation-only sort of thing, so start out with David and wait for an invite. It won't take long."

"Do you have any siblings?" asked Charlie.

"Yes," she said, "I have two younger sisters: Ellie, who's a senior in high school, and Grace, who's seven. Ellie loves all things theater and drama, and just auditioned for a musical her high school is putting on in the spring; Grace…well, right now Grace loves baking, but it basically changes every month. The only things that've stuck around are coloring and the violin."

"Okay," said Charlie, "and what do your parents do?"

"My mom is an interior designer and my dad," she said, taking her eyes off the road to stare at him with an ear-to-ear grin on her face, "is an architect."

"What!?" Charlie exploded in anxiety as he buried his face in his hands and thought out loud. "Why didn't you tell me? I could've reviewed my notes, come up with things to talk about—"

"Charlie," said Katie softly as she placed her hand on his knee. When it was safe to do so, she took her eyes off the road to look at him. "You're going to do just *fine*. You have nothing to worry about."

"O-khay," said Charlie on an exhale as he took three deep breaths.

Katie pulled the car into the driveway of a white colonial-style home with navy blue shutters. The house stood two stories tall and had four large, double-hung, French-paned windows on either side of the front door, which was covered by a small rounded pediment supported by two Corinthian columns. Hanging from the center of the pediment was a lantern-style porch light that gave direction to visitors at night.

"Okay," Charlie said again as he took two more deep breaths, working up the nerve to open the door.

Katie just laughed as she opened her door and got out.

Suppressing his anxiety just long enough to get out of the car, Charlie opened the car door and stepped out, one foot, then the other, holding his bottle of Spanish cabby in hand and desperately longing to down a glass of its red, grapy goodness and calm his nerves.

Katie had parked the car in front of a two-car garage that was part of a wing that looked like a later addition to the home, added long after the home was first built.

As Charlie stood in fear looking at this gorgeous home, cowering at the countless nightmares of how this day might go wrong, he felt Katie's hand wrap around his, and he turned to gaze into her eyes like a young boy taking a dreaded trip to the dentist.

Her face wore a smile that expressed both a concern for him and sheer amusement at the silliness of his fear. "You ready?" she asked.

Charlie took another deep breath. "Yeah," he said on an

exhale. "Let's do this. Just promise you won't dump me if this doesn't go well."

Katie laughed, leaning into him as she playfully touched his chest with her free hand. "You have nothing to worry about. Everything's going to go just fine," she said.

Charlie's nerves did not let up as the two made their way up the concrete walkway to the vintage red brick steps of the front porch. Together, they stepped up onto the porch, one heavy step after another, and Katie opened the door.

"Mom, Dad! We're here!" Katie hollered as she stepped inside and removed her shoes. Charlie took his cue, stepping inside and removing his as well. Still hunched over as he untied his shoes, Charlie began to look around. The floors were hardwood, made of naturally colored oak. Inside the door on either side of the small, glass panes that encased it, were four tall, knotty alder cabinets with dark knobs as handles, two on each side, that Charlie guessed were cubbies to store backpacks and other things.

Further inside the door, starting where the cubbies ended, were metal hooks, dark in color that were attached to a long piece of the same knotty alder wood. From these hooks hung a large variety of coats and scarves, and on the floor underneath them were piles of shoes, including some that Charlie had seen Katie wear.

"Oh, my goodness!" came a voice that sounded oddly like Katie's. Charlie looked up from the piles of shoes to see a woman about as small as Katie, with strawberry blonde hair and bright blue eyes. She had Katie's freckles scattered across her nose and cheekbones.

"You must be Charlie," she said excitedly as she snuck past Katie and wrapped him in a warm embrace. Charlie was not used to this kind of friendliness from people he'd just met, but his guard quickly crumbled as his arms found their way around this small, kind-hearted woman.

"Uh…" he stammered. "And you must be Angie," said Charlie cautiously. She pulled back from their embrace to look up at him. In her eyes Charlie could see Katie's familiar compassion and depth.

"We've heard *so* much about you!" she said.

Charlie just smiled, unsure of what to say.

"Oh, come come!" she said, pulling him by the hand out of the entryway and into a hallway that led into the kitchen. On the side of the hallway opposite the entry was a carpeted staircase with a beautiful railing that had white posts and a rich handrail made of mahogany with a volute at the bottom just to the right of the entryway, where the staircase made a two-stair jaunt out into the hallway.

Angie dragged Charlie past Katie, and Charlie looked at her, confused and desperate for help. Katie just laughed.

"I," Charlie started. Angie paused at the bottom of the staircase and turned back to face him, not letting go of his hand. Charlie could now see the kitchen behind her.

"I brought this," he said, lifting the bottle of Spanish cabernet in his hand to show her.

Angie smiled warmly as her face turned from the bottle in Charlie's hand to look him in the eye.

"Thank you, Charlie," she said, giving him yet another hug.

She took the bottle of wine, admired it again in her hands, then turned and continued to pull him into the kitchen.

"C'mon," she said as she pulled him along behind her. (This was a familiar experience for Charlie.) "You've gotta meet the rest of the clan."

Katie was following in their wake, grinning as she watched Charlie being sucked in by the love and warmth of her family, unsure of what to do.

Angie finally let up on her pull once she and Charlie stood inside the family kitchen. The kitchen was long, running from the back of the house to the front, on the righthand side, with rich cherrywood cabinets on either side of a large island the middle. At the end, situated between two windows that looked out on the river, was a large stainless steel six-burner stovetop.

The floors from the entryway to the kitchen were made of the same naturally colored oak, and gave a brightness that countered the warmth provided by the dark color of the kitchen cabinets. The cabinets and drawers were crowned with brushed nickel knobs and handles, and the entire kitchen had new stainless steel appliances and white marble countertops.

Standing hunched over an open oven door with a basting brush in hand was a man who Charlie presumed to be Katie's father. He wore a pair of dark, navy blue dress pants with a caramel brown sweater, and seemed quite focused on the large turkey that sat in a pan on a shelf that had been pulled from the oven. The savory-sweet aromas of rosemary, thyme, and something Charlie couldn't quite put his finger on made his stomach growl in lustful yearning for the meal Katie's family had prepared.

"Honey," said Angie, "this is Charlie."

"Charlie!" David said, standing up as he turned coolly around. He was holding a basting brush in one hand and a bowl in the other. "I was just bastin' the bird," he said as he set the bowl and brush on the counter then extended his hand to Charlie.

"Not a problem at all, David," said Charlie, trying to project confidence as he took David's hand and shook it.

"Call me Dave," he said, still holding Charlie's hand as he gazed into his heart with Katie's chocolate brown eyes.

Charlie's eyes glazed over with a layer of tears as he struggled to comprehend the welcome of this family he barely knew.

"Don't worry," said Dave, dawning a large smile as he looked at Katie, wondering if she'd told him. "It's a good thing. Only my friends call me Dave."

"I—" Charlie stammered for words. "Katie told me," he said softly, smiling back at Dave.

Dave released Charlie's hand and pointed behind him. "Grab a seat," he said. "Can I get you anything to drink?"

"Uh, I think I'm alright, thank you," Charlie said, still struggling to take it all in. "But I brought some wine, if you'd like a glass."

"Thank you, Charlie," said Dave, smiling at him with heartfelt sincerity. "I think I'd better focus on the cookin' for now. You do *not* wanna taste my drunk cookin'—unless of course you, too, are drunk," he said, his face morphing into Katie's mischievous grin. "But I will definitely enjoy a glass later!"

Charlie nodded in affirmation, smiling as Dave turned around, picking up his tools and returning his attention to the bird. "Just lemme know if you change your mind," he said, his voice fading as he turned around.

"Oh, and Charlie," said Dave, turning back around to face him, "please make yourself at home."

Charlie stood speechless at the loving welcome showered on him by this family he'd only just met. "Th—thank you," he said, struggling to find the words as he lightly choked on the tears he was fighting back. Dave just smiled at him, affirming the sincerity of his words, then turned around to continue his work on the turkey.

Charlie then felt a familiar hand graze his lower back as Katie nestled against his side. He put his arm around her and together they turned in the direction to which Dave had pointed. There, behind them, was a large, naturally colored knotty alder table that matched the cabinets in the entryway and ran perpendicular to the length of the kitchen under the window at the front of the house. It had five chairs around it and a bench on the side nearest the kitchen. On the bench sat a young girl who had Angie's strawberry blonde hair and held a blue Crayola crayon in her hand as she pressed it to the pages of her coloring book.

When she saw that Charlie and Katie were now paying attention to her, she took a break from her work and climbed off the bench. She walked over to Charlie and wrapped her arms around his legs. "I'm Grace," she said, tilting her head sharply back to look up at her sister's boyfriend.

"Hi Grace," said Charlie as he squatted down to look her in the eye, "I'm Charlie."

"I know," she said as if she could write an encyclopedia about him. "Katie's told me *all* about you."

"Has she now?" asked Charlie, tilting his gaze up toward Katie.

"Yup! She told me that you have *gorgeous* brown hair that she *loves* to play with, and that you go to *school* with her and that you're gonna be an architect just like Dad."

Charlie laughed.

"Oh, and she *also* says that you're a really good kisser."

"*Grace!*" said Katie, embarrassed by her sister's lack of filters. Angie, who had started preparing the sweet potatoes, let out a reflexive chuckle as Charlie again turned his gaze toward Katie, beaming with satisfaction. Katie's cheeks had turned bright red.

Grace, however, was unfazed by her sister's embarrassment as she sat back down to resume her coloring. "Do you wanna color with me, Charlie?" she asked, turning back around to look at him.

Charlie stood up and found Katie's hand as she fought to hide her embarrassment. "I'd love to," he said, stealing a kiss from Katie before the two made their way over to the bench and sat down next to Grace.

Grace slid the coloring book and crayons over as Charlie sat down next to her. She had been filling in the details on a picture of a unicorn standing in a meadow, and for a seven-year-old, she colored remarkably well.

Charlie picked up a green crayon and began to color the grass.

"No," said Grace. "If you do it *that* way, it won't look *real*," she said as she took the crayon from Charlie and began to color with small strokes in the direction the grass was pictured as bending.

"See!" she said, handing the crayon back to Charlie. "It looks better, doesn't it?"

Charlie turned nervously to Katie, unsure of whether Grace was really seven years old. "Yes, it does," he said as he stared at Katie. Katie was grinning ear-to-ear at Charlie's newfound acquaintance with her mini-me.

Charlie sat with Grace for a half an hour or so, learning to color as Katie looked on, her legs affectionately resting on top of his as she leaned into him and he wrapped his free arm around her waist.

Katie then stood up suddenly as though remembering she needed to do something, and made her way to the cabinets on Charlie's left.

Charlie took his eyes off the coloring book and gazed over his shoulder to see where Katie was headed.

"It's okay," said Grace, "you can go with her if you want. We've colored enough."

"Are you sure?" asked Charlie, turning his attention back to Grace.

"Yup, this one's almost done. And besides, I've taught you all I can anyway."

Blessed with the seven-year-old's permission, Charlie got up from the table as he lightly placed a hand on Grace's shoulder. "Thanks for teaching me how to color, Grace," he said, turning again toward the kitchen.

"You're welcome," she said without looking up from the task at hand. "You can color with me anytime, Charlie." Dumbfounded, Charlie turned his gaze back to Grace, who was still just as fixated on her task as she was before. Even the seven-year-old was welcoming Charlie into their home with exceptional love and warmth.

After a long stare at the wonder that was Grace Monroe, Charlie turned around to see Katie standing in front of him with a glass of wine. "Hi," she said, smiling brightly at him. "Figured you might want this," she said as she handed him the glass before stealing a kiss from him.

As the two parted lips, they noticed another girl standing in the doorway to the kitchen through which Charlie had been so warmly dragged. This girl had hair that had been dyed jet black, with the fair skin that characterized all the Monroe girls. Around her neck, holding her hair against her skin, was a large pair of headphones.

"Hey Ellie," said Katie. "This is Charlie."

"Hey," said Ellie, staring at Charlie for a few seconds before she stepped into the kitchen and made her way to the refrigerator to retrieve a soda.

"Do you wanna stay and hang out with us?" asked Dave.

"Nah," said Ellie, exiting the kitchen and walking back up the stairs as she lifted her headphones back over her ears.

"She's just a teenager," said Angie, attempting to reassure Charlie that it had nothing to do with him.

Charlie turned to look at Angie. She smiled, her eyes a bit somber because of her daughter's choice to remain removed from their family. She then went back to chopping lettuce for the salad.

"This is a beautiful home," said Charlie, his eyes surveying once again the masterpiece of a kitchen.

"Thank you, Charlie," said Dave as he opened the oven to check the turkey again. "We just finished with a pretty big remodel: kitchen, flooring, carpet, windows—the works!"

"Well it turned out very nicely," said Charlie as he smiled at

Dave. "I really like the design."

"Yeah, Katie tells me you're studying to be an architect," said Dave with excitement as he unwrapped some of the tin foil to take a gander at his bird.

"Yeah…" said Charlie, feeling uncomfortably vulnerable, knowing that this family already knew so much about him. And while he felt uncomfortable with the vulnerability into which he'd been thrust, he also felt immensely loved by this family that took such a profound interest in who he was.

"Get out while you can," said Dave, wrapping up the turkey and sliding the shelf back into the oven. He then tilted his head up at Charlie and winked.

Charlie smiled, then noticed Angie bustling away. "Can I help with anything?" asked Charlie.

"Nope!" said Angie. "You, Charlie, are *our* guest. You get to relax."

"Maybe Katie can give you the tour," said Dave as he opened the fridge and pulled out the stuffing. Charlie turned to Katie.

"C'mon," Katie said, gently leading Charlie by the hand. "We'll be back!" she hollered at her family as the two left the kitchen, heading down the hallway through which Charlie had been so affectionately pulled.

Katie stopped just outside the kitchen and opened a door on the right.

"This," she said, peering inside and flicking the light switch, "is the pantry, from which all good and delicious things come."

Charlie gazed around at the food-stacked shelves before Katie flicked off the light. It was clear that Katie's family loved to cook.

"And this," she said, pointing to an opening in the wall on the left as they took a few more steps down the hallway, "is the den, where my dad watches football. He's a big fan of the Cavaliers."

Charlie just nodded as his gaze moved from the leather couch on one end of the room to the large plasma TV on the other.

"Oh," said Katie, as she turned to continue the tour, "and my parents sometimes watch movies in there on weekends, so if you're ever here, just be aware that it's not always G-rated in there." She then looked back over her shoulder at Charlie with a grin on her face. "Shield your eyes," she said as she took a few more steps down the hallway, passing the bottom of the staircase.

"Hey!" hollered Dave from the kitchen. Charlie smiled at the dynamic of love and lighthearted humor that so clearly character-ized this family, knowing now that Katie's passionate concern for him wasn't a reaction to, but an extension of, her family.

"In here," she said, pointing to an open door on the far side of the entryway, "is the bathroo—"

Charlie had paused and was gazing up the stairs.

"You'll get to see my room later," she said, interrupting Char-lie's train of thought as she stared at him with a smile of affection-ate discipline, her smile and hips cocked to the left.

"How did you…" stammered Charlie, "I mean—"

"How long have you known me?" asked Katie rhetorically as she playfully smirked. Charlie's face conceded her point, and he slowly stepped in her direction.

"Spidey senses," she said, making spider legs with her fingers as she clawed in his direction.

Charlie chuckled as he began to see an even more playful side to his lover in the midst of her family. "Okay," he said, "so that's the bathroom."

"Uh-huh," said Katie, spinning around as she continued stepping to where the hallway opened up, "and this is the living room."

The hardwood floors continued past the entryway into an open seating area on the side of their home opposite the kitchen. On the far wall was a gas fireplace that was burning cozy hues of gold and orange. Running perpendicular to the fireplace under the window was a large dark brown leather sofa, with an oriental rug and coffee table in between it and two red upholstered armchairs.

The two then stepped to the right, wrapping around the staircase where there was a short hallway that opened up to the dining room.

"And this," Katie continued, "is where we'll be eating."

Charlie peered around the opening to gaze inside, where he saw a very large, long, dark brown dining table that looked as though it could seat as many as ten people and ran parallel to the width of the house. On the far end, the wall opened up into the kitchen. Charlie could see Dave working away at the stove. He turned to wave when he saw them. Charlie waved back.

On the end of the dining room nearest where Katie and Charlie stood was another fireplace. It, too, was ablaze with warmth. The hardwood floor ended at the room's entrance, and the dining room smelled like fresh carpet mixed with whiffs of the wandering scents from the kitchen. At each of the places on the table were bright white plates with matching napkins and shining silver utensils. Each of the place settings were accompanied by a crystal water glass and glasses for both red and white wine, and in the center of the table was a large, beautiful bouquet of fall colors.

"This is incredible," said Charlie as he stared through the double French-paned doors on the far side of the dining table. The doors opened onto a brand new deck overlooking the river, whose calm waters flowed gently by, grazing the grass leaves that cloaked its banks as if they were waving at them and offering a regal "Hello."

"C'mon," Katie said, squeezing the hand she now clasped. Together, they walked out of the short hallway outside the dining room back to the open seating area that formed the living room then down a slightly longer hallway that ran up the side of the house opposite the kitchen, separating it from the wing that jutted out to form the garage.

"This," said Katie, knocking on the closed door nearest the seating area, "is the garage. Nothing special in there," she said, her voice fading as she continued down the hallway.

At the end of the hallway was another French-paned door that opened out onto the deck. Charlie could again see the river in the distance, blocked only by some trees that grew on the east side of the home, behind the wing that jutted out to the left. They looked like a mix of oak and elm trees, peeking around the corner as though they were curious to see what was going on inside.

"And this," said Katie, opening another closed door on the same side of the hallway and turning on the light, "is my parents' office."

Charlie gazed in to see two large maple desks facing each other, each with one side flush against the wall. They were both accompanied by large, black leather chairs, and both had computers on them; one desk was considerably messier than the other.

"My dad's the slob," said Katie, noticing where Charlie's eyes had settled. "Must be a thing with you architects," she said as she playfully nudged him with her elbow.

Charlie smiled as she closed the door and then turned around.

"Finally," said Katie as she turned toward the open door opposite the office, "we have the guest room, complete with its own bathroom." Charlie turned and stared into the room, standing shoulder to shoulder with Katie.

"C'mon," she said, stepping into the room.

Charlie stepped in after her. The wall to the left of the door had two windows looking out over the deck and the river. In the corner, flush against the exterior wall and the wall opposite the door was a four-post queen-sized bed made of naturally colored pine with a fern green comforter, stacked with an abundance of pillows that made it look comfy and inviting; and in the corner opposite where the bed had been pushed was a small fireplace that was also lit.

"Do you guys usually light the fire in the guest room?" asked Charlie, puzzled.

"Not usually," said Katie, walking back into the hallway. "Do you want to see my room?"

Charlie's heart leapt at the idea, and he hurried after her, forgetting all about the fireplace. The two of them made their way back down the hallway to the living room and over to the staircase.

On the wall at the top of the stairs hung a large portrait of Katie's family. It looked recent. To the right of the portrait was a hallway that had a window at the end, and to its left was a door that led to the master bedroom. Charlie took a peek inside.

"That's my parents' room," said Katie from behind him. "You can go in if you'd like."

"No, no, I was just curious," said Charlie, still staring into the room as he felt Katie sneak behind him.

There was a short wall on the left just inside the door that ran for maybe six feet and then took a sharp turn toward the front of the house. Just beyond where the wall ended and the room opened up, Charlie could see the bottom half of a large bed, perhaps king-sized, and on the far side was another fireplace. Charlie could not see whether it was lit, but he suspected that it was.

Charlie then turned and saw Katie, smiling as she stood to the right of the staircase, in a hallway that took travelers toward the bedrooms above the kitchen.

"You ready?" she asked, extending her free hand to him as she held her half-drunk glass of wine in the other.

"Yup," said Charlie as he took her hand in his and the two continued walking.

"So, this is the bathroom that Grace and Ellie share," said Katie, opening the door to Charlie's right and letting him peek inside.

The bathroom was messy, but not cluttered, with one towel shoved over the towel rack, unfolded. The bathroom had a tub with a multi-colored polkadot shower curtain on the left and white cabinets with a dark, quartz countertop that ran along the right-hand side to a toilet at the far end.

On the exterior wall, next to the toilet, was a double-hung

window with French panes like the rest of the house. The panes of this window, though, were smoked glass, to ensure the privacy of Ellie and little Grace.

Katie then gently pulled him along. After taking a short jog to the left, the hallway continued to the point that was just over the kitchen, and there, it stopped. Just before it stopped were two doors, one on either side.

"The room on the left is Grace's room," said Katie, pointing in the direction of the open door, "and Ellie's room is the one on the right." The door to Ellie's room was closed, depriving the hallway of natural light it would otherwise enjoy, but a light could be seen under the door, and the recorded sounds of a musical could be heard coming from Ellie's bedroom.

Before Charlie could venture down the hallway for a peak into Grace's room, Katie pulled him along and he agreeably followed, knowing there was only one room left to see.

Katie led him back in the direction from which they'd come, past the master bedroom and down the hallway to the right at the stop of the stairs, with natural light spilling in from the double-hung window at its end. It had two doors opposite each other. Katie gently pulled him down the hallway, and Charlie's heart fluttered with excitement.

Standing closer to the window now, Charlie could again see the river and its calming waters from a higher vantage point. It looked even more peaceful and regal from this view.

Charlie stood gazing out the window when his thoughts were interrupted by Katie's voice.

"This," she said, opening the door on the right, "is my bathroom." Charlie peered inside to find a very neat and tidied bathroom, except for the straightener on the countertop that had its cord wrapped around it.

"And this," said Katie from behind him, opening the door on the left, "is my bedroom."

A shot of adrenaline pulsed through Charlie's heart as he turned around to find a queen-sized bed with a black metal headboard flush against the lefthand corner along the far wall. Katie's bed had a light baby blue comforter and was also stacked with pillows, and above her headboard hung a large canvas picture of the sun rising over a country landscape. To the right of her bed was a nightstand, adorned with a small alarm clock, a picture of Katie and her family, and a large lamp with a glass shade that had sunflowers painted on it.

"C'mon," said Katie, pulling him into her room.

Charlie's heart leapt and passion surged in his veins as she pulled him into her room. He knew from past experience that this was a de facto invitation to get between a girl's sheets. This time, though, Charlie felt odd about taking advantage of Katie's invitation with her parents downstairs.

But Katie's pull on his hand did not let up, and Charlie quickly gave in, stepping into her room as she pulled him toward her bed. She took his glass of wine from him and set it atop the antique chest of drawers with dark metal handles that was just inside her door to the right.

"Sit," said Katie, pulling him onto her bed. Charlie sat next to Katie, turning his torso to face her as she rested her arms on his shoulders and pressed her forehead against his.

She then closed her eyes and brought her lips gently to rest on his. The sparks of her tongue ignited the passion in Charlie's veins as he pressed his lips into hers and their hands began wandering over their thick layers of clothing, their lips interlocked in familiar rapture.

Charlie then leaned in, pushing Katie onto her back as his kisses moved to her neck and his hand reached under her sweater, grazing her bare midriff as he began to lift her sweater off.

"Charlie," said Katie softly.

Charlie lifted his gaze from her neck to stare into her eyes, which were now open.

"You don't want to do that," she said with a soft smile.

Charlie looked down at his pants and back at Katie. "No, I definitely do. Don't you?"

Katie sat up, and Charlie removed his hand from underneath her sweater. The two sat where they'd started, with torsos turned toward each other as Katie put one hand on Charlie's knee and wrapped the other around his lower back.

"Charlie," she said softly, gazing into his eyes, "what's your greatest fear?"

The passion was quickly fading from Charlie's veins with each passing heartbeat.

"Uh," he stammered as his mind rebooted, "abandonment."

"Right," she said. "You're afraid of losing the ones you love. So Charlie, why would you give yourself to me in the deepest form of intimacy the two of us could possibly have before I've promised you that I'm not going anywhere?"

"Well," said Charlie, staring out at the river as a hint of desire lingered in his veins, "you could just promise me *now*."

"Where there's no accountability?" said Katie. Charlie turned to face Katie. She was smiling gently at him, not wanting him to feel ashamed while wanting his highest good. She cared about him, more than he knew.

"Charlie," she continued, "you deserve a woman who's going to promise before God and all of her family and friends that she's not going anywhere, because then there are people to hold her to that promise. I may one day be that woman for you, but please don't sell yourself short of what you deserve by giving away what you cannot take back; not without that promise."

She gave his knee a gentle squeeze. "Okay?"

Charlie nodded. Despite Katie's effort, Charlie felt somewhat guilty about his lust, and found himself suddenly rethinking the many times he had given himself to women over the last seven years. Had he been selling himself short, depriving himself of what he really needed?

"Kids, dinner's ready!" came Dave's voice from downstairs.

The two of them started to get up. "I'm sorry," said Charlie somberly.

Katie grabbed both of his hands in hers and made him look deeply into her eyes. "There is absolutely *nothing* to be sorry for," she said. "Charlie, I want it as much as you do; believe me. We could have given ourselves to each other right there, and maybe it would've worked out; maybe neither of us would have left when things got hard.

"But Charlie, I care enough about you to say no to my desire just as much as I'm saying no to yours. So please don't hear that as me judging you in any way. There is no reason to feel guilty. I feel the same way."

Katie released his hands and wrapped her arms around his waist, pulling him in tight without breaking their gaze. "Okay?" she said, her face clearly worried about the condition of her lover's heart.

Charlie nodded, feeling better. "Okay," he said, wrapping his arms around her and pulling her in close as she melted into him. They held each other for several seconds before relinquishing their embrace and turning toward the door.

The two grabbed their glasses of wine and stepped out of Katie's room to make their way down to the kitchen. Their journey came to a halt when they ran into Ellie at the top of the stairs. She just stared at them.

"What have *you* two been doing?" she inquired, having noticed that they were coming from Katie's room. Only then did Charlie notice the static nature of some of Katie's hair.

"Oh, ya know," said Katie with Charlie standing in her wake. "Just taking advantage of him," she said, gently squeezing Charlie's hand to remind him of where her heart truly lie.

Ellie just smirked, shaking her head, and together, the three of them made their way down to the kitchen, where large white bowls and serving pans were now sitting on the island, filled with food.

Dave emerged from the dining room with empty hands, then grabbed a large platter that had thick slices of ham on it and spun around to head back into the dining room. Angie emerged shortly after him with empty hands, and she, too, grabbed another dish and headed back into the dining room.

With all the nonchalance of routine, the Monroe children began grabbing dishes of steaming food from the countertop and carrying them into the dining room. Grace grabbed the basket of rolls, Ellie the yams. Katie grabbed the stuffing.

"What should I do to help?" Charlie asked, unsure of how he fit into the picture.

"Mmm," said Katie. "Maybe bring the cranberry sauce?"

Aside from a few mixed cooking utensils, the bowl of cranberry sauce was the only thing left on the island to carry. Charlie grabbed it and followed everyone else into the dining room.

He paused, though, when he noticed that the oven was still set at four hundred degrees. He set the cranberry sauce back down on the counter, and after opening the oven to ensure that nothing was inside, turned it off and again picked up the dish he'd been asked to carry.

As Charlie rounded the corner at the end of the fridge to head into the dining room, he saw the entire Monroe family, bustling around the table to get everything set in its proper place. There was now much more than just place settings on the table.

On the end nearest the fireplace, resting on a large white platter and looking even bigger now that it was removed from its pan, was Dave's perfectly browned turkey; and on the end nearest Charlie was a slightly smaller platter that had large slices of ham on it. In between was no shortage of Thanksgiving foods, all of them in matching white dishes, save for the basket of rolls that Grace had carried in.

Whether mesmerized by the wonder of the table before him or this beautifully cohesive family, one cannot be sure, but as Charlie stepped into the living room carrying the bowl of cranberry sauce, he did not notice the lip at the edge of the hardwood floor where the ground transitioned to the Monroe's newly installed white carpet.

Charlie's toe caught on the lip as he stepped into the dining room, and he stumbled forward, spilling the dark red cranberry sauce from the bowl in his hands onto the unblemished fibers of the brand new white carpet. It hit the floor with a splat, sending tarty splatter flying. Charlie froze, staring down at the cranberry sauce he had just spilled. If there were any way this day with Katie's parents could have gone wrong, *this* was it.

Still frozen, Charlie cautiously turned his head to see the entire Monroe family staring at him, their eyes squarely fixed on their guest. Yet in all of their faces, anger was not to be found.

Charlie stammered for words, choking on the stomach now in his throat. "I'm, *so*, sorry..."

Dave smiled at him without even looking at the carpet. "Are *you* okay?" he asked. Charlie was startled by Dave's response. Who *were* these people? Where was the fit of anger from Dave at Charlie's stupidity? Where was the shrill of grief from Angie as she rushed to the kitchen to get the carpet cleaner?

"Well, yeah, I'm okay...but your carpet," said Charlie.

"It's alright," said Dave. "Don't sweat it."

"Well here," said Charlie, turning back toward the kitchen, "at least let me clean it."

"Nope," said Angie, moving behind Charlie to block his return from the kitchen. Charlie had no sooner turned to face Angie than she reached out, taking the bowl from him. "You just relax."

She then grabbed a serving spoon and began to scoop the sauce back into the bowl, exposing the bright red spot in the carpet underneath. When she'd finished, she stood up and carried the bowl and the spoon into the kitchen. The room felt unusually quiet.

"What can I do to help?" Charlie called after her.

"Nothing, dear," said Angie. She then turned to look back over her shoulder at him. "Except to eat."

"C'mon, Charlie," said Dave, standing at the head of the table, nearest the fireplace. Charlie turned to face him. "I saved you a seat," he said, opening his hand to the empty chair at his right, between him and Katie.

As kind as the family's response to Charlie's spill had been, Charlie was nevertheless terrified to sit next to Dave in the wake of his mistake. Slowly, he inched his way to the open chair, stepping around his glaring red blemish as he made his way up the table to the empty seat.

Angie returned to the dining room as Charlie passed Ellie, who was seated at Katie's right. Charlie paused his journey to what he felt was certain doom, and turned back to Angie, looking for something he could do to make up for his clumsiness and avoid what he was sure would be Dave's wrath. He saw Angie drop a white napkin over the large red spot on the carpet before she turned to look at him.

"See?" she said, her face beaming. "All better. Now let's eat." This woman's joy did not seem at all tempered by Charlie's misstep.

Charlie nervously scooted the chair next to Dave out from

beneath the table, sliding into it and expecting dragon fire to spew from Dave's mouth now that Charlie was in range. Katie's hand found Charlie's arm and slid down to wrap around his sweaty palms.

"Dad," she said, "do you wanna do the honors?"

"Sure, sweetheart," he said, turning to Charlie. "Charlie, we're gonna say grace. Is that alright with you?"

Charlie was not sure how to respond. Never before had someone asked him for permission to pray.

"Uh, sure," said Charlie cautiously, still expecting dragon fire.

Dave then gently clasped Charlie's free hand under the table as Ellie reached across and locked hands with Grace. Together, the Monroe family prayed.

"Father," Dave said, "we thank you so very much for the many blessings you have showered on this family. We thank you for each other, for delicious food and delightful company. And most of all, we thank you for Charlie. May your love and grace radiate from this house, today and every day.

"Amen," said Dave with a gentle squeeze of Charlie's hand. Charlie sat speechless as the Monroe family began to dish out the food. Never before had Charlie heard someone pray to the Almighty without Thee's and Thou's, much less *thank* God for him.

"I—" said Charlie softly, his eyes glazing over with tears as he stared at his feet, "I really am so sorry about your carpet." Dave had stood up to begin carving the turkey. He sat back down.

"Charlie," he said, putting his hand on Charlie's shoulder. Slowly, Charlie found the courage to look him in the eye. "Are *you* okay?" he asked.

"Well, yeah, I'm okay. But your carpe—"

"I don't *care* about the carpet," said Dave, staring intensely into Charlie's eyes. "I care about *you*. Carpet can be cleaned or replaced. *You*, Charlie, are irreplaceable."

Tears began to fall from Charlie's eyes as he sat, gaze locked with Dave while Dave kept his hand firmly on Charlie's shoulder. Embarrassed, Charlie slid back in his chair and stood up, hurrying out of the room.

He found solace in the family's living room, where he stood gazing out the window at Katie's car as tears flowed freely down his face, his soul overcome by the love showered on him by this family he barely knew.

He stood there not more than ten seconds until he heard a familiar voice from behind him.

"Hey…" came Katie's soft tone as she came and stood at his side, looking not out the window, but at him. "What's the matter?"

Charlie sniffled with a silent double sob as he turned to look at Katie. "Why does your family love me? They don't even know me."

Katie smiled a brokenhearted smile as she grabbed both his hands. "C'mere," she said, pulling him over to the leather sofa. Together, they sat.

"You know," she said as she began to wipe away his tears, "after our hike up Shady Side, I got together with some of my friends to catch up, and when I told them that I had been on two dates with Charlie Shaw, they freaked. One of them even called my mom and told her *all* about it."

Charlie looked at her, now even *more* afraid to return to the table.

Katie continued. "When I got home that night, my mom and dad were sitting in the den waiting for me. They told me they had concerns I was dating you. Given your reputation in this town as a —well, a ladies' man, they wanted to know what I saw in you."

She paused as Charlie looked at her with even more fear, knowing now what the people sitting in the dining room knew of him.

"Do you know what I told them?" asked Katie, unfazed by Charlie's worry.

"Do I wanna know?" asked Charlie, sniffling again as he brushed his nose with his hand.

"I told them that you were one of the greatest guys I knew, a man with impeccable courage; a man with a wounded soul who was desperately in need of love. I told them about the Charlie Shaw that *I* knew."

Tears again flowed down Charlie's face as he paused, struggling to take in what Katie was telling him. "But how can they love me when they know who I am; when they know that a guy like *me* is dating their daughter?"

Katie was quick to wipe away his tears with her sleeve. "Because they know what it's like to have love poured out on them when they do not deserve it. So when they heard about the Charlie Shaw that *I* was dating, the Charlie Shaw that *I* knew, they were no longer worried about their daughter."

Katie chuckled. "They were actually *excited* to meet you and show you that same love that's been poured out on them."

Tears were now streaming down Charlie's cheeks as he looked at the opening leading into the dining room.

"Charlie," said Katie as she continued to tend to his soul, wiping away his tears, "this love that you're feeling here—it's a love that shakes the soul. So this, right here, these tears, this is *good*.

"And it is certainly not something you should be embarrassed about. I promise you that my parents, my sisters, we've all cried these tears. We get it. So don't let yourself be embarrassed, okay?" she said as she waited for him to look her again in the eye.

Charlie turned his tear-stained face to Katie. "Okay," he said, barely able to get the words out as he smiled a broken smile. In her chocolate brown eyes, he found nothing but concern and compassion for him.

"Now," said Katie, wiping away the rest of his tears, "should we go eat some turkey?"

Charlie smiled, his soul still reeling from the love in which it had been so abundantly immersed. "Yeah," he said, and together, the two of them got up and slowly returned to the dining room to find the Monroe family seated around the table talking quietly, the food untouched. Charlie felt guilty. "Oh," he stammered, "I didn't mean to make you wait."

"Nonsense!" said Dave, turning to look at him with a beaming smile. "Souls trump things in this house, Charlie—even food—and it seemed to us like your soul needed some tending." Charlie's face found a smile as he basked in the warmth of Dave's grin. "Good thing we have a nurse on hand, huh?" he quipped, winking at Katie.

Charlie chuckled at Dave's sense of humor, filled with that boundless love that characterized this one-of-a-kind family, as he and Katie returned to their seats.

Dave stood up to begin carving the turkey. "So, whaddya say, Charlie, you a man of the breast or the thigh?"

"Whatever's easiest," said Charlie softly as he gazed up at Dave, his eyes still aching from the tears.

"I've got the best knife in the world," said Dave. "It's whatever you want."

Charlie's face dawned a smile that spoke of the tearful joy spilling out of his heart. "Breast meat, please," he said, softly.

"Oo, he's a keeper," Dave said to Katie, who was resting her hand on Charlie's leg.

"I know, huh!" exclaimed Katie with a gentle squeeze of Charlie's knee, proud of what she'd found in him.

"Here you go," she said, handing Charlie the stuffing as Dave laid a huge piece of turkey on Charlie's plate.

Angie, who had vanished into the kitchen when Charlie and Katie returned, reemerged with a white bowl in hand.

"Who wants *cranberry* sauce!?" she said, singing as she carried the bowl in and set it on the table.

Charlie looked up, startled with unbelief. Had it all been just a bad dream?

"What…how did you…?" he stammered, looking at Angie as though the bowl of tarty dark red sauce now set on the table in front of Katie weren't real.

"Oh, Charlie," said Angie, beaming at him. "Katie eats like a horse! Haven't you learned by now that we like our food? We always make extra, especially on Thanksgiving!"

Charlie smiled as a fresh batch of tears welled up in his eyes, remembering the meat-lover's pizzas and half-pound bacon cheeseburgers that Katie had ordered on their dates. Somehow, the love of this family overshadowed Charlie's glaring red blemish in every way, making it as though the mistake had never even happened.

"See," said Katie softly in his ear as her hand found his, "I *told* you you were going to do just fine."

Charlie stared into the eyes of his brown-haired beauty as the tears pressing against the banks of his eyes rolled down his cheeks.

"Here," she said, releasing his hand and grabbing a bowl from the table. She then lifted the large silver serving spoon out of the bowl and knocked it against his plate as she looked him in the eye, her face smirking with mischievous joy.

"Have some cranberry sauce."

Later that evening, after the meal and the pie were finished, the Monroe family sat around the fire in the living room, enjoying each other's company. Dave and Angie asked Charlie the same kind of probing questions that Katie had first asked him in Charming Beard almost two months before—questions not about where he worked or what he was majoring in, but about his deepest motivations, his hopes and dreams.

Charlie and Katie sat cuddling together on the couch under the windows while Dave and Angie sat cuddled up in one of the armchairs across from them. Grace sat with them, curled up in the other armchair and immersed in her coloring book. Ellie had retreated to her room after dinner.

"Oo! Oo!" said Katie excitedly as she looked up at Charlie then at her parents. "I've got one. What's your favorite Disney character?" she asked, looking up at Charlie.

Charlie looked down at her, smiling as he played with her hair. "Uh, I guess I'd have to say Simba," he said. "I loved the Lion King growing up."

Katie's eyes were beaming at him, almost as though her soul fed off the knowledge of who he was. She knew that Charlie related with Simba, having lost his family when he was far too young. Charlie then turned to Dave and Angie.

"What about you, Dave? Favorite Disney character?" asked Charlie.

"Mm…Goofy," said Dave as he smiled before taking a sip of the wine Charlie had brought. Somehow, Dave's answer seemed to fit so well with who he was, and it made Charlie smile even more.

"How about you, Angie?" he asked.

"Minnie Mouse," she said as she looked from her husband to Charlie, smiling.

Charlie then looked down at the beautiful woman resting her head in his lap. When the silence had lingered long enough, Katie looked up at him with playful innocence in her eyes.

"What?" she asked.

"Oh, no no," he said. "You're not getting out of answering this one." Charlie then turned to Dave and Angie. "Do you know that for our first three dates, Katie asked me countless questions but wouldn't let me ask her any?"

Dave and Angie chuckled. "Sounds about right," said Dave.

Charlie turned his eyes back to Katie, who was still looking up at him. "Well?" he said.

Katie smiled at him as she took a deep breath and exhaled.

"Okay, fine," she said. "But just this once!"

Charlie grinned as he continued to play with her hair. "We'll see," he said.

"Tigger," she said. Charlie looked at her with intense interest in her answer. "You know," she said, "always bouncin' around, full of energy…it fits, doesn't it?"

Charlie chuckled. "Yeah," he said, "I guess it does." Charlie then noticed that Grace was sound asleep in her armchair, her crayon still in hand.

"Oh, wow," said Charlie. "I didn't realize how late it is. I should probably get home."

Dave and Angie looked at each other, confused, then turned to look at Katie. Charlie's face contorted into a puzzled look as he, too, turned to look at the woman still laying with her head in his lap. As she turned her face from her parents to Charlie, he saw that she was wearing her usual mischievous grin.

"You haven't asked him?" said Dave.

Eyes still locked on Charlie, her playful mischief bursting at the seams, Katie popped the question. "Do you wanna spend the night?" she asked.

Charlie suddenly felt terribly awkward. Not only did her parents know about his reputation, but their daughter was now asking him to spend the night in her bed.

"Not in *my* bed," said Katie, reading his mind as her mischievous grin turned to an oh-brother smirk and then to a low giggle. "In the guest room!"

Charlie then remembered the fireplace he'd seen earlier, warming the room that on most days was empty.

"I'd love to," said Charlie softly, "but I didn't bring any of my things."

"That's not a problem at all, dear," said Angie. "We've got plenty of toothbrushes and fresh tubes of paste. Plus, we even give you a brand new pair of pajamas to remember your stay with us!"

Charlie beamed at her as his eyes again glazed over with tears, his heart melting in the warmth of this family's continued welcome.

"No one should be alone on Thanksgiving, Charlie," said Dave, his tone firm but soft. "If you have no home to go to, then *this* will be your home."

Charlie looked from Angie to Dave as the glaze over his eyes softened and began to run down his cheeks, his soul reeling more than he ever thought it could from this family's unthinkable love for a man they had only just met.

"Okay," said Charlie, smiling at them, "I'd love to."

"Wonderful," said Angie, her eyes filled with the compassion and warmth that had become all-too-familiar to Charlie. "Katie'll get you all set up. Just holler if you need anything, okay?"

Charlie nodded, and together, the four of them got up. After giving Charlie a warm hug, Dave and Angie made their way to the stairs, pausing as Dave scooped Grace up in his arms. Although Grace was now sound asleep, she did not let go of her crayon, even as her dad carried her up to bed.

Katie then led Charlie to the guest room, where the fire was still lit, warming the room with hues of red and amber. Charlie paused at the door, and when she noticed that Charlie was no longer with her, Katie turned around, her face confused and a little worried.

"What's wrong?" she asked.

Charlie stared at her, his eyes still wet with tears. She smiled warmly as she patiently waited for an answer.

"Thank you, Katie," he said, softly, scared to look her in the eye.

Katie was quick to step toward him and wrap him in her arms. "Thank me?" she said, gazing up into his tear-glossed eyes. "For what?"

"For all *this!*" said Charlie, tilting his head to point to the room in which they now stood. "For bringing me into your family and giving me a place to—" Charlie paused, unsure of where his brain intended to take the thought he had begun to voice.

"A place to?" asked Katie gently as she looked up at him, still wearing her warm smile.

"A place to call home," said Charlie, choking on his words as fresh tears began to run down his cheeks.

Still smiling at him, Katie reached up and began to wipe away his tears. "You will always be welcome here, Charlie," she said as she wrapped her arms around his waist. "And I mean that."

Charlie just smiled at her. He did not know what to say. "Thank you," he exhaled in what was barely a whisper. He pulled Katie in close and the two stood for several minutes, saturated in the warmth of their embrace, before Katie showed Charlie the bathroom, where there was a drawer full of new toothbrushes and miniature tubes of toothpaste. She then got his room ready for him, pulling down the comforter and tidying up the pillows while Charlie brushed his teeth and changed into the fresh pajamas he'd picked out.

Charlie climbed into bed, and Katie tucked him in tightly.

"Now," she said as she made sure the sheet and blanket were tucked securely under the mattress, "*no* sneaking up to my room in the middle of the night, okay mister?"

Charlie smiled at her. "K," he said softly, his face grinning. Katie stole a kiss from her lover's lips before moving to the doorway. There, she leaned against the doorpost as she pulled the door closed, leaving only her head poking through.

"Goodnight, Charlie Shaw," she said as she smiled before flicking off the light and closing the door. She had left the fire burning to keep him warm.

"Goodnight, Katie," said Charlie softly after the door had closed. After staring for several seconds at the closed door, faintly illuminated by the flickering of the fireplace, Charlie rolled over in bed and gazed at the river flowing by outside his window, its still waters shimmering in the evening moonlight.

As the weight of evening sleep slowly overpowered his eyes, Charlie thought back with a heavy yet healing heart on all of the love that had been so abundantly showered on him that day. For the first time in over seven years—perhaps for the first time in his life—Charlie felt fully known and truly loved. For the first time in quite some time, Charlie felt at home; and that night, he slept more soundly than he had in years.

9

Confessions

Charlie stood tall in the bathroom of his apartment as he tied a red silk tie around the white collar pinching his neck, with nothing but the incandescent shades of the vanity light to guide his effort. It was dark outside in Charlottesville. Winter had settled in over this small college town, and the sun was now setting in the western sky over the Blue Ridge Mountains a few minutes before five o'clock each day.

It had been exactly a week since Charlie spilled the cranberry sauce, and tonight he and Katie were joining the Monroe family for a concert at Grace's school to celebrate the advent of the Christmas season.

Charlie let the tie fall and pulled it in tight around his neck before turning his shirt collar down to cover it. The bottom point of his tie came to just above his belt buckle, exactly where he wanted it.

That night would be Katie's first time seeing Charlie all dressed up, and he knew how important it was that she not be disappointed. He had spared no expense in busting out the suit he hadn't worn in over three years and getting it tailored for his big debut.

Satisfied with his tie, Charlie rotated his shoulders several times in the mirror to reassure himself that he looked as good as he thought. He then returned to his bedroom to grab his jacket.

"Hoo! Damn, son!" said Michael, laughing as Charlie exited the bathroom. "She's not gonna be able to keep her hands off you!"

"That *is* the hope," said Charlie as he spun around, grinning ear-to-ear while walking backwards into his room.

"Say, when do I get to meet this girl?" asked Michael.

"Uh," said Charlie, looking at the watch he wore around his wrist. It had a plain face with a small window near the three o'clock mark that gave him the date, and was held around his wrist by an old, beat-up brown leather band. It was nothing special, save for one simple thing: the watch had once belonged to his father, and it was something Charlie only wore on very special occasions.

The time was 5:40pm. "Tonight, if she's here already," he said, disappearing briefly into his room to grab his jacket.

Michael stood up from his football game, his gazed fixed on the words that had just come from Charlie's mouth. He was far less interested in the football game than he was in the prospect of meeting the girl who had so captivated his roommate's heart. It had not yet been two months since an unexpected thunderstorm forced Charlie into that coffee shop, but it was already clear to Charlie's roommate that something was different about this girl— quite different.

Charlie returned from his room as he pulled his suit jacket onto his shoulders, folding down the collar. He then buttoned the top button and looked up at Mike.

"C'mon," he said, passing Mike on his way to the door. Michael hurried excitedly after him.

Charlie stepped out into the frosty winter darkness and looked down at the curb below, to the place where Katie usually picked him up. There was her white, four-door sedan, parked curbside. Katie, however, was nowhere to be seen. Charlie figured that she was inside the car keeping warm, and it made him much happier knowing that she was comfortable than if she were waiting for him out in the cold.

As Charlie and Mike descended the final staircase to the sidewalk that led to the curb, Charlie heard the pop of Katie's car door and saw his brown-haired beauty climb out and walk around to greet them.

His heart skipped more than a few beats, and whether because of her beauty or the tie cinched around his neck, Charlie was not sure, but when Katie came into view, he struggled to catch his breath, slowing his pace as he gazed open-jawed at his lover. She wore a long-sleeved red cocktail dress that had a large, matching red bow on her waist. Her thick brown hair shimmered in the moonlight and the pop of her black closed-toed heels echoed off the walls of Charlie's apartment building with every step she took. She wore hardly any makeup, and held a black clutch in her left hand as she walked. As much of an effort as Charlie had made to woo her with his attire that night, she had far outdone him.

"Hi," she said with bright red lips that parted to form a smile as she gazed at Charlie with her familiar chocolate-brown eyes, her breath visible in the frosty air.

"Who's this?" she inquired as she looked at Michael.

"Um, oh," said Charlie, blinking several times as he snapped out of his trance, his heart and lungs catching up as his manners returned to him.

"This is Mike, my roommate. He wanted to meet you, and I figured we had enough ti—"

"Well hi, Mike!" exclaimed Katie, cutting off Charlie's excuse. She did not need excuses when it came to people. She loved them, whenever, wherever she was. "I'm Katie," she said, extending her hand with a bright smile on her face.

Michael did not bother with a handshake, instead lowering his torso and wrapping his arms around the beautiful Katie Monroe.

"Uh. *Oh!*" said Katie, laughing as Mike lifted her slightly off the ground, squeezing her tight.

"Thank you," he said as he set her back down, still holding her closely in his embrace.

Katie laughed as she leaned back from their embrace, looking Mike in the eye. "Thank me? For what?"

"For lovin' on Charlie so," he said as he placed his giant hands gently on her tiny shoulders.

Katie looked at Charlie with that familiar tenderness in her eyes. "He makes it easy," she said. Charlie smiled with gratitude at the undeserved love Katie continued to shower on him. How had he been so lucky to find such a woman, a woman with so much beauty and such incredible depth?

Katie then turned her gaze back to her new friend. "So Mike, tell me about *you*!" she exclaimed, gently nudging him with her fist.

"Uh," said Mike, unsure of how to respond to such enthusiasm. "I play football," he said.

"*Do* you now?" said Katie.

"Yeah," he said, bashfully shuffling his feet. He did not understand why Katie was taking such an interest in him.

"This is Mike Ross," Charlie chimed in with a smile.

"Wait, seriously?" asked Katie, turning back to Mike. "*The* Mike Ross? The guy who throws would-be rapists through walls?"

"'Fraid so," he said, averting her gaze in an ill-fated attempt to hide his embarrassment at her admiration.

"We *love* you!" she said as she took a step toward him and, standing on her tiptoes, wrapped her arms around him to give him another hug. Her arms could not reach all the way around big Mike, but she hugged him all the same.

"Uh…oh," said Mike, unsure of what to do as he cautiously wrapped his arms around her.

"Monroes are big huggers," said Charlie with a tone that reeked of experience.

Katie then released Mike and stood gazing up at him as she started to shiver, rubbing her arms. "It was *so* nice to meet you, Mike!"

"Yeah, uh, nice to meet you, too," said Mike.

"Alright, Mike, we're gonna get going," said Charlie. "You want another hug?"

"Nah, I'm alright," said Mike. Charlie chuckled.

"K, I'll be back later."

"Alright," said Michael, raising his voice as he turned cooly on his heels to head back up to their apartment. "You keep your hands off her now, Charlie!" he said, laughing as he hustled up the stairs to the warmth of their apartment.

"Oh, don't worry, Mike," Katie shouted back through shivering teeth as she pulled Charlie in close by his tie and stole a kiss, "it's gonna be *me* who has a hard time keeping my hands off of *him*."

She then released him slightly as she concealed her bottom lip with her teeth, staring longingly at his lips.

"Hoo! Damn. Ha-*ha!*" said Mike as he continued his ascent, slowing briefly to watch Katie pull Charlie in close. "Well you kids have fun, then!"

"Oh, we will," whispered Katie as she stole another kiss, gently holding Charlie's lips captive as she closed her eyes and wrapped her arms around his waist. Charlie's eyes closed, his heart soaking in the ecstasy and the warmth of their embrace as she held him close. The light scent of Katie's perfume slowly found its way to Charlie's nostrils, and his soul followed it as it carried him off to that place where time stood still and love reigned.

Charlie was brought back to reality with an unwelcome jolt as Katie's hands slapped his hips. "Now come on, my legs are freezing!" she said as she hurried around the front of the car and opened the door on the other side.

Charlie opened his eyes, blinking several times as he swallowed hard. He smiled. He had been brought back to reality, but the foretaste of the eternity to which their passion took him left him desperately longing for more. Katie knew how to romance this man of hers, and he gladly welcomed her initiative.

"You okay?" she asked, staring across the hood of her car at her starstruck lover.

"Yeah. Yeah!" said Charlie as he hurriedly opened his door and climbed inside to where the heat was blowing. He knew that it was warmer inside the car than outside in the frigid air of Charlottesville's winter, yet somehow he did not feel as warm as he felt when immersed in Katie's embrace.

The two of them drove again through the streets of downtown Charlottesville and into the neighborhoods on the north side of town. Katie let out an enormous yawn as she drove.

"Huhhh-*HUM!*" came the noise from Katie's mouth.

"Little tired, are we?" asked Charlie, smiling as he looked at her.

"Yeah!" said Katie. "And it's weird, too. I got like twelve hours of sleep last night. I think I'm just beat with finals and everything coming up. I keep feeling like I can't get enough sleep."

"Hmm," said Charlie with a facade of concern. "Well, I mean, I'd be happy to come spend the night in bed with you if you think it'd help you sleep better."

Katie's head snapped in his direction as she glared at him with a playful smirk on her face.

"If! I said if!" said Charlie, protesting as he, too, smiled. Katie just shook her head, still smiling as she turned off the road into the parking lot of Indian Hills Elementary School. It was an older school, nestled back in the protection of one of Charlottesville's smaller hills. On the side of its red-brick building hung a banner advertising the school's seventh annual Christmas concert, and bright lights shone through the windows of the school into the darkness of the outer world.

The parking lot was packed, but by some luck, Katie managed to find them a spot not too far from the building, and together, they walked arm-in-arm up a small set of concrete stairs and down the long sidewalk to the school's double-doored entrance.

The inside of the school smelled a dollop of stale carpet with a dash of sweating children. The short benches and small hooks fixed to the walls along the hallways took Charlie back to his youth, running with his friends through the halls of Bennion Elementary School out to recess and to the lunchroom, with Mrs. Larsen affectionately yelling at them to stop running in the halls as she followed in their wake.

Inside Grace's school, there was a long hallway that ran its width along the front of the building, with open glass on one side and smaller hallways that led to classrooms on the other, branching off from the main hallway every thirty feet or so. Up and down the hallways, covering almost every square inch of the walls and even hanging from the ceilings was the artwork of the school's many children, much of it themed for the Christmas season.

Katie led Charlie to the right as they stepped inside the school's main doors, down the long hallway to where it teed, branching off to the right and to the left. At the end of both of these branches, on the wall furthest from the school's main entrance, were a pair of double oaken doors that fed into the auditorium.

When Katie and Charlie reached the end of the main hallway, Katie steered the two of them to the right, down the short hallway to one such pair of doors. They were propped open, and a younger woman with straight black hair greeted them, welcoming them as she handed programs to Charlie and Katie. Together, they both stood in the doorway while Katie gazed around the room in search of her family. The auditorium was packed full of students' family and friends, all of them socializing while they sat in anxious anticipation of their sons' and daughters' performance that evening.

After surveying the auditorium, Charlie joined Katie in her search, and not more than ten seconds had gone by before he spotted Angie's flailing arms in the third row of the middle section.

"There they are," he said, nudging Katie as he pointed in the direction of Angie's here-we-are dance.

Katie turned and smiled at him, then hand-in-hand, she and Charlie made their way across the back of the auditorium to the aisle that divided the middle section from the right wing of chairs, then up the aisle to the third row, where they apologetically scooted by two elderly couples as they made their way to the block of seats where Katie's parents stood waiting to receive them. Ellie sat next to her parents, seemingly tuned out to Katie and Charlie's arrival.

"Oh, Charlie," said Angie as she hugged him, giving him a kiss on the cheek. "How are you, dear?"

Charlie laughed at the amount of warmth that radiated from this small woman. "I'm good," he said, smiling at her. "And you?"

"So much better now that you two are here," she confessed as she stole another warm hug from him before passing him on to Dave.

"Charlie," said Dave enthusiastically with a small growl in his voice. Charlie went for a handshake, but Dave would have none of it. He wrapped his arms around Charlie in a firm yet affectionate man-hug.

"Oh, go on and sit next to Katie," interrupted Angie as the lights dimmed. "The show's about to start, and I just *know* you two are gonna wanna cuddle."

Charlie gazed over his shoulder at Angie, his face slightly panicked at her words, given all that she knew about him. Angie just winked at him, still smiling as the dim light turned to darkness in the auditorium.

Charlie quietly and anxiously scooted to his seat and plopped himself down next to his lover. He had barely managed to unbutton his jacket when she leaned into him, resting her head on his shoulder as the school's principal took the stage to welcome them all to the evening's performance.

The principal was a black woman who wore no colors but for the bright red polish on her nails. Her skirt and blazer were both made of a fine wool that had been died black—or perhaps a very dark gray—and she had straight black hair that was combed neatly over to the left as she stood proud on the stage in a pair of black patent leather pumps.

"Good evening, everyone," she said. "My name is Diana Swallow, and as the principal, it is my distinct honor to welcome you all to Indian Hills Elementary School. I want to say what an honor it is to teach your children each and every day here at this school. As you'll see tonight, every one of these wonderful children has so much talent and potential, and it is truly an honor to be a part of the process by which they realize that.

"So, without further adieu, let me introduce our first act, a solo by our very own Grace Monroe!"

Diana stepped off the stage as the curtain withdrew to the sides, revealing little Grace standing with her violin. She, too, had gotten dolled up for the evening, and looked positively adorable standing on stage at just under four feet tall in a pair of black Mary Janes, with her strawberry blond hair lightly curled, falling over her shoulders.

Katie sat up as Grace was introduced, whistling and clapping loudly for her little sister. Charlie, too, put his hands together for the wonder of little Grace Monroe. When she spotted her family seated so close to the front, Grace smiled at them, her face beaming with delight at their loving support.

She then tucked her violin under her chin and began to play "O Come, O Come Emmanuel." Her bow hand and her fingers moved with impeccable harmony, the taut horsehair of her bow bringing to life the notes she fretted with her tiny hand as she sailed effortlessly through the melody of this deeply moving carol.

Katie and Charlie both leaned forward in their seats. For Katie, this was just Grace; but for Charlie, this was a true marvel. Grace Monroe was a talented colorer, yes; but the way her hands moved so effortlessly in consonance with one another as she danced the notes of this familiar song brought Charlie to the verge of tears.

When Grace had finished the four counts of the final note, she released the instrument from her chin and, holding both bow and violin at her side, grinning ear-to-ear, she took a bow as the audience erupted in applause. She was given a standing ovation, and Charlie knew that night that he had seen something very special in the performance of Grace Monroe.

After Grace stepped off the stage, the performance continued as the second grade class took the stage and stood on some risers behind where Grace had played so effortlessly, and together, they sung an especially upbeat form of "Deck the Halls." But Charlie did not notice much of the remaining performances, as children from every different grade and all walks of life took the stage to celebrate the season that had befallen Charlottesville. His mind and his heart were caught up instead by the wonder and emotion of Grace's almost perfect performance.

The concert finished with an immaculate rendition of "We Wish You a Merry Christmas" by the school's sixth grade class, each of them with beautiful voices that coalesced together in melodious harmony and served as a lovely send-off into the holiday season for the family and friends of all the school's students.

Afterward, parents and families mingled in the main hallway as they waited for their children to find them and be taken home.

The Monroes managed to stake out a spot in the intersection where the main hallway teed, and Charlie stood with his arm wrapped around Katie as Dave and Angie mingled with the parents of other students. Ellie stood to Angie's left, leaning against the wall with her hands behind her back as she stared at her feet. She wore a pair of comfy black flats with a black linen skirt and white cotton blouse. It was clear that Ellie Monroe did not enjoy dressing up, certainly not as much as her older sister.

"Hey Ellie," said Charlie, acknowledging the only family member to whom he had yet to say hello.

Ellie looked up from her feet, staring at him before uttering a solemn, "Hey." She then returned to staring at her feet.

"Charlie!" came another, smaller voice from behind him. No sooner had Charlie turned around than tiny Grace lunged into his legs, wrapping her arms around him as Katie laughed at Charlie's surprise. Charlie felt butterflies tickling his soul as this beautiful girl showered him with a love that was so common in this family.

"Hi, Grace," said Charlie, squatting down to face her eye-to-eye. "That was quite the performance you had there!" he said as he placed a hand on her shoulder.

"Thanks, Charlie," she said bashfully as she looked at her feet and swung her dress from side to side with her hands hidden behind her back.

"I'm very proud of you," said Charlie. "Now, gimme another hug!" Grace leapt at the idea, and threw herself again into Charlie's arms as Charlie stood up, lifting her off the ground and holding her in his arms. "Look what your dad got for you," he said as they turned to face Dave.

Dave smiled, stealing a kiss from his youngest daughter's cheek as he handed her the bouquet of flowers he'd been carrying and told her how very proud of her he was. Charlie then handed little Grace off to Dave, and together, the six of them walked out into the parking lot to make their way to the Lawn for a ceremony that, although fairly new, was fast becoming a tradition in Charlottesville.

"Can I ride with Charlie?" asked Grace as the six of them stepped down the small set of concrete stairs in front of the school.

Both of her parents laughed as they looked at Charlie. Charlie shrugged, unsure of what it was that the seven-year-old saw in him.

"Yeah, sweetie, you can ride with Charlie," said Dave, setting her down. Grace ran to Charlie, who squatted down to meet her, then lifted her into his arms.

"Okay," said Dave, "so we'll see you guys there? Where do you guys wanna meet?"

"Uh," said Charlie, emitting the hum of his braincells as he looked to Katie, "how about by the Jefferson statue? I hear that's a good meeting spot," he said as he winked at Katie.

"Sounds good!" said Dave. "We'll see you there." He and Angie then took Ellie to their car while Charlie walked with Katie to the parking spot they'd been so lucky to find, holding Grace in his arms as she tiredly rested her head on his shoulders.

"I'm glad you came, Charlie," said Grace, still resting her head on his shoulder. Charlie turned to look at her, his heart melted by the warmth of the child in his arms.

"I'm glad I came, too, Grace," he said, remembering her spectacular performance.

When they got to Katie's car, Charlie opened the back door and let Grace climb inside. He then closed the door and turned to his lover, who was standing behind him looking beautiful as ever, even in the musty yellow hues of the parking lot's overhead lights. She was beaming at him, her eyes filled with adoration for the love Charlie had for her youngest sister as she leaned in to steal a kiss from him.

"You mind if I ride with Grace in the back seat?" asked Charlie as the two parted lips. "I think it'd mean a lot to her."

"Okay," said Katie, gently pulling him in close by his tie, "but later tonight, I get you all to myself," she said as she stared longingly at his lips.

Charlie smiled as he gazed down at the strands of Katie's hair. "I like the sound of *that*," he said softly. She tilted her head back to stare into his eyes as she stole another kiss before releasing her grip on his tie and walking around the front of her car to the driver's side while Charlie climbed in the back with Grace, who was overjoyed to have him sit with her.

Charlie discussed a number of important topics with the young Grace Monroe while Katie chauffeured the two of them into downtown Charlottesville, including new movies she'd seen and all of her latest coloring projects.

In the last week alone, Grace had finished *eight* whole pictures, including a picture of two deer standing in a meadow, one of an elephant, and another of three zebras in some tall African grass.

"*That* grass was very hard to color," said Grace, "but I figured it out. I'll teach you how to do it the next time we color, okay Charlie?"

"That would be wonderful, Grace," he said.

Charlie glanced up at Katie several times during their conversation. She kept looking at him in her rear-view mirror, beaming as he showed such an intense interest in Grace's life. It was clear that Katie herself had a very special relationship with Grace, but this was no surprise to Charlie: Grace had the same confidence in who she was and what she could do that Katie had, albeit with a little less humility. Grace and Katie were like two peas in a pod, and it melted Charlie's heart to think that Grace, much like her sister, had found something to love in him.

After about twenty minutes of driving, Katie found a parking spot near a small boutique that was two doors up from ol' Ben's bookstore, and together, the three of them got out of the car and made their way toward University Avenue. Katie and Charlie each held Grace's hand and lifted her off the ground as they walked, swinging her back and forth as she laughed with all the joy and the innocence of childhood.

"Hey, Grace," said Charlie as Grace recovered from a swing. The three of them now stood on the sidewalk outside Crossroads Bookstore.

"Yeah, Charlie?" asked Grace as her feet settled on the ground and she gazed up at him.

"That's where I work," said Charlie, pointing inside the bookstore's large front window.

"Really!?" said Grace as she ran to the window to peer inside, pressing her nose against the glass.

"Yeah, really?" asked Katie as she stared unbelievingly at her lover.

Charlie laughed. "Yeah. Why?"

"We've known Ben for years," said Katie. "He's been a friend of our family since before I was born."

A small chill ran up Charlie's spine as the words rolled off Katie's lips. He wondered if it was any accident that he happened to duck into Crossroads Bookstore on that fateful day his freshman year. Even in a town of forty thousand people, the odds that Katie and Charlie could have been so close for so long were approaching astronomical. He remembered their conversation about chance in the Shenandoah forest, and wondered if maybe, just maybe, there might be Something—or Someone—behind all of this.

"Okay!" yelled Grace, having had enough of the bookstore.

"Let's *go!*" she said as she came and stood between Katie and Charlie, grabbing each of their hands.

Charlie looked at Katie, shaking his head and smiling incredulously at the confident leadership of this small, energetic little person. They continued their journey to the Jefferson statue, swinging Grace in their arms as they arrived at University Avenue and the statue came into view.

"Oh, there they are!" came Angie's voice faintly from across the street as she turned and pointed in their direction.

After looking both ways, Charlie and Katie escorted their precious cargo across the street, continuing to swing her playfully in their arms. Once on the other side, though, Grace pulled at their arms, wanting to be released. Charlie and Katie let her go, and little Grace ran into her papa's arms as Dave picked her up and swung her around.

"Did you have a fun time with Katie and Charlie?" asked Dave.

"Yeah!" said Grace. "*I* got to see where Charlie works!" she boasted.

"Oh yeah," asked Dave, turning to Charlie, "where's that?"

"He works at Ben's bookstore," Katie said before Charlie could answer. Both of her parents looked at Charlie with faces that echoed the chill that had earlier pulsed up Charlie's spine.

"Who knew that all this time you were so close to us, Charlie," said Angie as she came and gave him a warm hug. "I'm so glad we finally got to meet," she said softly, nestled in their hug.

Charlie was overwhelmed by Angie's words, which gave voice to the emotion spurned by his inner dialogue about the relationship between chance and Creator. He was barely able to hold it together as he stood for almost a minute in the warmth of Angie's embrace; yet Angie did not seem to mind their prolonged hug, almost as if she knew about the waters of emotion churning in his soul.

The sound of thousands of voices intermixed with the harmonious coalescence of one of the university's a cappella groups echoed from the far side of the Rotunda, reminding them of why they'd come. Together they turned, and as they started to walk in the direction of the party, Katie snuggled into Charlie, wrapping her arm around his waist as he wrapped his arm around her. He held her close as they walked while his mind once again questioned whether this was all just happenstance.

As they stepped out onto the Lawn amid the shadows and silhouettes of thousands of university students and Charlottesville residents, Grace jumped insistently at Dave's side, her arms stretched high as she pleaded to be lifted up and see all that was going on. Dave obliged, lifting Grace high above his head and onto his shoulders.

The six of them came to rest in the middle of the crowd about thirty yards from the Rotunda, and Charlie pulled Katie around to his front and draped his arms over her shoulders, pulling her in close to keep her warm as they swayed back and forth to the a cappella rendition of Eartha Kitt's "Santa Baby." Charlie felt as he usually did with Katie in his arms, only it seemed more amplified this time around, now that he stood with not just her, but her entire family.

The a cappella group finished their performance with an augmented exhortation for Santa to hurry down the chimney that night, and after taking a bow to resounding applause, the group left the stage while a balding man with an egg-shaped head and round spectacles walked up the small set of stairs on the side of the stage and stood at a boom that held one of the microphones.

"Hello, and good evening," said the man, who was British. "My name is Richard Wilson, and I count myself highly fortunate to serve as the president of this great school. Residents of Charlottesville, my dear students, it is my great honor and pleasure to welcome you all out this evening as we celebrate together the holiday season that is once again upon us with the annual Lighting of the Lawn. As many of you know, this ceremony did not start in a time of joy but one of sorrow, as our nation sought to recover from one of the most heart-wrenching and devastating blows it has ever been dealt.

"And yet tonight we do not gather in sorrow, but in joy, for with the magic and wonder of the holiday season comes the promise of hope, the promise of a better world. Tonight, that is what we celebrate. Tonight, we look forward with longing anticipation to the better world of tomorrow.

"Now, if you will all please join me in counting down… Ten! Nine! Eight!…"

Charlie and the Monroe family echoed the balding man's countdown with thousands more as the tension steadily mounted in the crowd around them.

"Four! Three! Two! One!"

In a flash, the Lawn and the Rotunda lit up brightly with Christmas lights that were wrapped around every column and draped along every rooftop. Lights had even been woven up and between the trees, draping over the large expanse of grass on which they all now stood. Students and residents alike gazed up in wonder at the beauty all around them as the school's jazz band broke out in a celebratory performance of "Joy to the World."

Charlie and Katie wore ear-to-ear grins as they gazed up at the light that now radiated from all around them, and as they turned around to see it all, something caught Charlie's eye that gave him pause. Katie looked at him, then in the direction he was staring.

For the first time that Charlie had ever seen, Ellie Monroe was smiling, her face lit up with awe at the splendor that shone all around her. She then noticed Katie and Charlie staring at her, their faces wearing even bigger grins, having seen the joy of this girl who rarely if ever showed emotion; but Ellie's smile did not fade as she stared at them, and as the three of them stood, gazes locked, something deep within Charlie's heart began to change. For the first time in almost as long as he could remember, he felt at though he had once again been given what had so tragically been taken from him.

There, at the Lighting of the Lawn on that chilly night in early December, as Charlie stared at a beaming Ellie Monroe, the lone holdout to welcome him into the Monroe clan, Charlie felt for the first time in well over seven years that he had at long last been given what his heart had so desperately yearned for: a family.

The Monroe family stayed on the Lawn for as long as they could bear, celebrating the advent of the holiday season with their fellow Charlottesville residents. It wasn't long before Grace grew tired, and went from sitting on her daddy's shoulders to being held in his arms, where she collapsed in a deep slumber, her head resting on her papa's shoulder; and that's when the Monroe family knew it was time to go. Even in her sleep, Grace exercised leadership of those around her.

Katie and Charlie said their goodbyes to the rest of the family at the Jefferson statute, then made their way back in the direction of Katie's car, holding each other close as they walked.

"What happened with Ellie tonight was incredible," said Katie softly. "I can't remember the last time I've seen her smile like that."

"Yeah," said Charlie, his heart still caught up in the wonder of it all as his mind danced through the evening's events.

Whether because of his silence or a deeper connection the two of them shared, Katie sensed that something was wrong and halted their pace, turning to look up at him. "Are you okay?" she asked as she looked into his eyes with her hands on each of his arms.

"Yeah," Charlie lied. "I just," he started, unsure of whether to share with her what he was really feeling. By now, though, Charlie knew that he could trust Katie with what he felt. From the very beginning, she had overlooked even his worst qualities to see in him something that no one else ever had, and through her persistent love, amplified by her family's warmth and acceptance, she had shown him that she was not going anywhere. It was safe for him to tell her how he felt.

"I—for the first time tonight," he started, his eyes welling up with tears as he put to words the feelings of his soul, "for the first time tonight, I felt as though I had a family again." The waters of his soul began to run down his face as he confessed to her the feelings at the center of his being.

Katie smiled as she looked warmly into his eyes, and tears began to run quietly down her cheeks as she, too, felt both his pain and his relief, pulling him in close. Together, soft droplets of joy drenched their faces as they stood outside ol' Ben's bookstore, rocking back and forth in each other's arms.

Later that night, the two of them sat together in Katie's car outside Charlie's apartment building. It was silent, save for the heater blowing on their feet as their bodies unthawed from the frigid night's air. Charlie remembered his earlier promise, and he knew that Katie would not enforce it without some assurance, not with what Charlie's heart had been through that night.

"So," he said, breaking the silence, "do you still want me all to yourself?" he asked as he turned to look at Katie with a grin of excitement on his face.

Katie snapped her head in his direction, her face wearing its usual grin of mischief. She was excited at the prospect of once again journeying with him to the place where time stood still.

The two popped open the doors to her car, exposing themselves to a torrent of cold air. Together, they hurried up the stairs to Charlie's apartment where they knew they would be warm again. Outside the door, Charlie fumbled with his keys, his whole body shaking from a combination of cold and excitement.

He finally managed to get the door open, and the two of them stepped inside, pausing by the kitchen table as Charlie closed the door behind them.

"So," he said, "this is my apartment."

Katie looked around, gazing from the table, to the kitchen, to the sitting area as she nodded in silence, paying her dues to common etiquette. What she really wanted was him, all to herself, just as he'd promised.

"That's where Mike watches football," said Charlie when he saw that Katie's gaze had come to rest on the seating area to the right of the door.

"Speaking of Mike," said Katie softly, "is he awake?"

"I…don't know, actually," said Charlie.

Together, the two tiptoed through the main room and down the hallway that led to Charlie's room. They paused outside Mike's room, and stared in at the sleeping lump under the covers, then at each other, their faces dawning grins of excitement. Charlie gently closed Mike's door as the two continued down the hallway to Charlie's room with Katie in the lead, pulling him by the hand.

"And this," said Charlie as they stepped inside, his voice now very soft, "is my room."

Katie stepped into the middle of his room, gazing around at his neatly made bed, his small desk, and the open door to his messy closet. Charlie closed the bedroom door behind them, and no sooner had he turned around than Katie jumped him, pushing him against the door he had just closed as she pressed her lips firmly and passionately into his, not letting up as she removed his jacket and loosened his tie.

Charlie finished the job, removing his tie and unbuttoning the top button of his shirt as the two of them fumbled their way over to his bed, where they both lay down, Charlie on top of Katie, as they continued to drink in the sparks on each other's lips.

With any other girl whose lips Charlie was savoring in the privacy of his room, Charlie would not have hesitated to begin removing her clothes, letting his hands wander up her dress as he invited her into his bed. But Charlie remembered his conversation with Katie on the day he spilled the cranberry sauce, and much though Charlie knew Katie would not push him that far because she knew he deserved the mutual promise of unwavering commitment, Charlie also knew that this girl, even more than he, deserved just such a man, a man who would not allow her to give herself to him without first promising before God and men that he was not going anywhere. And Charlie had resolved that he would be such a man, that he *could* be such a man.

That night, the two lay in Charlie's bed, partaking of each other's lips in the ardent ecstasy that left them both yearning for more. It was only a little over an hour until Katie sat up, fixing up her hair and putting her shoes back on her feet.

"Really?" Charlie whined, disappointed that their time in a place where there was no such thing had already come to a close.

Katie looked at him, smiling as she held up her hair. She then gave him one more kiss on the cheek. "I need to get going before I fall asleep here."

Much though Charlie wanted to protest, insisting that she stay the night in his bed, he knew what Katie's answer would be.

"Alright," he said, his tone conciliatory as he, too, put his shoes back on and retrieved his jacket. Katie looked at him.

"Al*right*?" she said, her face both confused and intrigued. "No sly comment that I'd already warmed your bed and might as well stay the night?"

Charlie smiled at her. "You deserve a man who'll promise he's not going anywhere first. I'm trying to be that man for you."

Tears glossed over Katie's eyes as she looked at him, then with but a few quick steps, she buried herself in his arms. Charlie pulled her in close, kissing the top of her head as the windows into his soul shimmered with his own tears. Somehow, in the less-than-two months that he had spent with Katie and her family, Charlie Shaw's heart had been changed. He did not want a girl who would warm his bed for a weekend; he wanted a woman he could cherish for a lifetime.

Together, the two of them then walked out, down the stairs from Charlie's apartment to Katie's small, white sedan. They paused in front of her car for one last goodnight hug.

Katie made her way around to the driver door and opened it. Charlie stood still at the front of her car, a blank stare on his face.

"Katie," he said softly as he turned to look at her.

She turned her gaze from the inside of her car to meet his eyes. "I—" Charlie paused, fighting the urge to look away as he reminded himself once again that he could share with Katie all that was in his heart.

"I love you," he said. Never before had Charlie uttered those words to a woman. They were almost foreign to his lips, and yet he knew in that confession that he had given truest voice to the rivers of emotion flowing in his heart.

"I know," said Katie as she smiled at him from the driver side of her car. She then closed her door and walked over to him, wrapping her arms around his waist as she gazed up into his tear-filled eyes. "And I love you, too."

10

Sanctuary

THE NEXT NINE DAYS OF Charlie and Katie's life were insanely hectic, as both of them prepared for and took their final exams, wrote and submitted final papers, designed and presented final projects. All this work kept these two from seeing each other until an even colder Saturday morning in mid-December, when all of the semester's work had been done.

With school out of the way, Katie and Charlie now had four whole weeks to spend immersed in each other's presence, relishing each other's lips and sharing the deepest feelings of their hearts; and Katie had decided they would start their time together with a morning run.

She picked Charlie up outside his apartment at a few minutes before nine that morning. Exhausted, Katie had slept another twelve hours the night before, recovering from her exams. When they saw each other at long last, they ran into each other's embrace on the sidewalk between building and curb. Charlie lifted Katie off the ground and spun her around in his arms, their hearts full as they nuzzled close, pressing their noses together while staring deeply into each other's eyes.

"G'morning, beautiful," said Charlie as he stole a kiss, his hands resting on her cheeks.

"Mm. Hi," said Katie, smiling back at him with the warmest grin on her face.

A small wisp of frigid air reminded these two lovers of their need to get going, and they hurriedly raced to Katie's car, where it was considerably warmer. When Charlie made it to her car, Katie was already halfway in on the other side. She did not like the cold.

Charlie opened the door to the backseat on the passenger's side to set his suitcase inside. He had once again been invited to spend the night with his newfound family, and not just one night, but every night for the duration of his winter break. After laying his suitcase atop Katie's back seat, Charlie closed the door to the rear and opened the passenger door, then climbed inside.

"Are you ready for our run!?" asked Katie excitedly.

Charlie looked at her, his heart overjoyed to see her again. He leaned in to steal another kiss, then held her there, noses and foreheads pressed together as he gave his answer. "I'm ready for anything with you."

Beaming, Katie stole another kiss from him and the two of them journeyed home once again, making their way through the streets of downtown Charlottesville into the neighborhoods on the north side of town.

It didn't seem like long before Katie was again pulling in to the familiar driveway. Charlie gazed out the window at the home that had become something of a sanctuary for him, a place that held the greatest desires of his heart. He had missed this place.

"You comin'?" asked Katie cheerfully as she opened his door. "Or are you scared that a *girl* might outrun you?"

Wearing the softest of ear-to-ear grins, Charlie turned his gaze from the house to his beloved. He had missed her dearly. "Definitely scared," he said as he stared deep into her eyes, hoping for another kiss. Katie leaned in, supporting herself with one hand on the roof of her car.

"Well, don't be," she said as she gave him what he hoped for. She kept their noses close as she gave him some reassurance. "I won't rub it in *too* much." She then giggled and spun around, practically skipping up the sidewalk that led to the front door.

"*That's* reassuring," said Charlie as he climbed out of the car and retrieved his bag from the seat behind him. Katie just laughed.

"C'mon, scaredy cat," she said playfully as she opened the front door. Charlie followed in her wake, shaking his head with nothing but the sheer joy of his soul painted across his face, as though his spirit were dancing to a never-before-played melody bellowing from the world around him.

"Oh, Charlie!" came Angie's familiar voice as he stepped inside the family home. Charlie turned around from closing the door to see her making her way toward him, sneaking passed Katie to give another one of her cozy hugs. "I'm *so* glad you're coming to stay with us," said Angie, her face beaming at him.

Charlie looked from Angie to Katie, whose face echoed her mother's sentiment. "So am I," said Charlie.

He then made his way to the guest room with his suitcase, setting it inside before walking back through the living room to the kitchen where Angie and Katie stood talking.

"Where's Dave?" asked Charlie.

"Oh, he's out meeting with a client, dear, but he'll be back this afternoon; don't worry," said Angie.

"On a Saturday?" asked Charlie.

"The perils of self-employment," said Angie as she returned to the coffee pot for a refill. Charlie then noticed an open coloring book on the kitchen table with crayons scattered across it. He pointed at it, turning his face to Katie and Angie as he did so. Katie laughed, then proceeded to fill him in.

"When Grace heard you were going to be staying with us for *four* weeks, she could hardly contain her excitement. She dropped her crayons on her coloring book and ran around the house yelling, 'Charlie's coming! Charlie's coming!' And then she crashed. *Hard.* She's still asleep upstairs, but she is going to be so excited to see you when she wakes up."

As he took his first sip of the coffee Angie had poured for him, wrapping his hands around the ceramic mug, Charlie's heart was warmed by the thought of his favorite seven-year-old being so overjoyed to see him.

"So," said Angie, "I hear you two are going for a run."

"Yeah," said Charlie, sipping his coffee, "Katie's gonna kick my butt." Katie laughed, turning to her mother.

"It's true," she said, her voice matter-of-fact. "I am."

The three of them laughed as they continued to share each other's company, catching up on the last nine days of each other's lives. Charlie and Katie then laced up their running shoes and stepped outside the front door into the frigid late-morning air.

Both of them were wearing sweatpants and hooded sweatshirts, and yet both of them still felt the chill of the winter that had settled in over this small college town. Charlie shivered in the cold.

"Are you sure about this?" he asked. "I mean, there are other things we could be doing…"

"Don't worry," she said. "You'll warm up once we get going. Besides, I need to keep your ego in check." She winked at him as they made their way to the end of the driveway.

"Alright, fine," Charlie conceded, standing behind her. "Lead the way."

"You just wanna stare at my butt the whole time," said Katie without turning around.

"Well, yeah," said Charlie matter-of-factly, his gaze fixed. "Where else is my motivation gonna come from?"

Katie looked at him over her shoulder. She was smiling as she shook her head at him.

The two of them then took off on their run. Charlie's chest tightened and his breathing hastened as he remembered just how out of shape he was. It seemed easy for Katie, though, just like their hike through the Shenandoah forest.

They made their way down the old country roads on the north side of Charlottesville, crossing the main road that led back to town and making their way to the small mountains on the other side. Charlie's sides began to cramp. He remembered what his freshman year gym coach had taught him: in through your nose, out through your mouth. Slowly, he began to breathe in accord with his coach's instructions, and his side-cramps lessened.

Charlie then saw where Katie was taking him, as the road turned and banked up the side of a small mountain. His mind dreaded what was ahead as he quickly forgot his gym coach's instructions and his side cramps returned, his face contorting with exhausted anxiety as he saw the ascent in front of him. When Katie turned around at the base of the ascent, though, Charlie's mind quickly snapped out of it, playing it cool as the muscles lining the sides of his abdomen cried out from their torture.

"Race you to the top!" said Katie, smiling.

"You're on!" said Charlie, briefly forgetting just how out of shape he was. Katie turned around and took off, sailing with ease up the hill that to Charlie was so utterly grueling.

Breathing in through his nose and out through his mouth, Charlie put one foot in front of the other, straining with all his might to keep up with his love. He knew that if she beat him to the top, he would spend the next four weeks hearing about it.

But beat him to the top she did. Charlie was still twenty-five yards off when Katie reached the top, but even from a distance, he could see that something was wrong. Katie was bent over, heaving, trying desperately to catch her breath as she supported the weight of her torso with nothing but the hands on her knees. Even from a distance, Charlie saw what happened. His chest tightened with a shot of adrenaline as Katie's eyes rolled back in her head and she collapsed in a heap on the asphalt.

"Katie!" Charlie's side cramps were gone, and with newfound energy he raced desperately to her side. "*KATIE!?*" he screamed, kneeling at her side as he picked her up in his arms, tears streaming down his face. "Somebody *HELP!*" he shouted, looking around at the empty neighborhood.

His gaze snapped up from his lover when he heard the sound of the door to a nearby house opening. A small, rounded Hispanic woman with black hair emerged from the doorway.

"CALL 9-1-1!" Charlie yelled. The woman, seeing Charlie with Katie lying unconscious in his arms, did not pause to ask questions. She hurried into her house to retrieve the phone and call for help.

After what felt like hours to Charlie, she emerged again from her house. "Thank you. And please hurry," Charlie heard her say as she hung up the phone.

Charlie knelt down on the asphalt as he held Katie in his arms, rocking her back and forth as he whispered to her to hang in there, begging her not to leave him.

"Oh my goodness, it's Katie!" said the woman, having finally seen her face.

Charlie gazed up at her, his cheeks drenched in tears. She wasted no time turning on her heels and heading back to the house. After several minutes, she emerged again with the phone to her ear and a Rolodex card in hand.

"Hi, Angie. It's Mary Sanchez," Charlie heard her saying as the sirens drew near. Through tear-fogged, devastated eyes, Charlie stared down at the limp body lying in his arms as the sounds around him grew faint. He almost fought the paramedics when they arrived and pushed him back. He did not want to leave his Katie. He did not want to lose her.

Charlie rode with them in the ambulance, holding Katie's hand as he sat sniffle-sobbing while the paramedics monitored her vital signs. Several minutes later, they pulled into the emergency bay of the university's hospital and quickly hurried Katie out. Charlie followed in their wake.

"Twenty-one-year-old female, passed out while jogging…" Charlie heard them say as a team of nurses and a doctor met them and wheeled the gurney into the E.R. He kept pace with them as they walked with haste down the long hallway to the emergency room. His eyes were fixed on Katie, filled with a desperate hope that she would just wake up and it would all be okay.

"Do you know anything about her medical history?" asked the doctor. Charlie turned to realize that the man was staring at him.

"Uh," said Charlie, trying to pull together a decent thought. "Uh, no, I'm sorry." He began to choke on his tears. "I don't know."

"Okay, what's her name?" asked the doctor.

"Katie Monroe," said Charlie.

The doctor turned to walk away, then paused, taking note of Charlie's emotional state. He turned back, placing a hand on Charlie's shoulder as Charlie looked through tear-stained eyes at the middle-aged brown-haired man.

"We're gonna do everything we can to help her," he said. Charlie nodded, and the doctor left.

Charlie then took a seat next to Katie's bed, holding her hand as he gently rubbed it with his thumb. The nurses had hooked her up to all sorts of machines to help them monitor her status. For Charlie, it only served to amplify the gravity of the situation. He did not like seeing his Katie hooked up to machines.

Unable to sit still, Charlie paced back and forth at the foot of Katie's bed. The doctor returned after minutes that felt like hours to Charlie. "Okay," he said, looking at a thick silver metal clipboard. "Has Katie been sluggish at all lately? Has she been excessively tired, or—"

"Yeah!" said Charlie. "Yeah, she's been sleeping for like twelve hours a night."

Just then, the curtain brushed back. "Oh, Charlie!" said Angie, her voice heartbroken as she ran to embrace the young man she had come to love so much.

"I'm sorry," said the doctor, "are you Katie's parents?"

"Yes," said Dave, his face and tone quite serious as he locked gazes with the doctor, waiting for news.

"Perhaps we'd better talk somewhere private," said the doc.

"No, no," said Dave, looking to Charlie. "Charlie's family."

"Okay," said the doctor, hesitating with the news. "Well, based on what Charlie told me, I suspect that Katie's pre-B ALL is back." Dave and Angie's faces darkened.

"What's pre-B ALL?" asked Charlie.

"It's a form of leukemia," said the doctor. "It usually affects children. Katie had it when she was fourteen…" Charlie did not hear the rest of what the doctor said.

Leukemia. Cancer. Charlie felt sick to his stomach. He stared off blankly into the distance. Everything in his world now seemed terrifyingly uncertain. The doctor continued to talk, but his words were a muffled blur to Charlie.

Unable to take the news and desperately wanting to rebuild

the walls that had so forcefully crumbled before Katie on that fateful day in early November, Charlie pushed the doctor aside and walked away with haste. To where, he was not sure. To what, he did not know.

"Charlie!" he heard Dave cry out from behind him. But Charlie did not stop, his speed hastening to a jog as he wiped away the tears rolling down his cheeks. Deep in his heart, Charlie feared that he would once again lose the only person he had let himself love in over seven years, and his wounded soul could not take the agony.

Charlie sat hunched over in the gray upholstered chair he'd been lucky enough to find in a room that was both secluded and dark, save for the light softly creeping in through the stained glass windows. Everything in him longed for certainty, but nothing in him knew how or where to find it.

"Hell of a sanctuary," came a familiar voice from behind him. Charlie jumped in his seat, startled by sound in the darkness. "Sorry," said Dave softly. "I didn't mean to scare you." He paused.

"Can I sit?" he asked quietly.

Charlie nodded, not looking up at Dave as he sat in the seat to Charlie's left. The two of them were silent for some time, while by some miracle Charlie's eyes continued to manufacture tears to roll down his cheeks.

"How did you know to find me here?" asked Charlie, his eyes fixed on a stain in the burgundy carpet.

Dave was in no rush to answer, taking his time to contemplate his response.

"I figured you'd be looking for certainty," he said, turning his face to meet Charlie's look of perplexity. It was a few minutes before Charlie spoke again.

"How am I supposed to do this?" asked Charlie, his voice gargled by his tears. Again, Dave paused. He saw no need to rush this conversation to its end.

"You know," he said as he folded his hands and rested his elbows on his knees, gazing up at the altar, "it took Angie and I three years to get pregnant, and every single night for those three years we pleaded with God to give us a baby." Now even Dave was choking on his tears.

"I'll never forget that day when Angie walked into our living room holding that test in her hands. It was Christmas Day, and when she said those magical words, I could not contain myself. I wanted to laugh and cry all at the same time."

Charlie smiled as he thought about his time with Katie over the last two months, how his world had become brighter, his soul more alive. It seemed Katie had been a mark of joy on more lives than just his, from long before she was even born.

"When Katie got sick," said Dave, "I had no idea what to do in that moment. Here was this child that Angie and I had prayed for, *longed* for, the first girl to ever call me 'Daddy,' and I had to stand face-to-face with the possibility that I might have to bury my own child."

Tears now streamed down Dave's face as he continued to stare at the altar. It was clear that Dave was reliving a pain that Charlie knew all too well, and Charlie found himself putting a hand on Dave's arm. Dave turned and looked at him, forcing a smile with eyes that were clouded with tears.

"How did you do it?" asked Charlie softly. Dave chuckled, sniffling as he wiped the tears from his cheeks.

"It wasn't me," he said, smiling. "It was Katie. After the doctor told us that Katie had cancer, I found myself in this very room, crumpled in a heap. I had no idea what to do, no idea how to be there for my family. I found every excuse to be away, running errands for Angie so she could be with Katie. When I brought Angie and Katie dinner one night, Katie asked me to sit with her. She then asked Angie to leave the room so that the two of us could talk.

"As I sat at her bedside, my fourteen-year-old girl grabbed my hand in both of hers and said, 'Daddy, I know this is scary for you. It's scary for me, too. But you cannot love what you're afraid to lose; and Daddy, I need you to love me right now, okay?'" Dave was now audibly choking on his tears as his voice cracked with pain.

Charlie sobbed in unison with Dave, their hearts throbbing together.

"So she's always been that way, huh?" quipped Charlie as he laughed a tear-stained chuckle.

Dave joined his chuckle. "Yeah. That's my Katie girl," he said, returning his gaze to the altar.

"I just," said Charlie, trying to put words to the feelings of his soul, "I want to be there for her, but I don't know how. I mean, Katie's been my rock…"

Dave turned his face to look again at Charlie with a broken smile. "Perhaps it's time to find a new Rock," he said, turning and nodding his head at the cross that hung above the altar between the chapel's two stained glass windows.

Charlie was silent as he stared at the symbol that for him had been the banner under which he had suffered so much of his pain and torment. Yet he knew that he did not have the full story. By her love, Katie had shown him that there was something more to the Man behind this symbol, and in his hopeless state, Charlie was desperate to know more.

"I don't even know how to start," said Charlie softly.

Dave again turned to look at Charlie. "It starts with believing that God knows your pain." In an instant, Charlie's mind raced back to his conversation with Katie on the red-brick pathway of the Downtown Mall, remembering the story of Lela and her infinite joy even in the face of unspeakable tragedy.

Charlie sat in silence as his mind recalled his conversation with Katie in happier times, trying to piece it together with the sorrow that now loomed in his heart.

"But how can God know my pain?" asked Charlie. "He's never lost anyone."

"Don't be so sure, Charlie," said Dave, placing a hand on Charlie's knee as he stared at the cross. "Jesus had friends—people he loved, and he lost one of them.

"You know what he did?" asked Dave, turning to look at Charlie.

Charlie shook his head.

"He cried," said Dave, smiling through his tears. "God, cried. And then he got angry, angry not at his friends or their mourning, but at death itself." Dave then turned his gaze back to the cross mounted on the wall. "God knows your pain, Charlie, and he didn't just get angry. By dying on that cross and rising three days later, he made sure that death will never have the last word. Of course, it says nothing of what'll happen to Katie here, and now. But it's a promise, for what the future holds. The question is, are you willing to trust him to see you through this pain, whatever that may look like?"

Charlie folded his hands like Dave, resting his elbows on his knees as he leaned forward, gazing up at the cross. "I'm gonna try," he said softly as tears again welled up in his eyes. It was more than just the present pain Charlie was feeling.

Dave turned again to look at Charlie, then put an arm around him, bringing his hand to rest on Charlie's shoulder with a gentle squeeze. He did not need to say it, but Charlie knew in that moment that Dave was proud of him for his courage. The two sat in the hospital's chapel for a while longer, staring in silence at the altar and the cross that hung above it.

"You wanna head back?" asked Dave, breaking their silence.

Charlie nodded, and together, the two of them stood up. Charlie was somewhat surprised when Dave spun him around and wrapped him in a warm hug that hinted of desperation. They were in this together, and together they walked out of the chapel into the hospital corridor. Charlie now noticed much more of the hallway than he had before, including a small gift shop across the way from the chapel. There, in the window on a glass shelf, Charlie spotted a small Tigger doll.

"Hang on," he said, stepping away from Dave as he crossed the hallway into the gift shop. He retrieved the doll from the shelf and took it to the small cashier's stand.

Moments later, Charlie returned to the hallway staring at the doll he'd purchased for the woman he loved. He looked up at Dave, who was beaming, though his eyes still betrayed his broken heart.

Together, the two of them made their way back to the E.R., where they both learned that Katie had been transferred up to the oncology ward. There, she would undergo her first rounds of chemotherapy on an inpatient basis. So they retraced their steps back in the direction they'd come, stopping at the elevators and making their way to the third floor.

When the elevator door opened, Charlie's nose was hit with a whiff of bleach-laden sterility mixed with the fresh wood paneling that lined the walls. Together, Dave and Charlie stepped off the elevator and walked in pace with one another down yet another corridor to Katie's room. But when they stood outside, Charlie suddenly paused with a slight panic. He had no idea what to say to the woman he had left.

Dave, however, failed to notice Charlie's pause and opened the large door. Determined not to run away again, Charlie stepped into the room with Dave and for the first time since her collapse, stared into Katie's eyes.

"Let's give these two a minute," Dave said to Angie, and the two of them hurried quietly out, closing the door behind them.

Yet even with the movement around them, Charlie and Katie did not break their stare. In what seemed like a flash, Charlie's senses returned to him, and he felt the soft fur of the doll he held in his hand.

"I—" he started, unsure of what to say as he took a few steps closer to her bed and held up the Tigger doll in his hand, "I got you this." He then handed her the doll. Katie held it in both of her hands, resting it on her lap as she stared at it before turning to look up at him with tear-stained eyes.

"I'm sorry," said Charlie, his eyes filling with tears again as he looked at the brokenhearted face of the woman he loved. "I shouldn't have left, and I won't leave you again. I promise."

Setting the doll in her lap, Katie lifted both her arms in Charlie's direction, sitting up for an embrace as Charlie leaned down, wrapping his arms around the woman he loved.

"I was so worried about you," Katie whispered in his ear. Her words overwhelmed Charlie's heart, and he began to sob on her shoulder. Even when her body was entrenched in a battle against cancer, Katie remained more concerned with him than she was with herself.

Katie then scooted over in her hospital bed and Charlie took his cue, climbing on next to her as the two wrapped themselves in each other's embrace, resting their heads on one another as they each closed their eyes, mourning the present darkness together as they saturated each other in the presence of their love.

Half an hour later, the door cracked open and Angie peeked through. Charlie looked up, meeting Angie's stealthy stare. Gently, he nodded, telling her it was okay to come in. The door quietly opened as Angie turned around and put a finger over her mouth. Katie had fallen asleep in Charlie's arms, and Angie did not want anyone to wake her. Behind Angie came Ellie and Grace, lightly tiptoeing into the hospital room.

Grace ran to the side of the bed nearest Charlie, lifting her arms up in the air in silence, telling the world around her that she wanted to be hoisted up. Charlie leaned back, turning over onto his back in Katie's bed while he maintained one arm behind Katie's head, holding her close.

Dave followed after his youngest daughter, lifting her up into Charlie's lap, where she quickly lay down, turning on her side to face her sister. Dave had brought Charlie's suitcase from the guest room at the Monroe home, and after lifting Grace onto Charlie's lap, he returned to the bag he'd left standing upright in the doorway, rolling it over and setting it down next to the bathroom. He turned his head in Charlie's direction as he did so to ensure that Charlie saw. Charlie nodded in affirmation, dawning a grateful smile.

"Hi Charlie," whispered Grace as softly as she could. Charlie smiled.

"Hi Grace," he whispered, stroking her hair with his free hand.

It wasn't long before Grace, too, had fallen asleep, resting her head on Charlie's chest, with one arm on her sister's tummy. Even in a moment as sorrowful and dark as this, time seemed to stand still, and as evening settled in over Charlottesville, Charlie found himself staring out the window of Katie's hospital room, watching the sun set behind an elm tree that stood tall and bare just outside.

11

Heat Rising

———— ❧ ————

THE DIM HUES OF EARLY morning gently rolled in through the window, causing Charlie to drearily lift his brow as he opened one eye, turning over just enough to stare through the glass and see the dull gray-blue sky announcing the imminent arrival of the morning sun. Charlie then turned back over to return to his slumber when he noticed that Katie was shivering. He reached behind him and pressed the nurse's button on the side panel of Katie's hospital bed.

A short and stocky nurse with curly blond hair wearing dark purple scrubs came into Katie's room. Seeing that Charlie was the only one awake, she walked quietly over and stood at Katie's bedside, not saying a word.

"Can we get some extra blankets?" whispered Charlie. "She's cold."

The nurse nodded and hurried out, returning moments later with two large blankets that the two of them draped over Katie in an effort to keep her warm. Satisfied, Charlie then laid his head down again next to Katie and drifted off to sleep. It had been four days since Katie's collapse, and he had not left her side since. He had not even left the room.

When Charlie next awoke, he tilted his head back and smiled. Katie was awake, sitting up in bed as she watched him sleep while gently stroking his hair.

"Hi," she said softly. Charlie groaned as he stretched his free arm into the air, not moving the arm that was still wrapped around Katie as he flexed his muscles and stretched in concert with a big morning yawn.

"Mm-hi," said Charlie as he recovered from his yawn, closing his eyes and laying back down on her shoulder. Katie's shiver jolted Charlie awake, his eyes open wide as dread poured into his heart.

"Are you *still* cold?" he asked, turning his gaze from the folded over blankets that covered Katie's legs to look her in the eye with a furrowed brow and worried eyes.

"Yeah," said Katie as she slid down under her blankets and snuggled against Charlie, "but it's okay. I'll warm up soon."

Charlie did not believe her, and lifted his free hand to her forehead. She was burning up. He rolled over in bed and again pressed the nurse's button. Moments later, a nurse arrived in the doorway of Katie's room. She was a different nurse than the one who had helped Charlie that morning. She had dark brown hair that had been pulled up into a bun and wore a pair of light blue scrubs with ruby red Dansko shoes. She, too, hurried to Katie's bedside to see what was the matter.

"She's had the chills for several hours now," said Charlie. "We put these blankets on her this morning, but she's still shivering."

"Okay," said the nurse, looking at Katie. "I'll be right back."

She left the room, and Katie tried to nestle into Charlie and get him to relax, but Charlie would have none of it. His mind was intensely focused on the nurse, and through the window that separated Katie's room from the corridor on the other side, Charlie could see her rummaging through the nurses' station, presumably in search of a thermometer. In Charlie's mind, it was not the time to enjoy the intimacy he had with Katie; he needed to make sure that she got well first.

The nurse returned a few minutes later with a thermometer in hand, the kind with the plastic cone on the end that fits in the patient's ear. She stuck the cone in Katie's ear and pressed a button on the side of the thermometer facing her, holding it steadily in Katie's ear until the thermometer beeped to signal to her that it was done.

"One hundred point nine," said the nurse. "You really are burnin' up, sweetheart. Let me go get Dr. Miller and see what she wants to do."

Julie Miller was the same doctor who treated Katie when she got sick the first time. Katie loved her, as she did everyone she met, but the two of them had a kind of bittersweet bond. To most people, Katie's doctor was Dr. Miller, but to Katie, she was just Julie.

Several minutes later, Julie came walking briskly into the room and stood at Katie's bedside, taking note of her vital signs before turning her attention to the patient she loved.

Julie was a shorter woman with wavy, dark brown hair, dark brown eyes, and a slender face. Like her nurse, Julie wore light blue scrubs under her white, embroidered lab coat. She also had Dansko clogs, although hers were bright sapphire blue.

"How's my Katie doin'?" she asked as she felt Katie's forehead. Katie laughed.

"Apparently I'm burning up. But aside from that, I feel just fine," she said, turning her head to look at Charlie as she softly scratched his back. "Just worried about this one."

"Well it sounds like he's just as worried about you, sweetie," said Julie. Charlie just smiled as Dr. Miller took the thermometer and did a second reading. "Wow. One hundred point nine," she said as she turned from the display on the thermometer to look at Charlie and Katie. Her face wore a deep sense of worry over this latest discovery about Katie's health.

"Okay, first of all—there's nothing to worry about. Yet," she said as she pushed the air beneath her hand further into the ground. "Okay?" Charlie and Katie had said nothing about being worried, but both of them nodded.

"The fever is almost certainly due to an infection of some sort, but it could just be the flu. We *are* entering flu season, after all," she said as she looked around nervously. "I'll run some tests just to be sure, okay?"

Again, Charlie and Katie nodded. Julie then turned to the nurse. "Let's draw some blood and have the lab run a culture, and let's get her started on six hundred milligrams of acetaminophen every four hours and seventy-five milligrams of Tamiflu twice daily, just in case this *is* the flu."

Dr. Miller then made the notes on Katie's chart and dropped the thick metal clipboard in the tray at the foot of Katie's bed before making her way to the door.

She paused in the doorway, turning back to look at Katie and Charlie, who went from staring into each other's eyes to looking at Julie. "Nothing to worry about," she said as she tapped the door frame. Her eyes said that she was lying, and Charlie knew it.

Katie smiled. "I know," she said as she ran her fingers through Charlie's hair, her body still shivering in random spurts from her fever. "Thank you, Julie."

Dr. Miller smiled again, then hurried out.

Katie closed her eyes as she nestled down into her bed, pulling her lover in close. Charlie obliged, but he did not close his eyes. Instead, he stared blankly into the corridor outside of Katie's room, his heart dreading what the tests might reveal.

In what felt like hours to Charlie, the entire Monroe clan arrived. Charlie sat up and looked at the clock. It had barely been thirty minutes since Julie left.

"Who wants *breakfast!?*" sang Angie as she practically danced into the room with a large brown paper grocery bag in her arms. Charlie forced a smile as Ellie and Grace followed Angie into the room, with Dave picking up the rear carrying two more grocery bags that looked heavier than Angie's.

"Katie!" said Grace as she ran to her bedside.

"Hi, my love!" said Katie as Grace climbed on, opening her arms to receive her little sister.

Grace then climbed up onto the bed without any help and knelt on her sister's lap, giggling and smiling at the woman she so adored.

Dave set his bags down on the chairs under the window, then noticed his oldest daughter shivering under her blankets. His gaze snapped to Charlie, his eyes putting silent words to the fear that now filled Charlie's heart. But he did not say a word.

Taking his cue, Charlie climbed out of bed. "Here, Grace, you can have my spot," he said.

"Is everything okay?" asked Katie quickly. She knew it was not like Charlie to turn down an opportunity to lie in bed with her. Charlie turned to look at Katie, forcing a smile as he nodded.

"Everything's fine," he lied. Katie's face told Charlie that she knew he had just lied to her, but Charlie paid her no mind as he and Dave stepped out into the hall, closing the door behind them.

"Why is she shivering?" asked Dave quietly.

"She has a fever," said Charlie softly, his voice and tone somber, "and Julie said it's nothing to worry about, but her face told me otherwise."

Dave looked through the window at Katie, lying in her bed playing pat-a-cake with Grace. Dave's worried stare told Charlie that he was just as troubled as Charlie was by the latest news about his daughter.

"What're they doing about it?" asked Dave.

"They're running some tests, and they've got her on some medicine—aceto-something…and Tamiflu," said Charlie. He, too, was now staring at Katie through the window when Katie turned her head in their direction, catching the two of them spying on her. They instantly averted her gaze.

"We better get back inside," said Dave. Charlie nodded, and together, they returned to the family.

"Okay," said Dave, "who's hungry?"

"Me!" said Grace, turning briefly from her game of pat-a-cake to glance in the direction of the bags that held her breakfast.

Dave then made his way to the bag Angie had carried in and pulled out six white ceramic plates from the Monroe family kitchen. Charlie was impressed. These were not paper plates, or plastic plates. These were *real* plates. Dave and Angie did not mess around when it came to food, even when it was on the go.

Dave and Angie began to pull large, glass containers of food from the remaining bags along with serving spoons and eating utensils. The sides and the lids of these containers were quite steamed up from the heat of the food they had inside.

As container after container was opened, Charlie suddenly found that the appetite that had so quickly abandoned him when he saw Katie still shivering just as quickly found its way back. He stood at the foot of Katie's bed, looking with a watering mouth at the small table in Katie's room as Dave and Angie opened the glass containers to reveal freshly cooked bacon, eggs, hash browns, pancakes, and more. Charlie butted in line, making a plate of food for Katie and taking her breakfast in bed.

Then, after letting Grace, Ellie, and Angie get their food, Charlie loaded up his plate and sat down in one of the chairs under the window. There he feasted, scarfing down helping after helping of the delectable food that Dave and Angie had prepared.

After helping himself to thirds, it suddenly occurred to Charlie that it was a Wednesday. "Hey," he asked as he finished a bite of food and pointed at Grace and Ellie, "why aren't you two in school?" Grace and Ellie both looked at him as though they'd been caught in the act of doing something wrong.

"This was far more important, dear," said Angie as she smiled at him, her face still brimming with warmth, even as her eyes held a dash of sorrow and dread. Angie's words reminded Charlie of why it was that he fell so in love with this family: people came before everything else, even school. With all the uncertainty that Katie's cancer brought with it, Dave and Angie knew that it was much more important that their girls spend time *together* than it was that they spend it in school, and Charlie smiled.

But his smile quickly faded when he noticed that Katie had barely touched her food. The girl who once could eat three or four slices of a meat-lover's pizza just two hours after lunch had lost much of her appetite. Charlie had pressed her just two days earlier to eat, but Julie quickly rebuked him, telling him that it was important that Katie not be forced to eat when she wasn't hungry. As much as Charlie wanted Katie to have her appetite back, as much as he wanted to know that things were going to be okay, it was moments such as these that reminded Charlie of the uncertainty of tomorrow, the possibility of losing this woman he had just begun to know.

His appetite gone, Charlie set his plate aside, then gathered his things and stepped into the bathroom to brush his teeth and take a shower. But even as the water warmed his body and loosened his muscles, Charlie found no rest from the noose of dread that continued to tighten around his heart.

When Charlie opened the door to the bathroom, he was somewhat surprised to find that all of the glass tupperware and plates from breakfast had been cleaned up. The entire Monroe family now sat at Katie's bedside, their eyes fixed on the TV in the corner of her hospital room by the window, just above the door to the bathroom. Dave and Angie were seated together in a large recliner to the right of Katie's bed. Angie sat on Dave's knee, resting her head on his shoulder with her right arm wrapped loosely around his neck, her elbow resting on his other shoulder as her fingers played with his hair. Ellie sat with the family to the left of the bed, and Grace sat where Charlie expected her to: in Katie's lap on the bed, leaning back to rest her head against Katie's chest.

With the sound of the bathroom door opening, the entire family turned their gaze from the TV to Charlie, and he felt strangely vulnerable being the center of their attention. The last time he stood in such a position was when he spilled the cranberry sauce, and although he now knew that this family loved him, Charlie's soul had lost its appetite for their warmth and acceptance.

"C'mon!" said Katie, breaking the silence as she patted the empty space on the bed, just to her right. "I saved you a seat."

Charlie again forced a smile as he took Katie up on her offer, making his way to her bedside as he slid behind Ellie's chair. He climbed into bed next to Katie and turned his head to see what they had been watching. The TV was tuned into one of the hospital's cable channels, which was hosting a marathon of one of Charlie's favorite sitcoms from his childhood. It was a show that Charlie had not watched since the days his family was still alive. Charlie turned his head, staring around at the people who sat watching with him. In ordinary circumstances, Charlie would have been brought to the verge of tears, unable to contain the gushing waters of his soul as he realized once again that he had found a new home, but the terror of tomorrow that came with Katie's cancer refused to loosen its vice-grip on Charlie's heart. Even as

Charlie wrapped his arm around the woman he loved and nestled in close to her, a growing part of him wanted desperately to push away, to return to where he was on that early autumn day, before that storm forced him into a coffee shop. Even as Charlie held this life-changing woman in his arms, his heart wanted more than anything to return to where it was safe.

The Monroe family sat watching television for the rest of the afternoon as they laughed together and reminisced of happier days. Charlie lost track of time as he sat staring not at the TV, but blankly into the distance. A part of him wanted out, to return to his old ways of chasing potential bed-warmers on the streets of Charlottesville, but a smaller part of him knew that he could not leave Katie—not now, not yet.

At some point that afternoon, Dave muted the TV and asked if anyone wanted lunch, but the family only stared at him in confusion. Although it was late in the afternoon, they were not hungry on account of their late breakfast, and decided almost instantly that they were going to pass on any more food before dinner. Charlie wasn't hungry anyway.

As the sun began to set again behind the Blue Ridge Mountains, throwing a tantrum of red, orange, and lavender into the sky as it went, all three of the Monroe girls began to fall asleep, with Grace in the lead, and the family knew that it was time for them to go. Dave and Angie stood up and started gathering the brown paper bags in their arms.

"Here, let me help you guys carry those out," said Charlie as he began to climb out of bed.

"No, Charlie, you stay there," said Angie, forcing a smile.

"Someone's gotta keep Katie warm."

Dave and Angie then left, taking Ellie and Grace with them as they promised to return later that night with dinner for Charlie and Katie. The two of them nodded, saying goodnight to Grace and Ellie as they went. It wasn't long before Katie had fallen asleep in Charlie's arms, but Charlie could not join her. His mind raced as he feared what the tests might reveal about Katie's fever, the noose of dread on his heart still tight as Charlie thought about Julie and the worry she had worn on her face earlier that day.

Even as Charlie stared at the sleeping beauty in his arms, the woman he professed to love, he did not feel the way he had just two weeks earlier as he held her under the frosty night sky while they gazed around the Lawn at the lights shimmering in every direction they looked. He felt numb, and a very real part of him desperately wanted to run.

Later that evening, when Katie was sound asleep, a new nurse came in and introduced herself to Charlie with a whisper. Her name was Cassandra. She had dark brown hair that was curled and fell to the middle of her back. Her face was adorned with hazel green eyes and a small nose, and she had a very nice chest.

As Cassandra stood bouncing on her tiptoes, attempting to write her name on the board that hung on the far wall, her shirt lifted just above the line of her pants, exposing her bare midriff. Charlie stared at her as the fuller parts of her body bounced in unison with the rest of her body. Her pants began to fall as she bounced, and Charlie desperately hoped they would complete their fall as lust surged in his veins. He longed to see what it looked like beneath those scrubs, and he began to devise a plan for how he might secure Cassandra's number and satisfy his longing.

But when Cassandra left, Charlie found himself suddenly aware of the sleeping woman he held in his arms. He felt as though someone had driven a frozen blade straight through his heart. Overwhelmed with guilt for who he really was, Charlie's eyes filled with tears as he brushed Katie's hair behind her ear and kissed her forehead. Here she was, battling cancer and God knows what else as she lay sleeping in the arms of a man who claimed to love her, while *his* heart darted off to its old desires for a weekend bedwarmer.

His chest filled with panic as he held her. Why was he returning to the man he once was, a man he thought he had left behind in order to truly love the woman he now held in his arms?

Charlie's introspection was interrupted when he heard the resonant thud of the door to Katie's hospital room as it unlatched. In walked Dave and Angie, carrying another brown paper grocery bag. When they saw that Katie was asleep, they tiptoed over to the chairs under the window and softly set the bag down. Dave then made his way to Katie's side of the bed while Angie came to Charlie's side and grasped his hand, giving it a gentle squeeze as she smiled at him.

Charlie forced a smile in return, his heart reeling as he thought about what Dave and Angie would say if they knew what was really in his heart.

Dave then leaned in, brushing back Katie's hair as he softly kissed her forehead.

"Mm," groaned Katie as she slowly opened her eyes. "Hi, Daddy," she said with a dreary smile.

"Hi, sweetie," said Dave as he continued to stroke her hair.

Katie then turned her head and saw Charlie sitting next to her, staring off in the distance. "Hey you," she said, placing her hand on his leg.

Charlie turned to stare at the woman he had just betrayed, forcing a smile to his face. "Hey," he said.

"You guys hungry?" asked Dave.

Katie stared at Charlie for a moment, looking deep into his soul before answering. She could tell that something was wrong, and Charlie absolutely dreaded the thought that he would not be able to hide from her what it was.

"Yeah, I could eat something," she said as she sat up in bed and pulled the table over. "Charlie?"

"Hmm?" Charlie asked, again brought back from his guilt-ridden introspection. "Oh, yeah, I guess I could eat something."

Dave and Angie then pulled four plates out of the bag and even more sealed glass containers filled with food. One by one, they again opened the containers and filled the room with the aromas of their culinary endeavor. To Charlie, though, the scents were duller now than they were before. He ate his food mostly in silence, avoiding eye contact with this group of people he had once called his family.

Dave and Angie had made chicken for dinner, with a rice pilaf and baked asparagus as sides, along with some dinner rolls. But as good as Charlie knew the food was, he could not taste it. He could barely eat. His stomach was tied in a knot over where his mind had wandered with the young nurse Cassandra.

Later that evening, Dave and Angie sat together in the recliner in the corner of Katie's room as the four of them watched prime-time television. Charlie did not notice what they were watching. He could hardly help but spend the entire evening drenched in a panic at what he had done to the woman he claimed to love, at who he really was.

Though once a man who had committed to change in order to give himself wholeheartedly to this woman who had done nothing but love him in return, even when he did not deserve it, when the time came that Katie actually needed him to be there for her, Charlie had failed her miserably, and his soul writhed in pain from the guilt. He had not really changed. At his core, he was still the same man, nothing but a skillful womanizer.

When the particular episode they were watching had finished and the television rolled to a commercial, Dave and Angie stood up. "Well, we'd better get going," said Dave as Angie leaned in to give her daughter a kiss goodnight. Dave then did the same while Angie made the way over to Charlie's side of the bed. Charlie sat up to give Angie a hug, but was startled when she put her hands on his cheeks and gave him a kiss on the forehead.

"Goodnight, Charlie," she said, looking warmly into Charlie's eyes as she unknowingly poured salt in the gaping guilt-wound of his heart. Tears welled up in Charlie's eyes. If only she knew.

Dave then followed Angie around, wrapping Charlie in a warm embrace before the both of them packed up the brown paper grocery bag and made their way to the door, bidding Charlie and Katie a final goodnight as they closed the door to Katie's room behind them.

The sound of the latch had barely hit their ears when Katie

turned over on her side, sitting up as she looked at Charlie, who had not laid down since his goodbye with Dave and Angie. "Okay, Charlie," she said to the back of his head with a tone he knew all too well. "What's wrong?"

Charlie's chest tightened. He did not want to tell her what it was that bothered him, because he knew it would spell the end of their relationship, and as much as a part of him wanted to return to chasing tail on the streets of Charlottesville, he knew that this, that *she*, was what he really wanted.

He turned his head to look at Katie with tear-glossed eyes. "I'm sorry," he said softly.

"For what?" said Katie, wearing a smile of concern on her face.

Charlie sniffled as his chest grew even tighter. He did not want to tell her but he knew he could not lie to her. "Earlier tonight—" he started, pausing to take a deep breath as his eyes averted her stare. This was it. He might was well get it over with.

"Earlier tonight, when you were asleep, the nurse came in, and I found myself thinking just like I used to, checking her out and not really caring about what she was wearing—" Charlie paused, waiting for an explosion of anger. When none came, he continued, still avoiding Katie's gaze. "My mind began to wander, filling in the blanks as I thought about how to get her number..." He was sure by now that a fit of rage was boiling in Katie's heart. "I'm not the man I told you I could be, Katie. I can't be there for—"

Charlie jumped when Katie's hand grazed his cheek. He expected a slap. He expected to be told what a jackass he was for thinking about banging the nurse when his girlfriend lay next to him in bed with cancer. He did not expect a soft touch from Katie's hand, but it gave him the courage to look at her again, his eyes now glazed with tears.

"Is that all?" she said, smiling a brokenhearted smile that held nothing but concern for him.

"What do you *mean* is that all?" asked Charlie as tears began to roll down his cheeks. "Here you are, laying in bed with *cancer*, and I'm off thinking about how I want to *bang* the nurse…"

Katie gently wiped away his tears, which only made Charlie cry all the more.

"How can you still *love* me?" he asked, his voice now muddled by his grief.

"Charlie," she asked softly as she continued to tend to his soul, "when was it that you first started chasing women for sport?"

Charlie's gaze was incredulous. Even as she lay in bed battling cancer and whatever the tests might reveal, even in the face of the sleaziest of betrayals by the man who claimed to love her, she was still tending to his soul. After blinking several times to ensure that this was not a dream, Charlie quickly began to rack his brain. "Uh…" he said, vocalizing the sound of his thinking as he remembered Abby Baird, a young freshman he had made out with behind the bleachers at his high school, feeling her up (and down) before dumping her the next day. "My sophomore year in high school, I think," he confessed softly as he stared down at the blanket on the hospital bed, ashamed to look into the eyes of the woman he was so sure would soon dump him.

"So, right after you lost your family?" said Katie, her tone tender yet matter-of-fact. She knew the answer. Charlie turned to look her in the eye as a legion of tears readied again for deployment. With the skill that had first cracked the dam holding back the waters of grief that had been welled up for years in Charlie's heart, this woman had again seen what Charlie could not.

Charlie nodded, again looking down at the blanket as tears fell from his eyes. Katie then gently lifted his head, inviting him to look into her eyes as she continued to wipe his tears with her thumb.

"I know this is hard on you," she said. "And I know that a part of you wants desperately to run, to retreat again behind those walls in the same way you ran from the pain of losing your family." Her words unleashed a torrent of tears as Charlie began to sob.

"But you don't need to *hide* that from me, okay? I *love* you, Charlie Shaw—*all* of you. I knew on the first day we met in that coffee shop and you were all wet from the rain, that chasing women for sport was not who you really were, and it's still not who you really are, Charlie."

Charlie was beginning to sob uncontrollably. Katie, too, had begun to cry. She was feeling what he felt.

"I don't need you to be here *for* me, Charlie. I've done this once before all on my own, and I can do it again." Charlie looked up at her, stunned by her words as he waited for her to turn this into a cruel joke, dumping him and telling him to get the hell out; but the empathetic tears that ran down her cheeks told him that his fears were unfounded.

"But I *do* very much want you here *with* me," she said as she wiped away his tears.

Charlie's soul writhed in pain at her words, the way an open wound screams in torment as healing ointment is lathered over and into it. He continued to sob as she looked deep into his eyes, both of them staring at each other through their tears.

"So Charlie, do *you* still want to be with me?"

Charlie nodded as he gargledly murmured, "Mmhmm. More than anything."

"Good," she said, wiping away his tears, "because I still want you here, and that's not going to change, okay?" Charlie again nodded.

"Can you promise me something?" she asked softly. Charlie looked into her eyes as he hesitantly nodded. "Can you promise me that from now on you'll talk with *me* about how you're feeling, instead of trying to hide it from me by, I don't know, darting out into the hall with my dad?" Her face now wore her usual grin of mischief as she smiled at him through her tear-stained eyes.

Charlie smiled as a small chuckle bubbled up through his grief. "I promise," he said.

"Good. Now come here," she said as she sat up in bed and wrapped her arms around him. Charlie sobbed into her hair as she held him close, rocking him back and forth.

As the waters of Charlie's soul slowly calmed, he softly whispered three simple words in her ear. "I love you."

"I know," said Katie as she continued to rock him back and forth. "And I love you, too. So much."

The two of them then laid back down together as Charlie continued to sniffle, recovering from the onslaught of soul-tears that had just drenched the world around him, including Katie's hair, although she didn't seem to mind.

"Hey," said Charlie, his spirit perking up a bit, "you know

what I just realized?"

"Hmm?" said Katie, smiling at the joy that had once again found his heart.

"I can't remember the last time you shivered!" he said gleefully. Katie smiled as she gently stroked his cheek with her thumb, her hand resting behind his ear as slumber began to take their eyes.

"I guess it was just the flu after all," she said, her smile persisting even as the weight of sleep overwhelmed her eyelids. It wasn't long before Charlie's followed, his heart happy that the worst had passed.

Charlie awoke the next morning to Katie's fingers playing with his hair. His head rested against her shoulder, with one arm underneath her and the other draped across her belly. He slowly opened his eyes to stare at the curves of her chest, smiling as he nestled further into the arms of his lover.

"Mm," he said, snuggling in close.

"G'morning, sunshine," she said as she continued to play with his hair. Charlie felt a soft tingling in the arm that rested underneath Katie, and he groggily opened his eyes and sat up in bed.

"Ahhh," said Charlie, flexing and stretching his fingers as the tingling sensation intensified. Katie laughed, apologizing for cutting off his circulation.

"Mm," said Charlie, stealing a kiss as he smiled, his body still waking up. "Totally worth it."

He then looked out through the window toward the nurses'

station to see Dave and Angie talking with Dr. Miller. Dave caught his eyes and pointed in at the two lovers who were both now awake. The door opened, and together, the three of them came walking in wearing somber looks on their faces.

Charlie and Katie, who were smiling moments earlier as they stared into each other's eyes, foreheads locked, quickly lost their smiles as their guests entered the room.

"What's wrong?" asked Charlie.

The three of them looked at each other, deciding who would be the bearer of bad news. Julie spoke up.

"Katie has a staph infection," she said.

Charlie looked at Katie, who quickly grabbed his hand, squeezing it tightly as a silent, "I'm here."

"What does that mean?" asked Charlie, turning his gaze back to Julie.

"Well, staph bacteria live on our skin, so anytime you get an open wound, some of the staph bacteria enter your system. It's normally not a problem; but in Katie's case, she probably scraped her knee or something in the last month or two, and because her immune system was already weak from the leukemia, well…"

"Is it treatable?" asked Charlie, with a twinge of panic in his voice.

"We're going to put her on an antibiotic called Vancomycin," said Julie. "It should wipe out the infection in a couple of days."

"Should?" said Charlie, noting Dr. Miller's choice of words. Julie looked at him with a discouraged smile. It was clear that she was doing all that she could, but Charlie knew that he could not lose Katie, not after all that they had been through.

"With Katie's immune system already weak from the leukemia, and now the chemo, it's hard to say what will happen," said Julie. "But there's no reason to lose hope yet, okay?"

Katie silently reassured Charlie with another gentle squeeze of his hand. Charlie looked at her. She wore a face that echoed Julie's words. He then turned to Julie and nodded.

"I'm sorry," he said. "I know you're doing everything you can to help her; I just…" Charlie turned to look at Katie. "I can't lose her."

"Well, let's hope the Vancomycin works," said Julie softly as she made her way to the door. "A nurse will be in to get you started on that in just a minute. Okay, Katie?"

Katie nodded, smiling at Julie. "Okay. Thanks for everything, Julie."

Dr. Miller then left the four of them alone. Angie and Dave stood staring off into the distance. Angie's usual warmth had vanished, and Dave's face was especially serious.

"It'll be okay," said Angie, forcing a smile as she looked at Katie and Charlie. "Katie's strong."

Charlie, too, was staring off blankly into the distance, but out of his periphery, he saw Katie turn and look at him.

"Guys, can you give us a minute?" she said to her parents. Dave nodded, leading Angie out of the room.

When they had closed the door, Katie turned to Charlie, grabbing both of his hands in hers.

"Talk to me," she said.

Charlie turned, still wearing a dumbfounded stare of numbness on his face. He was terrified of what this news meant for

Katie, of what tomorrow might bring. The night before he had fallen asleep in the hope that she was out of the woods, that the fever was nothing but a basic flu bug.

"I—" he started, unsure of what his next words would be, "I just…I don't know what I would do if I lost you. I mean, you're my rock—"

In a flash, Charlie was taken back to the conversation he had with Dave less than five days before, and apparently he wore this sudden revelation as clear as day on his face.

"What?" asked Katie, her gaze probing into his heart. Charlie again looked back into her eyes.

"How am I supposed to trust God with my pain," he started, as anger began to boil up from the depths of his heart, "when all he's ever done is take away the ones I love?" His eyes were now glossy with tears of anger and anguish.

Katie dawned a heavy-hearted smile as she held both of his hands in hers. "Do you remember our picnic?" she asked as her eyes thought back to a happier day than this.

Charlie nodded as a tear rolled down his cheek. He remembered.

"Do you remember the question you asked me?" she said softly.

Charlie smiled with painful realization as he remembered. "Yeah," he said. "Why wasn't Lela angry?" Katie nodded softly as she gently rubbed his hands.

"Even as Lela sat in our refugee camp knowing that she would probably never see her mother again, Lela held onto joy because she knew that God did not just understand, but actually knew her pain; she knew that he had *experienced* her pain.

"But Lela knew something else, too; something that kept anger from hampering her joy." Charlie looked into Katie's eyes, longing to know Lela's secret. "Lela also knew that God did not owe her, that there was nothing she could do to put the God who gave her life in her debt."

Charlie stared into Katie's eyes, his eyes filling with fear on account of her words as he processed their implication for his own life. It was a terrifying reality for Charlie to face: if God did not owe him then Charlie could not be angry with God if He took Katie from him; he could not be angry with God for *anything*. And yet the musings of Charlie's heart the night before had proved to him that when push came to shove, Charlie had done nothing to put God in his debt. Even when he had nobly vowed with the purity of his love for Katie to be a better man, he could not do it.

Katie's gentle squeeze of Charlie's hands brought him back to the woman sitting before him, staring into his eyes.

"I—" Charlie started, unsure of where his mouth was going. "I'm scared," he confessed, as tears rolled down his cheeks.

Katie wasted no time sitting up on her knees in bed. Charlie joined her, and she wrapped her arms around him, holding him close as this new reality sank into Charlie's heart.

"Me too," she whispered. "Me, too."

12

Resistance

———— ❧ ————

THE SUN WAS BARELY BEGINNING to rise over Charlottesville as Katie and Charlie sat cuddled up under the blankets of her hospital bed watching early morning cartoons. Katie was resting her head on Charlie's chest with one hand draped across his stomach while Charlie gently tickled her back.

When the thud of the door latch resonated through the wall, Katie and Charlie both lifted their heads, staring in the direction of the doorway. The door opened slowly and in stepped Tameka, pushing the door with her backside while carrying a tray that held Charlie and Katie's breakfast.

Tameka was another one of the nurses in the oncology ward, and she was Katie and Charlie's favorite by far. She was a short black woman, barely crossing the five-foot threshold, with a round face that seemed always ready to descend into a scowl. Today she was wearing a pair of dark, navy blue scrubs with a pair of coffee brown clogs.

"Alright, you kids. Who's hungry?" she said as she pushed the door open, stepping backward into the room. The two of them sat up in bed as Katie pulled the table over, impliedly answering the nurse's question. Tameka then sat the tray down on the table and lifted the two thick plastic lids off of the plates to reveal French toast and eggs that, although not from the Monroe kitchen, looked delicious all the same. "I had 'em make it special for you two."

Katie smiled at her, her face beaming. "Thanks, Tameka."

"You're welcome, sweetie. Now you kids eat up. I'll be back in a half hour or so for your sponge bath," she said as she made her way to the door.

"That's alright, Tameka," said Charlie with a mouthful of food. "I'll take care of it."

Katie and Tameka both stared at him. Tameka's face wore the scowl it was made for, while Katie just stared at him with her usual joyous smirk, shaking her head.

"See you in a half an hour, Tameka," said Katie without taking her eyes off of Charlie.

"Mm-*hmm*," said Tameka as she closed the door. It had been three days since Dr. Miller had started Katie on Vancomycin, and it seemed like it was helping. Katie was eating more (not that Charlie was tracking), and she seemed less weak and fatigued than she had before. Perhaps it was just Charlie's perception, but in any case, his spirits were high. It looked like Katie might just make it after all.

When the two had finished their breakfast, they lay back in bed together to continue watching cartoons. They had barely snuggled into each other when Katie shook with a shiver. Charlie's head darted from the TV, his muscles tightening with dread as he looked down at her and she up at him. Both of their eyes were filled with worry. Charlie was worried about losing the one he loved; Katie was only worried about Charlie's heart.

Charlie felt Katie's forehead. The fever had not abated. He wasted no time pushing the nurse's button, and Tameka was soon opening the door again, this time with her hand.

"Okay, sweetie," she said, "you ready for your sponge ba—"

"She's shivering," interrupted Charlie. Tameka turned her face toward Charlie and saw the worry in his eyes. She wasted no time getting the thermometer from the nurses' station, and returned moments later. She put the cone in Katie's ear, pressed the button, and waited for the beep to confirm what they all feared.

"One-oh-two point one," she said softly, her tone somber.

"What do we do?" asked Charlie, panicking.

"Uh," said Tameka, "let me go call Dr. Miller and see what she wants to do."

Tameka left the room, quietly closing the door as she went. Charlie and Katie looked at each other. They could not have cared less what cartoon was playing on the television behind them. The world around them seemed suspended, darker, muted by a shiver, as the fear of tomorrow overtook the day that had only just begun.

Their gazes snapped to the door when Tameka returned, opening the door and poking her head in with a solemn smile. "She's on her way in, but she wants me to draw some blood for another culture," said Tameka.

"Does she think there's another infection?" asked Charlie. "Why hasn't her fever gone away?"

"We don't know," said Tameka as she stepped inside, "and we

won't know until the culture comes back."

"Well when will that be?" asked Charlie.

"Not until tomorrow mornin'," said Tameka, staring into Charlie's worried eyes.

Tameka then turned around and began to retrieve some supplies from the drawers to the left of Katie's bed. She turned to look at Charlie. "This might be easier if you—"

"I'm not leaving her," said Charlie.

"Oh-kay," said Tameka softly as she made her way to the other side of the bed. Katie was quick to find Charlie's hand, grasping it with a tight squeeze as she turned to Tameka.

"Thank you, Tameka," she said softly as Tameka unhooked Katie from her IV. Tameka looked into Katie's eyes, her face sad, as she nodded. Tameka then drew two vials of Katie's blood, hooked Katie back up to her IV, and left without saying a word. She, too, was saddened by the morning's shiver.

Less than a half an hour later, Julie walked through the door. It was clear that she had gotten ready in a hurry: her hair, instead of draping over her shoulders, was haphazardly held up by a clip, and she wore no makeup.

"How we doin'?" she asked softly as she walked in the door. With sad faces, Charlie and Katie turned from looking at each other to looking at Julie. They needed no words. Julie just nodded. "How's your bladder, Katie?"

Katie and Charlie looked at Julie with faces that, while sad, were confused by the lack of respect for social boundaries that Julie had just exhibited, but Julie was quick to recover.

"I need a urine sample!" she insisted. "It usually works better when your bladder's full." Julie smiled, trying to bring a glimmer of sunshine into the darkness that had settled over their morning.

"I think I could pee," said Katie as she sat up to get out of bed. "I'll be right back," she said as she placed her hand on Charlie's arm, "I promise." Charlie looked into her eyes as the two of them paused, suspending the world around them to say what could not be said with words. Whatever happened, whatever news came in the wake of these tests, they were here for each other. Charlie nodded.

But he, too, climbed out of bed, standing between the bed and the window as he put his face in his hands. Yesterday seemed so much better, so much happier. Yesterday, there was certainty in Charlie's world again, but with a shiver, that certainty had all vanished, and Charlie was once again left with the tension in his heart that made him want to run, to return to where it was safe, to where things were certain.

Charlie lifted his face from his hands when he heard footsteps and laughter enter the room. Dave and Angie had arrived. They had their arms wrapped around each other and their faces wore grins of intimacy, but with one look at Charlie, their smiles vanished. They knew that things were not okay.

"What's wrong?" asked Dave, his tone serious as Katie and Julie stepped out of the bathroom.

The five of them were silent as Julie walked Katie back to her bed and helped her climb in.

"Katie still has a fever," said Charlie, still standing between the bed and the window as he stared not at Dave and Angie, but down at the tan linoleum floor of the hospital room, "and her temperature's higher than it was the last time."

Charlie caught Katie's stare out of the corner of his eye and turned to look at her. She had climbed back in bed and was sitting up, her legs covered by the bed's blanket. Julie was making her way to the foot of Katie's bed to stand by Katie's parents. With a heavy-hearted smile, Katie patted the empty space next to her on the bed, and Charlie stepped to the bedside and climbed in next to the woman he loved.

As much as the uncertainty that now weighed on Charlie's shoulders troubled his heart, and as much as that part of him still wanted to run, to retreat to where it was safe, the part of his heart that was committed to Katie, to loving her no matter what, was winning.

"I've ordered another blood culture and a urine sample," said Julie, holding the plastic jar filled with yellow liquid in her hand. "We won't know what's going on until the results come back."

"How long will that take?" asked Dave, his voice full of concern.

"I'm gonna put a rush on the urine test," said Julie, "so we should have those results by this afternoon, but there's no way to rush the culture. It takes a full twenty-four hours to grow, so we won't have the results of that test until tomorrow morning."

Anxiety enveloped Dave and Angie's faces as they looked at Julie. They did not want to wait until tomorrow morning to know what exactly was wrong with their daughter.

"I'm sorry," said Julie softly as she made her way past Katie's parents to the door.

"Thank you, Julie," said Katie softly. Julie turned to look at her, and Charlie thought for a moment that he saw a tear in Julie's eye, but he could not be sure. With a somber nod, Julie left.

"Well," said Dave, as he lifted the brown paper bag that had *Eva's* printed on the side, "we brought breakfast." Eva's was a local European-style bakery and café with an assortment of delicious treats. Charlie had been there once or twice, and he very much enjoyed their food; that day, however, Charlie knew that the food would not taste good. He was not even sure he could eat.

The four of them were quiet for most of the day as they sat watching whatever was on TV, their minds paying no attention to the images on the screen. Charlie and Katie's breakfast from Eva's became their lunch, but even then, they did not eat much. At five minutes to three that afternoon, Angie stood up.

"I need to go get the girls," she said, but no one listened to her. Julie had just walked into the room. She held a turquoise blue folder in her hand with a face that said she did not have good news. When Angie looked around and realized that they were all staring at the doorway, she, too, turned around.

"What is it?" asked Angie softly. Julie just stared at them, her face grave and unsmiling.

"Do you want the results now, or all together in the morning?" she asked softly.

"You wouldn't be asking us that if they were good," said Charlie. Julie looked at him. Her face confirmed that Charlie was right. The room was quiet.

"What did the test say?" asked Dave, piercing the silence. Julie turned to look at Dave. Her face said that she did not believe that Dave was ready to hear what she had to say, but when Dave did not change his mind, Julie opened the folder in her hands, staring down at its contents.

"Katie's kidneys are failing," she said as she attempted to hide her emotion with the folder in her hands. She paused as Charlie saw what he thought was a tear fall from her eye. When no one else spoke up, Charlie intervened.

"Well, can't she get a, a transplant or something?" he asked. Julie looked up at him. Her eyes were glazed over with tears as she forced a very sober smile.

"Because of the infection, she's not eligible for the transplant list." The room again fell silent as the family soaked in the anguish of the news.

"What if I gave her one of mine?" asked Dave. Everyone turned their heads to look at him, but he was only looking up at Julie, his eyes screaming of his desperation through a layer of tears. It was clear that he did not want to lose his oldest daughter, the first girl to ever call him "Daddy." When Julie did not respond right away, everyone turned their gazes back to her. It was clear that each of them was desperate for a dash of hope, but they found none in Julie's face. Tears were now running down her cheeks.

"With her body in the state it's in," she said, fighting to get out the words without breaking down, "she wouldn't survive the surgery." Dave's soul cried out in lament as he buried his face in his hands while Angie merely sat next to her husband, staring blankly at the corner of Katie's bed. This woman who was usually so full of warmth and love now seemed empty as she attempted to process the news.

Julie turned her gaze to Katie. Tears were now running freely down her face, dripping onto the folder she held in her hands. "I'm sorry," she whispered, barely able to utter the words.

Katie needed no words. She stretched both her arms out in Julie's direction, inviting the woman who had so faithfully cared for her to step into her embrace. Julie hesitated as she fought desperately to maintain composure, but she could not hold out from Katie's invitation. She stumbled toward Katie's bed as she dropped the folder on the floor, breaking down in sobs as she walked. Together, Julie and Katie met in overwhelming embrace as they shared in their grief.

Charlie just sat next to Katie in bed. His face, his heart, his entire being was numb as he stared off blankly into the distance. He did not, indeed he could not, cope with the reality that he was going to lose the only person he had truly loved in the better part of a decade. Yet Charlie was not angry. Something about Katie's words, spoken so truthfully yet tenderly just three days before, made it impossible for Charlie to feel anger. But with the void left in his heart by the absence of anger, Charlie was not sure *how* to feel in a moment such as this; and so he sat, numb.

Slowly, Charlie turned his head when he felt a hand grasp his own. He stared into Katie's tear-stained eyes as his vision quickly became crowded by the waters of his soul. In no time at all, it poured down his cheeks as Katie wrapped her arms around him and pulled him in close, refusing to let go in the same way she had on that cold November day.

"There is one *possible* option," said Julie softly as she wiped her face of its tear tracks, her voice muddied by her grief. Everyone lifted their heads in Julie's direction, frozen in their sorrow as their souls looked at Julie, thirsty for hope and desperate for the smallest bit of good news that might quench their thirst.

"Depending on the results of the culture, we *may* be able to start Katie on dialysis," said Julie with a sniffle, "which would perform the function of Katie's kidneys until she's healthy enough for surgery." She paused, taking a deep breath. "But if the staph bacteria are resisting the antibiotics…" Julie trailed off, staring out the window as another tear rolled down her cheek.

"But you're saying there's a chance she could make it?" asked Charlie. Julie nodded.

"Then we hold onto hope," said Dave, his eyes exhausted from sorrow. Julie turned to Dave, smiling at what seemed to her like hopeless courage. She knew Katie's chances, and they were not good, but to this family, it did not matter. They held onto hope all the same.

Later that night, Charlie was laying in bed with Katie, holding her tightly in his arms as tears ebbed and flowed from the lenses of his soul. Dave and Angie had gone home to break the news to Grace and Ellie. All of them knew that it would be especially hard on Grace if Katie did not make it, but Katie didn't seem at all worried about her little sister. She did not even seem worried about herself, but only about Charlie.

When Charlie had not spoken in over an hour, Katie tilted her head back in his arms, staring up at him with tear-stained eyes to see if he was awake. Charlie lifted his head from the pillow to meet her gaze, tears still rolling from the corners of his eyes.

"Talk to me," said Katie softly, her voice shaky with his grief.

"Guh," said Charlie on a gurgled exhale as he let his head fall back into the pillow. Katie would not take "guh" for an answer. She sat up in bed, wincing as she propped herself up with her hand and turned to look him in the eye. It was clear to Charlie that Katie did not feel well. Her body was shivering now more than it had before, even with the acetaminophen, but she did not care about remaining under the blanket. All that she cared about was making sure that he was okay.

Charlie knew that he was not going to get away with no answer, and he slowly attempted to put words to the heartbeat of his soul.

It took several minutes of thinking and processing before Charlie was able to give more than a sorrowed exhale, but Katie remained patiently gazing down at him, waiting for an answer.

"How do I trust Him with this?" said Charlie, turning his eyes to look up at his lover as tears rolled down the side of his face, dripping off his ear onto the pillow beneath his head. Tears began to roll down Katie's face as well, as she lay back down next to the man she loved, scooting herself up to bring her head to the pillow.

Charlie turned his head to the left, staring down at his brown-haired beauty as he pulled the blanket over her and held her close. With a devastated smile, Katie gently played with his hair, looking into his eyes.

"You know when I knew that *this*, that *we*, were something real?" she asked softly as she gazed into his eyes, the two of them drowning in grief-laden intimacy. Charlie forced a smile, but did not say a word.

"It was when you asked me if I wanted to know what happened to your family," she said as she wiped a tear from his eye.

"When you got up and started walking away from me that day, I thought I had lost you. I thought you were going to run back to where it was safe, chasing women for sport. But when you asked me if I wanted to know what happened, I knew then that this was real. You came back; and you've always come back.

"It's the same with Him as it is with us. You keep coming back, keep showing up, even when it hurts to do so. I *know* you can do this, Charlie; I know you can trust Him with this, because that very same courage that invited me to look into your soul that day on the Lawn still lives in you."

Tears were now streaming down Charlie's face as he turned his gaze back to the ceiling, inhaling a sob as he thought back on their relationship. It seemed to be so in vain now that this might be the end of their story.

When Katie's hand gently met Charlie's cheek, he turned his gaze again to look her in the eyes. "Promise me that you'll keep showing up, even when it hurts more than you think you can bear." She stared deep into his eyes as she wiped away his tears. "Promise me that."

Charlie took a deep breath, attempting to bring relief to his soul, and on an exhale, he gave his answer.

"I promise."

Charlie did not sleep well that night. In fact, he hardly slept a wink as he stared with dread at the holes in the ceiling tiles, colored as they were by the dark blue hues of the evening sky. It was easy for Katie to find sleep, as her body struggled to fight off such a grueling prognosis, and Charlie held her close as she slept, with both arms wrapped around her in a vain attempt to contain her shivering.

As the earliest light of morning dawned in the sky above them, Charlie's gaze shifted from the ceiling tiles to the tall, naked elm tree outside the window to Katie's hospital room. It was now four days until Christmas, and there was a very real chance that Katie would not make it even that long. But there was also hope: if the test results were good, Katie could be put on dialysis. She could still make it through this; she could still weather the storm.

"Mmm," came Katie's soft groan as she stirred in Charlie's arms, tilting her head back to look up at him with one eye open. They needed no words as she smiled at him. She had survived the night. There was yet another day of hope.

"Hey, beautiful," said Charlie as he gently pushed her hair behind her ear, his soul weighted with anxiety as his fingers grazed the heat of her forehead. Katie just smiled at him, nestling deeper into his arms as she again closed her eyes with a shiver. Charlie laid his head back down on the pillow, staring once again at the outside world.

When the familiar thud of the door latch echoed through the walls, Katie and Charlie lifted their head to see their visitor. It was Tameka.

"Oh-kay," she said, "how about we get you a sponge bath, Miss Katie?"

Confused, Charlie strained his neck to look at the clock on the bedside table. It was nine thirty in the morning. The clouds that hovered in the sky above Charlottesville had distorted Charlie's sense of time, or perhaps it was simply the worry that had kept him up all night.

In happier times, Charlie would have quipped that he could be the one to bathe Katie, but Charlie's soul had lost its sense of lightheartedness. This was no time for humor.

"I'll be right back," said Charlie as he kissed the top of Katie's head, lifting the blankets off of his legs. Katie looked at him with concern in her eyes as Charlie sat up in bed. Charlie looked back at her when he felt her hand grab his arm. She did not want him to leave. "I promise," he said as their eyes remained locked. Katie smiled. She did not know which promise he was reaffirming, but she knew that he would be back, and she let go of his arm.

Charlie then slipped on his shoes and stepped out of Katie's room. It seemed like a foreign world to him. He had not set foot this hallway since his trip with Dave back from the sanctuary in which he sought refuge when he first learned that he might lose the woman he loved.

After a minute of soaking it all in as he rubbed his eyes, Charlie remembered that the elevators were to the right. He had seen a small coffee shop on the main floor next to the gift shop, and Charlie knew that if he was going to make it through that day, he would need a very large cup of their most potent brew.

As Charlie walked toward the elevator, his senses slowly stirred, and he began to notice the people around him. They were giving him odd looks as they passed him, which confused Charlie. When an older doctor with gray hair and brown-rimmed glasses gave Charlie the third strange look in under thirty seconds, Charlie stopped and looked down at himself. He smiled. He had forgotten that he was wearing pajamas. It must have seemed very out of place to these doctors and nurses to see a person walking their halls in pajamas without an IV bag attached to him.

Charlie just smiled a painful grin, his soul still burdened with uncertainty as he stepped onto the elevator and pushed the "L" button. Again, he rubbed his eyes, trying to wake up as he listened to two nurses behind him talking about…something. Maybe her boyfriend…or was it her weekend? Charlie couldn't be sure, but in any case, Charlie knew that he needed a very strong jolt of caffeine as the elevator dinged while the doors opened to the floor that housed the coffee shop.

He stepped out of the elevator, looking around as he did his best to remember where the coffee shop was. He then noticed the sign on the wall, the kind that has a list of places in the hospital and arrows pointing patients and guests alike in the direction they need to go. One of the places listed on the sign was "Chapel," with an arrow pointing to the right. Charlie knew the direction he needed to go.

When Charlie arrived at the coffee shop, he saw a long line of patrons standing as they waited for their morning pick-me-up. His gaze then turned to see the chapel's open doors, and Charlie felt strange as he stared at them. It was almost as though Something were calling him closer. Charlie turned to look back at the long line of patrons, then shrugged his shoulders and groggily dragged his feet in the direction of the open doors.

He took a few steps inside the dark chapel, staring in the direction of the altar and the stained glass windows. He noticed the front row of chairs in which he and Dave had sat just ten days before. His words from their conversation echoed in Charlie's mind as he glanced around the room. He remembered Dave recounting his story of Katie when she first got sick: "You cannot love what you are afraid to lose, and I need you to love me right now, okay?" The words were just as relevant to Charlie as he stood in the chapel's doorway as they were to Dave back then.

Charlie then noticed a man sitting quietly in the third row from the front, off in the shadows. His hands were clasped together, resting on the chair in front of him as he gazed at the front of the chapel. Charlie followed the stranger's line of sight to see what he was staring at. His eyes landed on the bronze cross, centered above the altar between the two stained glass windows and illuminated by the incandescent hues of two spot lights. As Charlie stared at the object of this stranger's attention, Dave's words again flooded his mind: "Maybe it's time to find a new Rock."

As Charlie stood staring at the icon that for him had been the symbol of so much hurt and suffering, his mind was flooded with memories of all the conversations he had enjoyed with this woman who may very well not make it to Christmas: conversations about love and acceptance, about Lela and the real Source of her joy, about God and the God-man, about chance and creation. And as Charlie stood for several minutes staring at this emblem of so much of his suffering, he found himself slowly believing that there really was Someone more who was at work in all of this. As much as this icon had been the source of so much personal anguish for him, Charlie also knew that it was the symbol under which Katie and her family had so loved him, the same banner under which Lela suffered with joy, the same Name by which Katie had not dumped Charlie and told him to get the hell out, choosing instead to care for his soul with her tender love and concern when Charlie deserved anything but.

At the very least, Charlie knew that he did not have the full picture of the One for whom the cross stood as a symbol, the One that so many claimed to represent. Satisfied with his decision to believe, Charlie pressed his lips into a firm smile and nodded, turning from the chapel and stepping back into the hallway. There was now a Winnie the Pooh doll in the window of the gift shop where Tigger had once been, and it made Charlie smile a bit more.

Turning his gaze to the right, Charlie saw that the line at the coffee shop had dissipated, and he made his way over.

"Hi, what can I get you?" asked the woman behind the register. She was older, perhaps mid-forties, with curly red hair and pale blue eyes that were weary with the burdens of life.

"Hi," said Charlie, gazing up at the menu, "can I get a venti cup of your Columbian brew, please?"

The woman turned around in silence, pulling a large white paper cup from the stack and setting it under the coffee pot as she pulled the lever, releasing the steaming black liquid that would give Charlie the jolt in his veins that he so desperately needed.

"Two eighty-three," she said as she returned to the register, setting his steaming cup of coffee on the counter.

Charlie reached into the pockets of his pajamas. His chest tightened with an embarrassed panic as Charlie patted down his pajamas in a desperate search. His pockets were empty. He had again forgotten his wallet, and slowly, he turned his gaze to the woman behind the counter.

"It's okay," she said. "You need it. It's on the house." Charlie smiled at the woman's kindness, nodding as he took his cup of coffee.

"Thank you," he said softly. The woman behind the counter just nodded. Somehow, she understood the pain of Charlie's soul, and Charlie could not help but wonder as he made his way back to the elevator if the woman, too, had lost someone close to her, perhaps in this very hospital.

In any case, Charlie was grateful for the woman's grace as he stepped onto the elevator and the first surge of caffeine began to take hold in his veins as the savory black liquid swirled in his empty stomach. He pressed the button with the "3" next to it, and the elevator started up, taking Charlie back to his beloved.

By the time of the elevator ding, Charlie was already feeling more awake as he stepped off the elevator and began the journey down the corridor that led to Katie's room. Perhaps it was just the caffeine in Charlie's veins, but Charlie now walked with a bit of a spring in his step. The world seemed a little less darker now than it had before as he rounded the corner, stepping through the open doorway into Katie's room. But when Charlie saw what was on the other side, he froze.

Standing to the left of Katie's bed, between the bed and the window, was Dr. Miller. She had another blue folder and was holding Katie's hand as they stared at each other with tear-stained faces. Dave and Angie were also there, standing in the corner of the room near the TV, holding each other close as Angie buried herself in her husband's arms with a tissue in her hand.

Charlie's eyes welled up with tears as his gaze turned from Dave and Angie to Katie, who was looking only at him, her eyes drenched with tears and weary from crying. Charlie's hands trembled as he stared at his beloved, his vision clouding over with the weight of his tears. Inside Charlie's heart, another battle was being fought. A strong part of him wanted desperately to turn and run back out of the door through which he had just come. But it seemed now that reinforcements had been sent to provide tactical support to the part of him that wanted desperately to stay, and with the aid of that Reinforcement, Charlie stood both determined and enabled to mount a resistance to that lesser part of him that wanted to run.

Charlie's hand slowly loosened its grip on his coffee cup. It fell from his hands, hitting the floor with a loud thud as he slowly began to walk toward the woman he loved, speeding his pace as tears poured down his cheeks. He fell into her embrace, and together, they sobbed on each other's shoulder, holding tightly to each other in a desperate attempt to never have to say goodbye.

In that moment, Charlie stepped back into a darkness that he had not experienced in over seven years, since the very night on which he learned that his parents had been murdered. But this darkness did not seem as dark now as it was then. Like northern lights in the arctic sky, the darkness in which Charlie was now immersed seemed to shimmer with a faint hope. He was not alone in his grief. Someone else was with him.

13

Emmanuel

———— ❧ ————

ABOUT FORTY-FIVE MINUTES AFTER Charlie dropped his coffee cup, the hospital's janitor arrived with a mop and a bucket. He was an older man in a dark gray jumpsuit with a few strands of white hair left on his head and gray stubble on his face. He had tanned leather skin and wearied brown eyes. As he mopped up Charlie's coffee, he lifted his head to stare at the two lovers holding each other in Katie's bed. Katie had cried herself to sleep in Charlie's arms, but Charlie was still awake, and with tear-stained eyes, his gaze met the janitor's. The janitor smiled a most somber smile, and nodded before returning to his task. Charlie knew that he understood what it felt like to lose someone he loved.

Charlie did not leave Katie's bed for the rest of that day, not even to shower. He simply held her as his heart wallowed in anguish while she slept on his shoulder, the hospital bed holding the two of them upright.

As the light of dusk faded in the skies over Charlottesville, Katie stirred. She turned her head up to stare with a broken heart into the eyes of her lover. "You're still here," she said with a smile.

"I promised you I would be," said Charlie as tears welled up in his eyes, "and I'm not going anywhere."

Katie smiled as her eyes, too, flooded with tears. She closed them, forcing the tears down her cheeks as she nestled into his side.

Charlie's gaze then snapped to the doorway. The janitor was long gone, but Angie now stood in the opening, propping herself against the frame as she leaned inside. Charlie was confused, wondering why she didn't just come in.

"Is she awake?" whispered Angie. Wavering with confusion, Charlie nodded. Katie heard her mother's whisper and rolled over to look at the door.

"Mom?" she asked, her tone mirroring Charlie's confusion. Angie dawned the brightest of grins on her face as she stood back up and stared in the direction of the elevator, motioning to others with her free hand to come. Angie then stepped into the room, out of the way of the traffic, as people Charlie had never met came pouring into the room, each of them carrying something in their arms, from gifts, to food, to a small Christmas tree that was quickly plugged in and set in the corner of the room. Dave picked up the rear with a large brown box that looked quite heavy.

As people set their assigned item down, they turned and came to Katie's bedside, wrapping their arms around her. Although Charlie did not know anyone, they all knew Katie, and indeed, many of them seemed to know him as well, because after they hugged Katie, many of them would come to Charlie's side of the bed and wrap him in their arms.

When they had all finished hugging Katie and Charlie, they

stood to the side of her bed as Katie and Charlie stared at Dave and Angie with looks of perplexity.

Dave and Angie smiled at each other, then turned their gazes to face Charlie and Katie. "Under the circumstances," said Dave, "we thought we'd all celebrate Christmas a little early this year." Charlie and Katie could not contain themselves as a flash flood of tears rolled down their faces and they looked into each other's eyes.

Then everyone turned their gazes to the doorway as Ellie and Grace arrived. Ellie was carrying a large, heavy brown paper bag with both of her hands, while little Grace held a plastic grocery bag in one hand and a large black instrument bag in the other.

"Katie!" Grace said, dropping her things on the ground as she ran to Katie's bedside and lifted her arms up. One of their guests was quick to lift Grace onto Katie's bed, and Katie's youngest sister quickly snuggled against her side as Katie wrapped her arm around her while the strangers in the room chuckled at Grace's childlike affection for her older sister.

After setting her bag down, Ellie then shook her head and returned to the doorway to carry Grace's assigned things into the room, out of the way of any future guests.

"Okay," said Dave with a clap of his hands, "who's hungry?"

He did not wait for an answer, pulling not one, but two large serving dishes from the heavy brown box he had carried in. Each of them held a roast of prime rib. Dave then unwrapped the foil that encapsulated the serving dishes as Angie scoured the bags that had been carried in. After a minute or so, she found the carving knife, turned quickly around, and handed it to her husband. Angie then retrieved the plates of the Monroe kitchen from the bag that

Ellie had carried in, enough for each of their guests, as Dave readied the knife in his hands to begin his cut.

"Katie, sweetie, how hungry are ya?" said Dave as he looked at his daughter, beaming.

"It's Christmas," Katie said with tears streaming down her face. "I'll eat." With a radiant smile on his face, Dave cut off a large piece of prime rib for his eldest daughter.

"Charlie, how about for you?" asked Dave.

Charlie looked from Dave to Katie, his arm still wrapped around the woman he loved as he smiled. "Well," he said, "if Katie's eating, I better eat, too."

"Excellent!" said Dave as he cut off another large piece for Charlie, passing their plates to Ellie, who'd been busy unwrapping several other serving dishes, each of which were loaded with delectable sides to accompany the feast that Dave and Angie had prepared. Ellie then asked Katie what sides she wanted, and Katie opted for all of them. Even though the sickness overtaking her body had deprived her of an appetite, Katie was determined to celebrate Christmas one last time with her family. Ellie asked the same question of Charlie, and he, too, opted for all of the sides. Angie then took their plates, now loaded with food, and served each of them their Christmas dinners in bed; and together, Charlie and Katie ate, for what Charlie knew would be one of their last meals together.

One-by-one, Dave dished up thick cuts of prime rib while Angie and Ellie dished out the sides, handing the brimming plates to their guests. People smiled and laughed, joking with each other in merriment befitting of the season that had befallen Charlottesville.

"Oh, waitwaitwait," said Dave, holding up both of his hands when Charlie and Katie were no more than two bites into their food. (Dave was still holding the carving knife loosely in his hand.)

"We need to say grace! Who'd like to do the honors?" Dave asked, peering happily around the room.

When the awkward silence had lingered long enough, a brave soul spoke up. "I'll do it," said Charlie softly. Almost immediately, the entire Monroe family, including Katie, turned their gaze in his direction. Even little Grace sat up to look at Charlie.

"Thank you, Charlie," said Dave, choking on the tears in his eyes. He knew what a risk Charlie was taking in offering to pray to a God he was not yet sure he could trust.

With tear-filled eyes, Charlie opened his left hand to Katie and his right hand to a woman he did not know, who happily grasped it. When everyone in the room was holding hands, Charlie bowed his head and opened his mouth. What words he would say, he did not know, but words came all the same.

"God," said Charlie softly as a tear fell onto the blanket, "thank you for this time together, and for this delicious food that Dave and Angie have prepared." Charlie paused, attempting to swallow his grief as he continued.

"We thank you for family…and most of all, we thank you for Katie, for her love, for her kindness, and for these precious last moments that we get to spend with her." Charlie paused, sniffling as tears fell onto his lap. "Amen," he said, opening his eyes and looking at Dave.

Tears were now streaming down Dave's face, but his smile had not faded, as he echoed Charlie's sentiment. "Amen," he said with a firm nod. Charlie then turned to his love when he felt her gentle squeeze around his hand.

Her face, too, was drenched in tears as she brought her face close to his. "I love you," she said softly as she gazed into his eyes, "and I always will." She then kissed Charlie, and Charlie held her close, refusing to let her go. Charlie did not want to lose this woman that he so desperately loved as he pressed his lips into hers, longing for the bond between their lips to somehow save her from death.

But Charlie knew that it could not, and after what felt like hours to him, holding his lips against hers, Charlie pulled back, staring at his lover as she opened her eyes. Tears were still flowing down her cheeks, but Charlie was quick to wipe them away as he sniffled. Only then did Charlie feel the weight of everyone's stare, and he turned to see a room full of tear-stained faces looking at these two young lovers who would soon have to say goodbye.

Charlie smiled at the room full of people he did not know as he wrapped his arm around Katie. "C'mon, everyone, it's Christmas. Let's eat."

And with that, several smiles, and a few sniffles, the room full of strangers began to indulge in the meal that Dave and Angie had prepared for them while Grace nestled back into her sister's side.

"Grace," said Katie. Her sister looked up from the nest she had made between Katie and the side of the hospital bed. "Do you remember when we used to play the airplane game?" asked Katie.

"Yeah," said Grace as she sat up in bed. Charlie then noticed that even Grace's eyes were stained with tears, and it broke his heart to see this girl now broken with grief who not three weeks before was swinging so happily in the arms of Charlie and Katie as they walked to the Lawn.

"Well, here it comes," said Katie as she did her best to make an airplane noise, guiding her food-filled fork to Grace's mouth. Grace took the bite her sister had prepared for her, then snuggled back into Katie's side. It was clear that Grace was in no mood to eat.

With a heavy heart, Charlie smiled at the way in which Katie loved Grace, even now. He then returned to staring around at the room full of people who seemed to know him much better than he knew them. When an older woman with tanned skin, black hair and soft brown eyes caught Charlie staring at her, she immediately turned to him, finishing her bite of food with one hand over her mouth as she waited to introduce herself.

"Hi, I'm Vicky," she said, smiling as she extended her hand.

"Charlie," he said, extending his hand to clasp hers as they stared into each others' eyes.

"Vicky is my mom's best friend," came Katie's voice from behind Charlie's head. Charlie turned his head to face his lover as he let go of Vicky's hand. "She's just Aunt Vicky to me," said Katie as she took another bite.

Charlie then turned back to face the stranger he'd just met.

"Angie's told me so much about you, Charlie," she said with a smile that walked carefully around his grief. "She loves you, ya know."

Charlie's eyes glistened with tears as he stared back at this stranger. Silently, he forced a smile and gave a firm nod to his new acquaintance. He knew that Angie loved him. In a short period of time, she had become like a mother to him.

Only then did Charlie notice a younger woman standing in the doorway. She was Katie's age, with shoulder length dark brown hair and eyes that matched. She held the straps of her purse in front of her with both hands as she stood patiently waiting for the moment where Katie would meet her gaze.

As Katie finished a conversation with an older man to her left, she paused, having too noticed the stranger in the doorway.

"You here to lose your butt in Scrabble?" asked Katie as she smiled. The stranger in the doorway matched Katie's grin with tears in her eyes as she hurried to Katie's bedside to meet her in a warm, prolonged embrace as the two of them cried together.

"Charlie," said Katie with a sniffle as she and the woman released each other and the stranger stood at Katie's bedside, "this is my lifelong best friend, Sammy. She goes to school in New York."

"Hi," said Sammy, extending her hand to Charlie. Charlie wiped his hand on the hospital blanket, then grasped Sammy's hand in his, shaking it as he stared into her warm gaze.

"I'm Charlie," he said after swallowing his bite of food.

"Sammy," she said, still smiling warmly as she held his hand. "Katie's told me so much about you." Charlie simply smiled and nodded as he turned to Katie, raising his brow in pleasant surprise.

"So you play Scrabble, huh?" he asked.

"Oh yeah," said Katie, "and I *always* kick Sammy's butt."

"Yeah," said Sammy, "but it's only because she cheats."

"Lies," said Katie, smirking with a mouth full of food.

"I had no idea you played!" said Charlie, his eyes ablaze with a sudden excitement. "It's my favorite game. The three of us'll have to—" Charlie paused, catching himself, his soul again reminded that the only certainty tomorrow would bring is that Katie would not be there. He sat in silence, staring off blankly in the distance as fresh tears covered his eyes. "Sorry," he said.

Katie wasted no time finding Charlie's hand and grasping it with a firm squeeze. Charlie looked at her, his vision cloudy, then to Sammy. Both of them had cloudy vision, too.

"Hey Grace," said Dave. His youngest daughter perked up from her nest at Katie's side. "Why don't you play a song for us?" he asked. Charlie was not sure if Dave had noticed his moment with Katie and Sammy, but he suspected as much.

"Okay!" said Grace excitedly as she climbed out of bed and hurried over to her violin case. Katie wiped Charlie's tears from his eyes as he did the same for her. They then smiled at each other, bathed in their mutual affection, and turned to listen to Grace play a song for them.

At the first note little Grace played, Charlie was taken back to his seat next to Katie in the auditorium of Indian Hills Elementary School. Again, Grace's fingers sailed effortlessly through the melody of "O Come, O Come, Emmanuel" in concert with the hand that held her bow, and Charlie was again moved to tears. But somehow, the melody of this classic Christmas carol seemed more real to him now than it was before, and it was not long before tears were streaming down his cheeks as his entire being seemed to echo the melody of this cherished song.

When Grace finished the last note, she untucked her violin from her chin and did a small curtsey as the room erupted in applause. When Charlie had finished lauding young Grace with praise, he suddenly noticed Dr. Miller and Tameka standing in the doorway, though his eyes were still cloudy from his tears.

"Hey," he asked, staring in their direction as the applause died down, "I thought you two had left for the day?"

"Well," said Julie, looking at Tameka, "we had, but we couldn't miss this." Charlie's efforts to keep his vision clear seemed in vain as he again looked around the room, staring at all the people who loved Katie so much—not that it surprised him. He knew very well why they loved her, but something about having so many people gather around her to say goodbye warmed the depths of Charlie's soul. He thought about the legacy that Katie was leaving behind, a legacy of love and deep friendship, and Charlie vowed to himself that his legacy would be the same as hers. He did not yet know how, but Charlie Shaw vowed that night that he would learn to love as deeply and as well as Katie had.

Later that evening, the party died down. All of their guests had left, save for Dave, Angie, Grace, Ellie, and Sammy, who sat with Katie and Charlie as the seven of them watched *It's a Wonderful Life* on the TV in the corner of Katie's hospital room. It was not long before Katie fell asleep in Charlie's arms, but he did not mind it in the least.

When the movie finished, Dave and Angie kissed both Katie and Charlie goodnight, and then Sammy and the Monroe family tiptoed out quietly, trying not to wake the sleeping beauty in Charlie's arms.

That night, despite getting almost no sleep the night before and having been through the most emotionally taxing day of his life, Charlie could not find rest, and lay back in bed staring at the ceiling tiles as he reviewed the day in full, starting with his affirmation in the chapel that morning and ending with *It's a Wonderful Life* that night.

But as Charlie's mind reviewed his experience that day, it could not shake the sentiment he felt when he turned the page of the day's review and landed on Grace's performance. Yes, her performance in the auditorium of Indian Hills had deeply moved his soul, but that was only because he was amazed by Grace. Tonight, the very melody of that song had echoed in his heart, and it left Charlie wondering why.

"Hmm," came a groan from Katie's mouth as she stirred, turning her head to stare up at Charlie. "Why are you still awake?" she asked.

"Shh," whispered Charlie as he gently brushed her hair behind her ear, "go back to sleep." But Katie refused to listen to him, sitting up in bed as she positioned herself for a conversation. Charlie could see in her eyes that it was a struggle for her even to do that. "No," Charlie pleaded with her. "*Sleep.*"

"This is more important," said Katie, determined to have this conversation with him. When Charlie realized he wasn't going to win this battle, he, too, sat up. "Now," she said, having sat up enough to look at him, "talk to me."

Charlie stared back into her eyes, her face nothing but a shadow, save for the deep blue waters of nightfall trickling in through the window. He did not consider the thoughts of his mind or the pondering of his heart to be worth the discomfort she was enduring to have this conversation, but the look in her eyes, visible even in the dark, told Charlie that he was not going to escape it.

"When Grace played that song tonight—" started Charlie as Katie reached for his hands, "when she played it, I just…I *felt* it. Ya know?"

Even in the darkness that flooded their room, Charlie could see Katie's warm and gracious smile on her face. "C'mere," she said as she turned to lay back down in bed with him. Charlie took his cue, happy that she was returning to a position in which she was comfortable, and laid down next to her as he wrapped his arms around her and pulled the blanket over her. Katie turned on her side to snuggle with him as they continued their conversation.

"Do you know what 'Emmanuel' means?" asked Katie.

"No," said Charlie softly as he played with her hair.

"It means 'God with us,'" she said, tilting her head back to smile at him, "and so by calling Jesus 'Emmanuel,' what people were really saying is that he is God *with* us, God-who-knows-our-pain."

Charlie continued to play with Katie's hair as his mind considered what she had just told him.

"So, why do we still sing for Emmanuel to come, if Jesus was Emmanuel? He's already come, hasn't he?" asked Charlie. Again, Katie tilted her head back to stare into the eyes of her lover with a smile.

"Do you know *why* God became a man?" she asked softly, her face still wearing her warm and gracious smile.

"No," confessed Charlie. It was true. He did not know much about this God, except that he did not know much about this God; that much had been made clear to him by Katie and her family.

Katie laid her head back down on Charlie's shoulder. "When Jesus came and announced that he was the One they'd all been waiting for—that he was Emmanuel—everyone thought that at last, here was a man who would save the Jewish people from the oppression of Rome, and when Rome put him to death on a cross, many assumed he was just another fraud.

"But three days later, when he rose victorious not over Rome but over death itself, slowly, people began to see that freedom from Rome was never the purpose of Emmanuel. That was too small."

Again, Katie paused, this time propping herself up in bed as she stared down at her lover, her thick, messy brown hair draping over her shoulders.

"Do you remember our hike up Shady Side?" she asked him.

"I'll never forget it," said Charlie, swallowing hard.

"Do you remember our conversation about the cry deep within every one of us," said Katie, "that death should never have been a part of this world?" With tears in his eyes, Charlie nodded. That conversation, once just a theoretical dialogue, was now very real to Charlie. With every beat and tremor, his heart longed for a world in which Katie would not die from the sickness that had so quickly conquered every part of her body. Desperately, he longed to not have to say goodbye.

"Charlie," said Katie softly as she wiped away his tears, "*that's* the hope of Emmanuel: a world in which all pain and suffering, all sickness and even death itself, is no more. If Jesus did not rise from the dead, then he was just a crazy person who thought he was God; but if Jesus really *did* rise from the grave two thousand years ago, then it means that death does not have the last word—that *this* is not goodbye, not really."

Tears were now streaming down Charlie's face as he began to sob. Katie was quick to tend to his soul, gently wiping away his tears before laying down next to him, wrapping her arms around him and pulling him in close as she shivered.

"It doesn't surprise me that you felt that song tonight, Charlie. It's the heartbeat of your soul."

14

Snowflakes

———— ❧ ————

Charlie awoke the next morning as daylight poured in through the windows. Clouds hovered high in the sky above Charlottesville. It looked as though a storm were coming. Charlie turned over when he felt fingers running through his hair and saw Katie, sitting up in bed next to him, having propped herself up on two of the hospital's pillows. She smiled at him when she saw him, and although she looked beautiful as ever, it was clear to Charlie that she did not feel well.

"G'morning, beautiful," said Charlie groggily as he rolled over and nuzzled his head into her side.

"Hi," said Katie as she lovingly chuckled, shivering as she placed her hand on the back of his head.

"I need to say goodbye today," she said, her voice somber and her tone very grave. Charlie wasted no time sitting up in bed and looking at her. He could tell that her eyes were fighting back tears as she said those words. She was desperate to hang on for one more day, but in Katie's eyes, Charlie saw that Katie knew she could not hold out for much longer.

"I asked my parents to invite everyone who I want to see one last time to come here," she said. "They're coming in an hour if you want to showe—"

"No," said Charlie, "I'm spending every minute with you that I've got." The temporary hardness in Katie's face cracked, letting tears rush to the front of her eyes as she stared at him. She nodded, and Charlie pressed the button that raised the hospital bed up. Together they sat, arms wrapped around each other for the rest of the morning, until Katie's first visitor arrived at the door.

She was an older woman with golden brown hair and bright blue eyes, and when she knocked, Charlie turned not to look at her, but at Katie. Leaning back from their embrace, Katie met his gaze, pressed her lips into a firm smile, and nodded.

Charlie climbed out of bed, slipped on his shoes, and stepped into the hallway, closing the door behind him. Today was the day he had been dreading for almost two weeks, and he was not sure if he was ready to face it at all.

"Charlie!" came Angie's voice from behind him as she and Dave made their way from the elevator. Angie wrapped him in one of her warm hugs and held him close. Charlie melted in her arms and began to sob, but much like her daughter, Angie did not let go —refused to let go—as she held tightly to this brokenhearted son of hers. It was not long before Dave joined in their embrace, wrapping his arms around the both of them as they mourned the imminent loss of a woman they all adored.

With a sniffle, Dave leaned back from their hug. "How is she today?" he asked, wiping his eyes.

"Not well," said Charlie, wiping the tear tracks from his face. "She knows it's time."

Dave then turned his head to look through the window of Katie's room, watching her say goodbye to a woman who Charlie did not know.

"Who is she?" asked Charlie.

"That is Melinda Johnson," said Angie, "Katie's high school English teacher. One of the few teachers who Katie remembers to stay in touch with."

Charlie stood watching as the woman standing at Katie's bedside slowly broke down in tears at Katie's words. She, too, loved the woman in the hospital bed, and it broke her heart to know that one of her students was going to die before she'd even graduated college.

It was not long before some of the nursing staff brought chairs for Charlie, Dave, and Angie, and the three of them sat mostly in silence as, one after another, visitors came to say goodbye to the woman they all loved. Some of the visitors were people Charlie had seen the night before, but most of them were people he did not know.

Charlie sat in a daze, unsure of what to feel. He could no longer be angry at anyone, certainly not at God, and the waters of his soul, it seemed, had been drained. But Charlie became suddenly alert when he saw a familiar face walking from the elevator. The man stopped at Katie's room, smiling at Dave and Angie as he knocked on the door. When he was not given an immediate invitation to enter, the man came over to say hello to the three somber faces sitting by the nurses' station.

"Hi," he said, his voice raspy but not old. He was a younger man, with a straight, well-kept beard, brown in color, and he had a chocolate-colored flat cap on his head with a pair of black, rounded-square-rim glasses over his eyes. He wore a forest green t-shirt that had a naked tree on the front, with a pair of dark, straight leg jeans and dirtied white sneakers.

"Hi Jake," said Dave, standing up to meet the man in a warm, yet somber embrace.

"I'm so sorry for you guys," said Jake, recovering from his hug with Dave only to meet Angie in another embrace. When Jake and Angie parted, Dave turned toward Charlie, bridging the space between Angie and Charlie with his arms.

"Jake, this is Charlie, Katie's boyfriend," he said as Charlie stood up, shaking the man's hand.

"Nice to meet you, Charlie," said Jake. Charlie just nodded.

"Jake is one of the pastors at our church," said Dave. "He was Katie's youth pastor in high school." Charlie turned with surprise to stare again at the bearded man, who was smiling at what must have been a dumbfounded look on Charlie's face.

"I know you from somewhere," said Charlie softly as he peered into the man's eyes. Jake's eyes darted as he smiled awkwardly.

"Been to church at all lately?" asked Jake with a chuckle.

"No…" said Charlie, continuing to rack his brain for the knowledge of where he'd seen this man before.

"Um, do you like coffee?" asked Jake. That was it!

"Charming Beard," said Charlie with a smile of accomplishment as he remembered with fondness the day he met—and there it was, a reminder of the darkness that loomed over their lives.

"Yeah," said Jake, "Katie was one of our best customers." Jake smiled a sober smile as a hint of tears lingered in his eyes.

The sound of the door to Katie's room opening was Jake's queue to say goodbye as he turned and made his way to her room while the previous visitor emerged with eyes that were exhausted with grief.

"Well," said Angie softly as the three of them stood there, "I'd better go get the girls. This is not going to be easy on them." Charlie and Dave were silent as they nodded at Angie's departure, fighting back tears of their own.

Dave and Charlie then sat back down in the chairs the nurses had brought for them, staring through the window into Katie's room as they watched her say goodbye to Jake while Angie took off in the direction of the elevators.

"I was really proud of you last night," said Dave as they both stared straight ahead. "I know what a huge step that was for you, saying grace." Dave then turned to look at Charlie, who, though he still looked forward, now held tears in his eyes.

"Yeah, well," whispered Charlie through his tears, "Katie made it easy." He paused as tears rolled down his cheeks onto the linoleum floor with a soft splatter. "I don't know what I'm gonna do without her," Charlie confessed as the dam holding back his sorrow crumbled and the waters poured down his face.

Dave was quick to put his arm around this man who was now very much a son to him, pulling him in close as he, too, broke into heavy-hearted sobs.

The two then looked up in the direction of the elevators to see Sammy walking toward them. No sooner had she seen the tears streaming down their cheeks than she, too, began to cry, running toward them as they stood up to meet her in mutual embrace, and together, the three of them sobbed over the woman to whom they would all soon say goodbye.

The sound of Katie's door opening served as a sharp reminder of the agony that was in store for each of them, and as the sound reached their ears, Sammy pulled back from their embrace and stared at Charlie and Dave with a look of dread in her eyes as her bottom lip quivered. Sammy did not want to face what was on the other side of that door any more than they did, but slowly, she turned, and the three of them watched as Jake emerged from Katie's room. His eyes, too, were red with grief as he looked at the three of them. He dawned a most somber smile before making his way to the elevator.

Katie then turned to look at Sammy through the window, forcing a smile on her face as she stared into the eyes of her best friend. The sun was setting in the window behind Katie, but with the clouds hovering above Charlottesville, there was no beauty in the sky that night, but only a dull-gray light that was slowly fading.

Dave placed a hand on Sammy's shoulder with a gentle squeeze, causing his oldest daughter's best friend to turn her gaze to his. Pressing his lips into a smile, Dave nodded. Sammy matched his nod, then turned and walked toward the open door to Katie's room. She closed the door behind her and slowly made her way to her best friend's bedside.

Katie and Sammy were in the room together for over an hour, their cries of sorrow audible even at the nurses' station. Dave and Charlie could not help but join in their lament as they sat together in the chairs the nurses had provided them. It was not long before Angie was walking back from the elevator with the girls.

"Charlie!" cried Grace as she ran to him. Charlie smiled through his tears, lifting little Grace onto his lap, where she snuggled up as he wrapped his arms around her. When he sniffled, though, Grace broke out of the ball into which she'd curled and lifted a hand to Charlie's face, wiping away his tears with her small thumb as she stared innocently into his eyes.

Awestruck yet devastated, Charlie stared at Grace, seeing in her a glimpse of the woman to whom he would soon say goodbye, and he only sobbed all the more, pulling Grace into his arms as he squeezed her tight. She accepted his embrace, curling back up as even she began to mourn the loss of her big sister and very best friend.

When the door to Katie's hospital room opened again, the five of them quickly turned their faces to see Sammy emerge and run into Angie's arms, sobbing as she ran. Angie met her in a sorrowful embrace.

"I guess I'm next," said Ellie, her voice stale and dead as she stared at the open door. Angie was quick to tend to her daughter, turning from her hug with Sammy to grab Ellie's hand.

"It'll be okay, sweetheart," said Angie. Without looking at her mother, Ellie began taking steps to Katie's open door, and was soon closing it behind her.

Charlie watched the interaction between Katie and Ellie through the window to Katie's room to see how this sister who had remained so removed from their family would respond to this moment of final goodbye. It was quite a few minutes before Ellie was visible again. Evidently, she had stayed near the door in something of a standoff with her older sister. But when Katie's lips moved, no doubt speaking those powerful words that struck at the heart, Ellie quickly came into view as she ran to Katie's bedside, wrapping her arms around the sister to whom she would soon say goodbye. Ellie then climbed into bed next to Katie, and the two of them had a long, heartfelt conversation; about what, Charlie could only imagine.

About forty-five minutes later, Ellie emerged from Katie's room, her face wrought with grief as she stood still in the doorway, staring at her family, then slowly took steps toward them. Dave was quick to stand up, his bottom lip quivering as his daughter increased the speed of her movement, walking briskly into the arms of her father. The two of them then sobbed together, sharing in each other's grief. The sound of this grown man sobbing only brought more tears to Charlie's eyes.

He then noticed Angie frozen, staring blankly at the open door to Katie's room. "I guess I'm up," she said, her voice dead to the world around her as she began to take steps toward the hospital room of her oldest daughter. Apparently Katie had decided the order well in advance, and everyone but Charlie seemed to know it, leaving him wondering where—and even *if*—he fit into it.

The five of them watched as the door closed behind Angie and she slowly, dreadfully, made her way to her daughter's bedside to say goodbye, sitting in a chair that she pulled close to the side rail.

It was not long before Angie had stood up from the chair and collapsed into her daughter's arms as the two of them shed the water of their souls together. There are many ways in which one might appreciate the bond between mother and daughter, but watching a mother say goodbye to her oldest daughter is perhaps the greatest, and Charlie sat in sorrowful awe as he stared through the window to Katie's room, watching these two women sob silently in each other's arms.

A half an hour later, the door to Katie's room opened once again, and Angie emerged with a tear-stained face and stood in the doorway, staring at them.

"Grace," said Dave. Grace pushed back from the ball into which she'd been curled in Charlie's arms as she emerged to look at her daddy. "It's time to go see Katie," he said through his tears. Grace then turned to look in the direction of Katie's room and saw her mother standing in the doorway, waiting for her. She looked up at Charlie with eyes that had clearly been crying.

Charlie forced a smile as he closed his eyes and nodded. "It's okay, Grace," he said with grief in his voice. Grace again turned in the direction of Katie's room, then climbed down from Charlie's lap and started to walk in the direction of her mom, who received her with open arms and walked with her to Katie's bedside, lifting her onto the bed next to her big sister. Grace did not snuggle into her sister's side, but instead sat on her knees near Katie's feet, staring at her sister with what appeared to be a standoffish look as Angie quietly left the room, closing the door behind her and returning to her family.

The five of them sat in silence, save for their sniffling, as they watched Katie and Grace through the window to Katie's room.

"Grace has never said goodbye to anyone before," said Dave,

choking on his grief. "I just wish this time wasn't her first." Charlie put a hand on Dave's arm, which was resting atop his knee as he sat stooped over in his chair, his fingers interlaced. Dave turned to look at Charlie.

"Grace will be okay," said Charlie. "She's strong, just like Katie." Dave smiled at Charlie as his bottom lip quivered, and an onslaught of tears mounted in Charlie's eyes as these two grown men mourned together.

"Look, you guys," said Angie, her voice garbled by grief. Charlie and Dave turned to look through the window to Katie's room. Grace had scooted closer to Katie, still sitting on her knees as Katie held both of Grace's hands in hers. Grace was smiling at Katie as tears streamed down her rosy cheeks, her small body moving in rhythm with her sobs as Katie said goodbye to her mini-me. It was not long before Grace stood up on her knees and collapsed into her sister's arms. Katie wrapped little Grace in a somber hug as the two of them sobbed in sorrow together.

Grace stayed in Katie's arms for another forty minutes or so, her little body spasming less and less as her soul emptied its sorrow onto the sister she did not want to lose. She then sat up, looking into Katie's tear-filled eyes as her older sister kissed her on the forehead and gave her one last, prolonged hug goodbye.

Grace then climbed down from Katie's bed and opened the door. Angie was quick to meet her youngest daughter, walking toward the door as Grace ran into the arms of her mother with tears streaming down her face. It broke Charlie's heart to see a girl normally so full of life suffering this agony.

Angie then returned to where the Monroe family had

gathered, holding a sobbing Grace in her arms as she, too, cried a river of tears. She stood staring to Charlie's right, and Charlie quickly realized that she was looking at Dave, who sat staring blankly off into the distance with dread in his eyes.

"Sweetie," said Angie softly with a sniffle. Dave turned his gaze toward his wife as his bottom lip again quivered. She smiled a brokenhearted smile, then extended her free hand to him, offering to help her already devastated husband to his feet.

Dave accepted her offer, grasping his wife's hand as he stood up tall, sniffled, and wiped his cheeks before beginning the journey to Katie's room for their final goodbye. When he reached the doorway, he took one last look back at his family with a grief-stricken smile before entering his daughter's room and closing the door behind him. It was a good minute or two before Dave reemerged in their view through the window to stand at his daughter's bedside.

As he approached, Katie extended her hand to his. Dave took it and kissed it, holding his baby girl's hand in both of his as he stared down at it, afraid to look her in the eye. When Katie's lips opened to say what looked like, "Daddy," her father quickly turned his gaze to meet his daughter's, and there, he broke down in silent sobs, his body visibly convulsing with anguish. Katie was quick to scoot over in bed, creating the space for Dave to sit next to her, and Dave wasted no time taking Katie up on her offer as he climbed onto the bed next to his daughter, the first girl to ever call him "Daddy."

For all the times where Katie had no doubt snuggled into her daddy's arms, that day it was her daddy who snuggled into hers as he sat next to her in bed, his heart broken and his soul in agony at the imminent loss of this daughter he loved so very much.

The two of them were in Katie's room together for almost an hour and a half. After the first half an hour, it seemed like Katie began reminding her daddy of all the good memories they had together, because the two of them would look at each other as they laughed through their tears; but their laughter would quickly revert to sobs as the darkness looming overhead refused to let loose its hold on their hearts.

When Dave finally emerged from Katie's room, he paused just outside the doorway, sniffling as he wiped the tears from his cheeks and attempted to regain some composure before making his way back to his grieving family. Grace had cried herself to sleep in the arms of her mother, who was now sitting where Dave had sat before his wife helped him to his feet.

"We can stay if you'd like," said Angie. Charlie turned his head to realize that Angie had spoken to him. Katie had included him after all.

Charlie forced a somber smile and shook his head. "I think I'll be okay," he said.

"Okay," said Angie, "we'll be back with dinner after we run the girls home." Charlie nodded, and Dave and Angie both kissed him on the forehead. After saying his goodbyes to Sammy and the Monroe family, Charlie turned to face the goodbye he dreaded the most.

Katie caught his eyes through the window and forced a smile as she stared at him. Charlie, too, smiled, and began to walk toward the open door to her room.

When he arrived, he closed the door behind him. The sun had long ago set over Charlottesville, leaving nothing but darkness in the world outside Katie's window. Charlie stared into the eyes of his lover, beaten as they were from the day's endless stream of sorrow; but it was clear that Katie was determined to get through this one last goodbye to the man she loved so very much.

"I didn't think I made the list," said Charlie softly. Katie's eyes shook with the breaking of her heart at his words.

"Of *course* you did," Katie said as tears rolled down her cheeks and she forced a smile. "I just had to save the best for last." Tears now let loose from Charlie's eyes.

"I don't wanna say goodbye," he said, sobbing as he began to walk toward her bed, increasing his speed with every step until he collapsed at last in the arms of his beloved, where their souls writhed in anguish as they sobbed together.

"Neither do I," whispered Katie through her tears.

It was not long before Katie scooted over in bed, Charlie climbed in next to her, and she wrapped him in her arms. The room was silent for over an hour, save for the occasional sniffling and sobbing of these two brokenhearted lovers.

"A storm's coming," said Katie, breaking their silence as whistling winds shook the naked elm tree that stood tall outside the window. Charlie just pulled Katie in closer, tightening his grip on the woman he did not want to let go as he remembered the storm that had driven him into that coffee shop to meet a girl who would change his life forever.

"I always loved the day after a good snowstorm, when the darkness of the storm has passed, and the sun shines so brightly in the clear, blue sky." said Katie. Charlie only squeezed her tighter. He did not like her choice of tense. "Even though the sun is further away, it shines brighter than it ever could on a summer day. Do you know why it shines so brightly?"

"Mm-mm," said Charlie, still refusing to let her go.

"Because like a mirror, every snowflake in that fresh blanket of snow reflects that light.

"Charlie," she said, loosening the arm that had been tightly wrapped around him. Charlie tilted his head back to look up at Katie, then took his cue and sat up next to her in bed, looking her in the eye as he wiped away his tears.

"I've been nothing but a snowflake for you," she said. Everything in Charlie roared in protest of her words, but no sooner had Charlie opened his mouth to give voice to his protest than Katie's finger met his lips, pressing softly against them. Silenced, he turned again to look into her eyes, not saying a word.

"You need to hear this," she said. A layer of tears again glazed over Charlie's eyes as he looked into hers. Slowly, he nodded.

"Since the day that storm drove you into Charming Beard, all I have done is reflect a Light that to you felt so far away," Katie said, exhaling her grief as she stared out the window.

She then turned to look into the eyes of the man she loved as she held his hand in hers. "And that Light is much nearer to you now. It's springtime," she said, "and I'm melting away."

Katie paused, inhaling a sob before she continued.

"Any goodness you have seen in me was nothing more than a reflection of that Light, Charlie. As much as I have known and loved you with everything that I have and am, He knows you far better than I ever did and loves you infinitely more than I ever could, like the Papa you never knew you had."

Katie was now sobbing softly as she reached up with the hand that had been wrapped around Charlie and began to play with his hair. Charlie's eyes, too, were welling up with a fresh batch of tears.

"He loves you, Charlie, and he's always been there." Katie paused, bringing her hand to his face as she gently caressed his cheek. "You're not alone. You've never *been* alone, not now and not even then." Katie paused, staring into Charlie's soul through the layer of tears painted on his eyes. The water of his soul began to gently roll down Charlie's cheeks as he stared into Katie's heartbroken eyes.

"He was there that night, Charlie. He was there in that room with you when your dad's partner told you your parents were gone. He was there with you when you and your sister were sent to your grandparents' house. And he was there with you when you lost your sister and thought you had no one else to turn to." At that, Charlie began to sob, but Katie did not stop telling him what he needed to hear.

"He's always been there, and believe me when I say that he was crying just as much as you were." Charlie's soul gasped for air as he stared into Katie's eyes, beat as they were from the endless flow of tears. Even though she herself was laden with grief, Katie did not stop tending to Charlie's soul, wiping the tear tracks from his face.

"There will come a day, probably soon," said Katie, "when you feel like you're alone. But promise me that when that day comes, even though you feel like no one's there, promise me you'll look for snowflakes."

Charlie smiled through his sobs as his spirit struggled for breath, then nodded. Katie smiled, and even though her smile was tainted with the sorrow of goodbye, her heart beamed with pride at the man she held in her arms. She knew how far he'd come, and even though the time had come for these two young lovers to say goodbye, Katie knew that whatever happened, Charlie would be in good hands.

Satisfied, Katie nodded, inhaling three sobs before she exhaled her grief and pulled him in close. Charlie gladly accepted her invitation, snuggling into her as he wrapped his arms around his brown-haired beauty. Katie pushed the button that lowered the hospital bed down so that they were now both laying flat. Dave and Angie, who were sitting outside the door by the nurses' station, were quick to notice, and Dave softly opened the door to turn off the light as the two lovers cried themselves to sleep.

Charlie awoke the next morning still snuggled next to Katie as he gazed out at the gray clouds swirling in the skies over Charlottesville, the wind gusting through the leafless trees both in and around the small college town. Charlie then strained his neck, looking through the window behind him at the nurses' station to see if Dave and Angie were still there. The two were not to be seen, and Charlie wondered if they'd gone to pick up the girls as he returned his attention to the woman lying next to him. Sitting up in bed, Charlie kissed her on the forehead as he gently brushed her hair behind her ear. She did not stir.

The door opened softly, and Charlie turned to see who it was as Tameka poked her head in. "Is she ready for a sponge bath?" she asked.

Charlie turned back to Katie, brushing her hair behind the ear in which he softly spoke. "Katie, Tameka's here to give you a sponge bath." He paused as he continued to caress her cheek with his thumb. "I told her I could do it, but she insists…"

When Katie still did not stir, Charlie's chest tightened and he shot up in bed. "Katie," he said, at a level much more audible than a whisper. "Katie!?" She still did not respond as tears welled up in Charlie's eyes. "KATIE!" Charlie yelled as he began to sob violently, his heart and his soul—his entire being—enduring more pain in that moment than he ever thought he could bear. Charlie could not take it, and collapsed onto his lover, resting the side of his face atop hers as he audibly sobbed.

Tameka was quick to step into the room, followed by Julie. They came immediately to Katie's bedside, staring at the monitors.

"Vitals are stable," said Julie as she lifted Katie's wrist, palpating it to ensure that the monitors weren't lying to her. Charlie continued his sobbing, but when he heard a sharp click, he turned to see Julie through the foggy lenses of his soul. She stared at him with tears in her eyes as she held in her hand a small flashlight that she had pulled from the front pocket of her lab coat.

"Can I look at her, sweetheart?" asked Julie. With a large sniffle, Charlie nodded, scooting over in bed to allow Julie to have a look.

Julie opened each of Katie's eyes, shining her light into one after the other before she clicked it off. She took a few steps back.

"What is it?" asked Charlie, still fighting the already lost battle of holding back tears.

Julie turned to look at the face of Katie's devastated lover, and when she saw his tear-drenched face, her heart broke.

"She's slipped into a coma," she said softly. Charlie's face contorted to the shape of his soul as his gaze fell from Julie to Katie's unnaturally still form. Tears rolled down his cheeks, falling softly on Katie's face.

"Will she come out of it?" asked Charlie without looking up at Julie.

When Julie did not respond, Charlie turned his head to see that tears had started rolling down Julie's face. She looked him in the eyes and shook her head. Sobs again overtook Charlie as he looked from Julie to Tameka, whose face was also drenched in tears.

Charlie then turned to stare down at his lifeless lover, whose chocolate brown eyes and warm, gracious smile he would never see again, as his tears continued to fall on her face and sobs shook his breath without relief.

"Let us know if you need anything," said Tameka as the two of them stepped quietly out of the room. "We'll call her parents and let them know." Charlie nodded, but did not take his eyes off of Katie.

Charlie sat with Katie for another hour or so, brushing her beautiful brown hair behind her ear and kissing her forehead as his thumb gently grazed her soft cheeks.

He would never hear her laugh again, or see the smirk of

ridicule she would give him when he quipped about helping her sleep or giving her a sponge bath. Never again would he taste her lips with the same sparks of passion that had once breathed life into the love the two of them felt for each other. Charlie did not ever want to say goodbye, but the time for goodbye had come far too soon.

When Charlie could shed no more tears, though he continued to sob, he gave Katie one last kiss on the forehead, then climbed out of bed and slipped on his shoes. In a grief-stricken daze, Charlie opened the door to Katie's room and stepped into the hallway by the nurses' station. Unnoticed, he turned toward the elevators, walking almost in a zombie-like fashion out of the hospital into the freezing cold air; but he did not feel a thing.

It felt like an eternity and no time at all before Charlie was standing outside the door of his apartment, only then to realize he did not have his key. Though his body shivered, Charlie did not feel the cold as he softly knocked on the door. He heard the sound of footsteps on the far side, and the door soon opened.

Mike stood in the doorway with a look of incredulous concern on his face as he stared at his roommate, shivering in the cold wearing nothing but pajamas.

"Charlie," said Mike, "I—I thought you were supposed to be with Katie…"

Charlie's sobs returned as his lips parted. "She's gone, Mike." Fresh tears rolled down Charlie's face as his sobs renewed their strength, aided by his shivering body. Charlie's roommate wasted no time at all stepping out into the cold and wrapping his grieving friend in his arms, bringing him in close as he rubbed his back up and down with his hands, trying to warm Charlie up as he sobbed in his arms.

After several minutes, Charlie's sobbing stopped, and Mike loosened his embrace. "C'mon inside," he said softly, stepping aside to let Charlie in where it was warm.

Mike closed the door behind them as Charlie stepped into what felt like a foreign world to him. Even though it had not yet been two weeks since Charlie last stood in this room, the time between now and then had seemed like a lifetime.

"What happened?" asked Mike softly.

Charlie turned. His eyes again flooded with tears as he stared at his roommate, whose face was wrought with heartfelt concern. "Have a seat," whispered Charlie as he moved over to the sectional in front of the TV. Mike was close behind him, taking a seat next to Charlie as he turned to face his friend. Mike then pulled a blanket from the back of the couch and draped it over his roommate.

Starting with the morning on which Katie had picked Charlie up to spend his winter break with their family, Charlie told Mike the entire story. He told him about Katie's collapse on their run, about their trip to the emergency room and Katie's relapse. He told him about the fever and the infection, and the devastating news that the test results had delivered when Katie did not respond to the antibiotics. He told him about the early Christmas party, and about Katie's goodbye.

"And when I woke up this morning," said Charlie, his voice cracking from the trauma inflicted upon his soul, "she was gone."

When Mike put a hand on Charlie's knee, Charlie turned from staring at their tan-gray carpet to look into the eyes of his roommate. They were glazed over with tears, and the tracks on his face told Charlie that Mike felt his pain. In silence, Charlie forced a smile, and together, the two of them nodded. Charlie did not need to be told that Mike was there for him. He already knew.

"What can I do?" asked Mike.

"Nothing, Mike," said Charlie. "At this point, I just need a shower."

"Definitely can't do *that* for ya," said Mike softly. Charlie smiled at his roommate's attempt to bring a small bit of lighthearted humor into the darkness that was now choking Charlie's soul.

Seeing that he could be of no more help to his roommate, Mike got up in silence.

"Thanks Mike," said Charlie without looking at him. Mike took a few more steps behind the sectional and put his large hand on Charlie's shoulder with a soft squeeze. Charlie again nodded in silence.

Charlie was not sure how long he sat on the couch in his grief-stricken daze, before getting up to head to the bathroom, where Charlie stared at himself in the mirror.

He was a mess. His hair was sprouting from his head in every conceivable direction, and his puffy eyes were a mix of red and pink, utterly exhausted from two weeks of what felt like endless tears. It did not matter to Charlie, though. Nothing did, really. At this point in his life, Charlie simply needed to put one foot in front of the other, so he got himself ready to take a shower.

Even in the shower, though, Charlie struggled to put one foot in front of the other, standing still for minutes at a time as water the temperature of which he could not feel ran down his body. His mind darted from flashbacks of his memories with Katie—making out between the bookcases of the Alderman Library, talking about God on the Downtown Mall and on a trail in the Shenandoah forest, being held in her arms as his soul writhed in anguish from her family's undeserved love for him—to wondering what his life would now look like without Katie in it.

When Charlie finally emerged from the shower, the small digital clock on the counter in the corner of the bathroom told him it was almost one o'clock in the afternoon. He dried himself off, then wrapped the towel around his waist and stepped out of the bathroom. Mike was standing out in the hall waiting for him.

These two friends stared at each other in silence. Mike's face told Charlie he was worried about him. "I'm about to take off and head home for Christmas," said Mike. "You wanna come, get away from all this?"

"I think I'm gonna stay here," said Charlie softly, as he stared out the window at the storm mounting over Charlottesville. Despite the agony that now had a vice-grip on Charlie's heart, he could not say yes to Mike's offer to flee. Not one fiber of his being wanted to leave.

"Mmk," said Mike, pulling cash from his wallet, "if you change your mind, there's a train that'll take ya down to Atlanta. This should cover your ticket."

Charlie took the cash from Mike, then stared him in the eyes as he nodded. "Thanks Mike."

"Sure thing," he said softly. "I'll see ya later."

"See ya, Mike," said Charlie as he watched his roommate head to the door where his packed duffle bag was waiting.

When the door had closed behind Mike, Charlie turned and walked down the hallway into his bedroom. His mind flashed back to the night of Grace's Christmas concert as he remembered the taste of Katie's lips and the breath-taking beauty of her in that red dress that had a large bow on her waste. Even here, Charlie could not escape the memory of the woman he'd lost.

After getting dressed in the few clothes he had left, Charlie slid Mike's cash into his pocket and sat down to write in his journal, attempting to calm his heart through writing, only to remember that the journal he had in his room was full. The new journal he had just purchased was sitting with most of his clothes, in a suitcase in Katie's room.

When Charlie realized he could not soothe his soul through journaling, he stood up, pausing when he saw the world outside his window. The light was fading in Charlottesville, as the first snow of the year fell on this small, college town.

Charlie was not hungry, and indeed, he could not eat. So, with nothing to do and fresh snow blowing in the world outside, Charlie unmade his bed, and not five minutes after he'd climbed under the blankets, a deep slumber took him, and he slept the entire night.

15

Charlie's Prayer

———— ❧ ————

THE NEXT DAY, CHARLIE AWOKE to very little light in his room. Wondering if it was too early to be up, he groggily turned over in bed to see that the snowstorm of the day before had not let up on Charlottesville, as thick white snowflakes continued to empty from the storm clouds above to the streets below.

Charlie sat up in bed, turning toward the window. As his bare feet hit the ground and he readied himself to stand up, Charlie felt something press into the sole of his foot. Curious, he reached down to see what it was, and as he picked it up, agony's vice-grip quickly took hold of his heart once more. It was one of Katie's bobby pins.

It was Christmas Eve, but Charlie knew he would not be celebrating. There was nothing *to* celebrate. In just two weeks, Charlie had gone from the excitement of spending his entire winter break with the woman and the family he loved, to being alone, left to bask in his grief on a day that brought hope to so many. A day that so many would spend laughing in merriment would be for Charlie one of the worst days of his life.

Having removed Katie's bobby pin from beneath his foot, Charlie stood up, staring at the memento in his hand as fresh tears rolled down his cheeks. Charlie then knelt down and pulled from beneath his bed a small box that held only the most special of items. He set Katie's bobby pin next to the bottle of his mother's perfume, inhaling a sob as a few of his tears fell in the box before he closed it and slid it back under his bed.

Charlie then turned, looking again at the thick snowflakes falling outside, and stepped to his closet to retrieve the warmest outerwear and boots he could find.

As Charlie pulled a thick coat from its hanger, he noticed a small package sitting in the corner of his closet. Holding his jacket in one hand, Charlie bent over and retrieved the stuffed cardboard envelope. In a flash, he was taken back to two-and-a-half months before, on the day that an unexpected thunderstorm had forced him into a coffee shop to meet the woman he would never forget. It was the package he had intended to mail that day: an application to one of the biggest architecture firms in New York. He had forgotten all about it, having lost any desire to leave Charlottesville on the day he met Katie Monroe.

With a sober heart, Charlie set the package on his desk, resolving to mail it when Christmas had passed. He then put on his jacket and made his way through the empty apartment, stepping out into the snowstorm as a gust of frosty wind grazed his cheeks. He barely felt it as he turned to head down to the bus stop that was just a few yards from where Katie would normally pick him up.

As he stood waiting for the bus, Charlie stared at the spot where on so many occasions his breath had been taken away by the woman in wait for him. He could almost hear her laugh as he picked her up and spun her in his arms before she stole a kiss from him. The waters of Charlie's soul overflowed their banks, this time freezing on his eyelashes as he sniffled his grief.

When the bus arrived, Charlie stepped on. The bus driver stared at him expecting either payment or a student ID card. Charlie panicked. His wallet sat tucked away in the suitcase on the floor of Katie's hospital room, but Charlie rummaged through his pockets anyway. He almost cried again when his fingers bumped against Mike's cash in his front pocket, and he quickly pulled it out and handed the driver two dollar bills, but the driver simply stared at him. In his eyes, the driver could see that Charlie was not okay, and he lifted his hand, shooing Charlie's money away.

"I'll take ya wherever you need to go," he said as he pressed his lips into a somber smile. With tear-clouded eyes, Charlie nodded.

"The Downtown Mall, please," he said softly.

"You got it, buddy. Have a seat," said this kind stranger.

Charlie took a seat behind the driver, staring blankly out the window of the bus. It occurred to Charlie that he had not ridden this bus since the night he was running late to meet Katie for their first date, and as his lips forced a smile, Charlie began to sob. He was not one for crying in public, but the darkness that hung over Charlie's world made everything else seem dead.

"This is your stop, son," came the driver's voice. Charlie snapped back to reality, turning his head toward the driver as he nodded and stood up to exit the bus and return to the snowstorm outside. He paused when the driver put his hand on Charlie's arm, and Charlie turned to look at him with tears in his eyes. "I'm sorry," said the driver.

Again, Charlie forced a smile and nodded. The driver released his arm, and Charlie stepped off the bus at the east end of the Downtown Mall. Workers for the mall raced around on small ATVs equipped with snow plows, desperately trying to keep the pathways of the mall clear for the day's last-minute shoppers. But Charlie did not care. He did not even know where he was going, but simply walked, putting one foot in front of the other as he climbed the stairs from the bus stop onto the east end of the mall.

With the ache of anguish weighing down on his entire being, Charlie continued to slowly put one foot in front of the other as he made his way west.

He passed the theater in which he and Katie had watched *Survivor*, the movie that spawned their first conversations about God and truth. He saw Julienne's in the distance, the restaurant in which Katie had first identified Charlie's greatest fear: abandonment. If only he knew then that *this* was how their story would end, perhaps he would not have asked for a second date. Even such a thought, though, brought tears to Charlie's eyes. As much as the vice-grip that agony had on his heart made the depths of his soul ache for relief, Charlie would not have had it any other way. He had loved Katie, in a way he had never let himself love before, and he could not let himself regret it.

Charlie stopped as he stared through the familiar bay window of Charming Beard. The patrons inside wore smiles of laughter and joy as they shared in each other's company on the eve before Christmas. Charlie longed for what he saw in their faces, but from the surface of his skin to the depths of his soul, such laughter and joy were nowhere to be found.

Charlie took a few more steps, following the bay window as it ducked back toward the shop's chocolate-brown door. He grabbed the large bronze bar that ran almost the height of the door and pulled it open, again flooding his ears with a discorded symphony of voices that now seemed hopelessly muted to him.

There was no line, and slowly, Charlie made his way to the counter. Jake stood behind the register, and when he heard the door close behind Charlie, he looked up to see his customer. When he saw that it was Charlie, he dropped what he was doing.

"Charlie," said Jake, walking quickly around the counter and placing his hands on Charlie's shoulders as he looked into his eyes. Jake's eyes told Charlie that he did not need to ask; he knew. And as sobs again overwhelmed Charlie's defenses, Jake wrapped Charlie in his arms, pulling him in close as he, too, mourned for the woman they had both loved and lost.

After several minutes, Charlie's sobbing had stopped, and Jake pulled back from their embrace, reaching under his glasses to wipe the tears from his eyes.

"What can I get for ya?" he asked as he forced a smile.

"What was Katie's usual drink?" asked Charlie as tears refused to let up. Jake looked at him with a face that was surprised, but eyes that understood.

"You got it," he said with a nod before he returned to his spot behind the counter and began to scribble on a pad of paper. Charlie pulled the cash from his pocket and began to pick out a five-dollar bill. Jake looked up just enough to see the cash in Charlie's hand, then returned to the pad of paper. "Put that away," he said. Charlie's hands froze as he looked at this pastor he barely knew. Jake then finished what he was writing and stood up, looking Charlie in the eye as he smiled a heartbroken smile. "This one's on the house."

Charlie forced a smile as tears welled up in his eyes. Even in the midst of his grief, snowflakes seemed to abound everywhere he looked, from the bus driver to the coffee shop.

"And a blueberry muffin, right?" asked Jake. Charlie looked at Jake through tear-laden eyes with a stare of incredulity. How had this man remembered what Charlie had ordered almost three months before, when he didn't even know him?

"That's what you like, isn't it?" asked Jake. As a tear rolled down Charlie's cheek, he nodded, dawning what was perhaps the first real smile in what felt like an eternity, tainted though it was by his grief. It was not Jake's love and kindness that Charlie was experiencing in the midst of his agony. He was not alone.

"Okay," said Jake. "I'll have it right up for ya. Go grab a seat, anywhere you'd like." Charlie turned around and almost immediately knew where he wanted to sit.

Two older ladies were getting up from the table next to the large fireplace, on the side closest to the bay window. Just like before, the fire was lit, casting its warm hues of amber and gold onto the patrons around it as Charlie quickly made his way to the table where he knew he needed to sit. This time, though, he did not sit in the chair, but on the bench with the tufted leather back where Katie was sitting on the day they met, in the very same spot.

Charlie had barely taken off his coat and sat down when Jake brought his coffee and muffin to the table. "Here ya go, Charlie," he said as he set them on the table. "Twelve-ounce extra pump soy vanilla latte. And your blueberry muffin."

Charlie looked up at the face of this man he barely knew and smiled. "Thank you," he said softly. Jake put a hand on Charlie's shoulder and waited until Charlie looked him in the eye.

"Of course," he said with a nod. "If there's anything else you need, anything at all, please let me know," Jake said as he placed his business card on the table. Charlie's gaze moved from the card to the face of this man Charlie barely knew. He nodded.

Jake nodded back, then released Charlie's shoulder and returned to his work behind the counter, wrapping up the food that had not been eaten that day. Charlie watched him go, then returned his attention to the business card Jake had set on Charlie's table. On the side facing Charlie was the familiar black-and-white cartoon sketch of a bearded Irishman wearing an Irish top hat, grinning as he winked. On any other day, this jolly-looking man would have brought even a small grin to Charlie's face; but not today. Today, the Irishman's jolly seemed out of place. Charlie's eyes moved from the card on the table to the white ceramic mug that held the drink he had never before tasted.

Charlie stared down at it, then lifted the mug to his lips, wrapping his hands around its glazed exterior as the warmth of the drink inside permeated his frost-bitten hands. He sipped it, and in some way, it was as though Charlie were tasting the memories of the woman he had loved so very much. The drink was especially sweet, and it surprised Charlie, given that Katie had always ordered beer instead of those sweet...and there Charlie's mind stopped.

Even his memories of such small things as Katie's preferences were now just that: memories. Katie did not prefer anything anymore. She was nothing but a body laying lifeless in a hospital bed. Her smiles, her laugh, the way in which she always knew just how to tend to his soul—everything that made Katie who she was, all of it was gone.

Charlie inhaled a sob, tears returning to his eyes as he lowered the ceramic mug to its plate with shaking hands, then picked off a bite of his muffin and put it in his mouth. Although he chewed and swallowed, he could not taste it. He was numb to the entire world.

And so Charlie sat in the seat once occupied by a woman whose beauty, body and soul, shone like the sun. Sobs and tears came and went as his mind darted back and forth between the memories of this woman he had loved so fiercely to the world in which he now lived—a world where she was no more.

In one of the undulations by which Charlie's mind returned to the present, it dawned on his consciousness that he was the only patron left in the shop. Charlie stared around the room. The sun had set on Charlottesville, and though the fire still burned next to him, warming a man that could not feel, there was not a soul to be seen. Charlie wondered if he'd been locked in, left by mistake, and then he saw Jake emerge from the back room. Jake had stayed well past closing to give Charlie the space he needed to grieve.

When Jake saw that Charlie was looking at him, he stopped and smiled. Charlie forced a smile in return before standing up and gathering his things, embarrassed that his agony had been such an imposition on this stranger.

Jake made his way to Charlie's table, but did not say a word as he gathered up the plates that held the barely sipped latte and the muffin that had barely two bites out of it.

"I'm sorry," said Charlie softly as he put on his coat. Jake stopped what he was doing and put a hand on Charlie's shoulder, waiting again for Charlie's tear-beaten eyes to meet his own.

"There's nothing to be sorry for," he said. Fresh tears glazed over Charlie's eyes as he stared into the soul of this pastor he barely knew. In that moment, as Jake gathered up what would be a wasted drink and muffin that he had given Charlie for free, Charlie knew that the Monroes were not the only people in this world who believed that people were more important than things. Katie's words from just two nights before about snowflakes and the distant sun echoed in Charlie's mind. Even as Charlie's snowflake melted in a hospital bed, the Light that was once so distant was quickly drawing nearer, becoming brighter in the world all around him, its glory radiated by snowflakes everywhere he looked.

Jake finished gathered up the plates and made his way to the kitchen while Charlie walked to the door, his speed still slowed by the weight of his agony. He paused with his hand pressed against the door, ready to push it open, and looked back at the counter to find Jake staring at him, still holding the plates in his hands. After several seconds, Jake simply closed his eyes and nodded.

Charlie nodded back before turning to face the door that led out into the wintery darkness. He was not sure how, but Jake's kindness toward him that day had lessened ever so slightly the vice-grip of agony on Charlie's heart, healing wounds that Charlie did not even know he had. Jake had not offered beaten-down clichés or a pious, "I'll pray for you." No, unlike many of the pastors who had tried to be there for Charlie in the wake of losing his family, Jake had a wisdom that knew when to speak, and when to let it be. Feeling slightly relieved as the once-so-distant sun that had drawn so quickly near began to thaw deeper parts of Charlie's soul than he ever knew existed, Charlie pushed the door open into the darkness that now loomed over the outside world, and a frosty chill slammed against his body.

The snow was still falling in Charlottesville, but the storm was nearing its end as Charlie made his way west toward the university. He was not sure exactly where he was going, but he kept walking all the same, putting one foot in front of the other.

Some time later, Charlie found himself seated on the steps of the Rotunda. The university was closed for winter break. Its sidewalks remained unplowed and its steps unshoveled, but that had not stopped Charlie from sitting on the same steps where he and Katie had first tasted the sweet sparks of passion between their lips.

Charlottesville was quiet, filled with nothing but the silence of snowfall as Charlie stared with weary, tear-stained eyes over the expanse of grass that was now buried in snow, where he and Katie had shared so many memories that were pivotal for the healing of Charlie's soul.

"Charlie!" came a familiar Scottish voice from the distance as the crunch of footsteps in the snow sounded from Charlie's left, near the corner of the Rotunda. "Charlie," came ol' Ben's voice, relieved that he'd found him as he slowly trudged his way through the deep snow that now blanketed the ground.

"Ben?" Charlie asked. Ben had now reached the bottom of the steps and was climbing toward Charlie at a faster pace. "How did you…I mean…?" Setting aside the fact that it was late on Christmas Eve and practically all of Charlottesville was in bed, Charlie was dumbfounded at how Ben had managed to find him *here*, in a snowstorm.

"Ah goot a call from Dav an' Angie. Thaur woorried aboot ya, Charlie," said Ben as he finished climbing the stairs and sat down next to the employee he loved, looking him in the eye. "So am Ah."

Fresh tears splashed against the banks of Charlie's eyes, flowing down his face as he turned from the gaze of the wise old sage sitting next to him to look out again over the Lawn. The burden of agony only doubled down on his heart when Charlie thought of Dave and Angie worrying about him. He could not for the life of him fathom why they loved him—and then he remembered: snowflakes.

"I—" Charlie started, shaking his head in dismay. "I know that God loves me, Ben, I do. Katie, Dave, Angie—even the bus driver…they've all shown me that. But I don't know what to do…I don't know how to get through this."

Charlie paused as he turned his head to look into Ben's eyes. They were filled with nothing but compassionate concern for the young man who had worked in his bookstore for the last three years.

"I just don't want this to be the end," said Charlie, his voice thick with grief as he began to sob, finally putting words to the agony that held so tightly to his soul. Charlie returned his gaze to the expansive snow blanket as he struggled to breathe under the weight of his grief. He leaned forward, resting his elbows on his knees as he brought his hands together, interlacing his fingers.

Ben mimicked Charlie, leaning in so that his head was on the same plane as Charlie's when he turned to look at this young man he loved. "Charlie," he said. Charlie turned his tear-frosted face to look into the eyes of this wise old sage. "D'ye believe in miracles?"

Charlie's mouth dropped and his brow furrowed in disbelief at the words of the sage sitting next to him; yet a part of Charlie desperately wanted to believe in a world where miracles were possible.

"I…" Charlie started, unsure of how to speak when two parts of him were pulling his mind to opposite extremes.

When Charlie could not give an answer, Ben continued. "Everythin' in ya wants ta believe tha this ain't the end, but noo part of ya wants ta believe it doosn't have ta be." Ben's voice shook ever so slightly with grief, not for the loss of Katie (for Ben did not seem to think she was really gone), but for Charlie, bound to a system of rules and a way of thinking that did not allow for a big God who could do big things. Although Charlie now believed that he lived in a broken world, Charlie struggled to believe in a God with the power to put it right. Like Katie, Ben somehow knew the deeper parts of Charlie's heart, but Charlie did not know how.

"Charlie," said Ben, placing a hand on Charlie's knee and looking out over the Lawn, "seems pre'y clear ta me that ye already troost in His no." Confusion took Charlie's brow as he stared at the side of ol' Ben's face, feeling strangely vulnerable.

"How do you…?" Charlie started, desperately wondering how

Ben knew anything about Charlie's newfound relationship with the Creator. Ben chuckled.

"D'ye remember the firs' time ye walked inta me bookstore?" Ben asked with a smile. "Ye were so confused when Ah harred ya on the spot." Ben paused, looking into the eyes of his employee. "D'ye remember what Ah said to ye when ye asked me wah Ah'd harr a man withoot even knoo-in' him?" Charlie shook his head.

"One does nah need ta knoo the facts aboot a man ta knoo his hart," said Ben, staring into Charlie's eyes. "Ye wood nah be here if ye din't troost in His no. Ye wood nah halve walked inta yer pain; ye wood've run as fast as ye cood from it." Charlie smiled, remembering his conversation with Katie about what it meant to trust Him with his pain. He had not taken the train to Atlanta. He had stayed. He had showed up, even when it hurt more than he thought he could bear.

"Miracles, Charlie," said Ben, "oonly happ'n when thoos who troost in His no darr to believe tha Goud mah joos' loov them enough ta change His no to a yes."

Tears flooded Charlie's eyes as the smallest ray of hope shone faintly in his soul. He began to sob as he turned his gaze and again stared out at the expansive snow blanket that now covered the Lawn. The two were silent for a few minutes before ol' Ben spoke again.

"Christmas is a taim of magic and woonder," said Ben. Again, Charlie turned to look at Ben as Ben stood up, pressing his weight onto the hand that still rested on Charlie's knee as he got to his feet. He took two steps down the Rotunda before turning back to look Charlie in the eye. "Doon't be afraid to as' for woonder, Charlie. Ye never knoo joos' wha' He mah say."

With that, Ben turned and made his way down the rest of the steps on which Charlie sat, as the young man who had worked for him for so many years turned his gaze from the wise old man rounding the corner of the Rotunda to the direction of the hospital in which Katie lay lifeless.

No sooner had Ben disappeared from sight than Charlie was on his feet, hastily making his way down the unshoveled steps of the Rotunda, across the blanket of snow that covered the Lawn, and out through one of the breezeways between the old student dorms onto University Avenue.

Charlie stood there, staring across the street at Bluegrass Pub. Why Charlie was going back to face the lifeless body of the woman he loved, pouring more salt into the open wound of his heart, Charlie did not know. He only knew that there was a chance, however small it may have been, that this was not the end of their story, and he had to know what was on the next page.

He turned, making his way in the direction of the hospital, the snow crunching under his feet as he walked with more speed than he had all day, almost as though the weight of agony was no match for the Force that propelled him back to where Katie's defeated body lay lifeless on a hospital bed.

Charlie paused at the hospital's doors. On a plaque with the title "VISITORS" was the message, "If you're visiting after 9pm, you will need to present your pass at the front desk." A small tremor of panic shot through Charlie's veins as he read the plaque and looked inside at the front desk. He did not have a pass, but he knew that he must return to Katie's room.

Cautiously and quietly, Charlie opened the door to the hospital and slowly made his way to the front desk, where he could see a security guard sitting, his face illuminated by the blue glare of the screen that hid most of his face from view. As Charlie neared the front desk, the guard's face came into full view, and Charlie saw that a deep slumber had taken the guard. He smiled, turning quickly to head to the elevators.

Once inside, Charlie pressed the button with a 3 next to it. The doors closed, and the elevator's motor started up, hoisting this young lover to the third floor, returning him to the woman he loved.

When the doors opened, Charlie stepped out into the familiar corridor and made his way back to the room where he had spent most of the last two weeks. As he approached, he could see that the room was dark inside, and the clock that hung on the column by the nurses' station told him that it was well past midnight. Christmas was here.

Charlie paused outside Katie's room, staring into the darkness at the lifeless body laying in the hospital bed as tears flooded his eyes.

"Sir, can I help you?" came the voice of a woman Charlie did not know. Charlie turned to see who it was, but before he could get even a glimpse, another voice intervened.

"He's fine, Nancy," she said. Charlie turned to see Julie, his vision clouded with grief as he smiled at her. She returned his smile. Charlie turned to the darkness that filled Katie's hospital room and stepped inside, gently closing the door behind him.

With the lingering storm clouds overhead, the only light in

Katie's room came from the monitors above her bed. Though her heart beat and her chest rose and fell with her breaths, she did not stir—she *could* not stir—as Charlie slowly stepped to her bedside.

Fresh waters from Charlie's soul splashed against their banks, spilling over as he gently brushed her gorgeous brown hair behind her ear, softly grazing her cheek with his thumb. Charlie's lip quivered, and his tears quickly turned to sobs as he gazed upon the lifeless body of the woman he so desperately longed to hold in his arms just one more time.

Charlie's body could not take the weight of the grief that had so quickly returned to his soul, and he collapsed, his torso falling onto Katie's bed as his soul violently gasped for air and the waters of his soul spilled onto her lifeless body.

When Charlie could sob no more, he just lay there, unable or unwilling to lift himself back up and stare again at Katie's face, devoid of life. Yet in all of this, Charlie was not angry—he *could* not be angry—at the One who could have done something to stop it.

The whistle of the wind blowing outside caught Charlie's attention, and Something in him gave Charlie the strength he needed to stand as he turned his attention to the window, staring at the elm tree that stood outside, its branches now covered in snow. As the wind continued to blow, the deep blue canvas of the night sky began to emerge, sprinkled with the evening stars, from behind the storm clouds above Charlottesville. The storm was over.

Charlie stared in awe at the crisp fabric of the evening sky, and it took him back to what he felt that night that Charlottesville lost its power, and Katie had dragged him to the Lawn to gaze at the stars above, ablaze with heavenly glory. Charlie smiled through his tears as he remembered the details of that night: the smell of Katie's hair, the warmth of her laying next to him, the wonder…

Charlie turned from gazing at the heavens above to the woman who lay lifeless on her bed, and as he sobbed fresh tears, Charlie sank into one of the seats under the window, his face falling into his hands. But it did not stay there long. His face lifted skyward as his hands pressed together, interlacing their fingers.

"I know you don't owe me," said Charlie as fresh tears splashed against his eyelids, "and I know that you love me, even if you say no…you've shown me that." Charlie began to sob uncontrollably. "But please don't let this be the end."

Tears continued to roll down Charlie's cheeks as his soul gasped for air, desperate for relief from this agony as his gaze turned from the woman who lay lifeless before him to the One who could do something about it. Charlie sat this way for some time, his gaze moving back and forth, until a deep slumber finally came, weighing on Charlie's eyes until it took them; and there, he slept.

16

Christmas Day

———— ❧ ————

CHARLIE AWOKE THE NEXT MORNING with a jolt as his leg spasmed and his mind came to. The weight of exhaustion still pressed heavily on his shoulders as he stared around the bright, sun-lit room, rubbing his eyes as he wondered for a brief moment where he was.

When he saw Dave leaning against the wall near the open door to Katie's room with a coffee cup in his hand, Charlie knew exactly where he was, and he turned his gaze to the woman laying in the hospital bed. The clock on the table next to her bed told him that it was not yet eight o'clock in the morning, but the sun shone so brightly through the window that it almost burned Charlie's eyes with its glory as it reflected off the freshly fallen snow. Katie looked almost heavenly in the morning light, her soft, fair skin bathing in its glory. But she still did not smile.

Charlie's face was somber as he stared at his lover, still laying in bed the way she had the night before. Wonder had not come, and with a sniffle of grief and budding tear drops, Charlie turned to look at Dave, who was not looking at his daughter but at his son. Worry plagued his eyes. Charlie forced a smile, and Dave returned the favor before nodding to Charlie's right. Charlie turned to see the gift to which Dave had nodded.

On the table to the right of Charlie's chair, next to the small Christmas tree, was a fresh cup of coffee, something Charlie knew he would need if he were going to make it through Christmas Day without any more sleep.

"Thanks," whispered Charlie as he wrapped his hand around the warm paper cup and lifted it to his lips. Though Dave's face still wore a forced smile, he was silent, his gaze having turned from Charlie to his daughter as he stood rather still with his coffee cup in his hand. Charlie had barely set his cup back on the table when he heard a sound that his ears could not believe.

His gaze snapped to Katie's bed to see her arm patting the bed around her in search of the side rail as she finished the long groan that had so captivated Charlie's attention. Charlie's bottom lip quivered, his eyes electrified with disbelief, fighting back a sob as he continued to watch Katie's movement, wondering if it was all just a dream.

When the groan had finished, Katie smacked her lips as she lifted her head slightly, looking at her father and then at Charlie.

"Can I get some water?" she asked. The loud thud of Dave's coffee cup hitting the ground shook Charlie from any delusion of a dream, and he raced to Katie's bedside as tears of greatest joy slammed against their banks, flowing down his face while his soul sobbed with joyful laughter. Katie laid her arm on the side rail, opening her hand to Charlie as he approached, and Charlie took it in both of his as he smiled through his sobs, almost unable to stand as he cherished the hand he held, gazing into Katie's eyes as drops of laughter streamed down his face.

"What?" said Katie quietly as she smiled at him, doing her best to speak with a dry mouth. "You didn't think you were getting rid of me *that* easily, did you?"

Charlie just laughed through his tears as he leaned in, dripping tears on her face as he kissed her forehead.

In no time at all a team of nurses rushed into Katie's room with Julie in the lead, one of them carrying a large, plastic mug of water with a straw poking through its lid. Julie seemed almost panicked at what she was seeing, shining her flashlight in Katie's eyes as she felt her forehead, unable to believe what was before her eyes. She then took the thermometer from one of her nurses as another nurse brought the plastic cup around to the side of the bed on which Charlie stood.

Charlie took the cup from the nurse as Katie sat up in bed and Charlie held the straw to her lips. She drank as Dr. Miller put the thermometer in her ear, holding it there until it gave her a confirming beep.

When Julie saw the read-out on the screen, she shook her head with incredulity, sticking the thermometer in Katie's ear again as she impatiently pressed the button and waited again for its beep. Again, it beeped, and as Julie looked at the second read-out, tears flooded her eyes.

"I don't believe it," she said before turning slowly to look at Dave and Charlie. "Ninety-eight point six."

Charlie looked at Katie, his face beaming. Even through his

relentlessly foggy vision, Katie looked immaculate, and the two of them smiled at each other with a joy that the world around them could not understand.

Katie then turned to look at her dad, and Charlie joined her, remembering that there was someone else in the room who loved Katie as much as he did. Dave's face was drenched in tears as he sobbed, almost afraid to believe what was before his eyes. His daughter wasted no time opening her free arm to invite her father into her embrace.

Dave took his cue, stumbling toward Katie's bedside as Julie and the nurses stepped back. He fell into his daughter's arms, sobbing tears of joy as he kissed her cheek and she held him close, wrapping one arm around him. Charlie let go of Katie's hand to allow her to wrap her other arm around her sobbing father, but Katie would have none of it. She held onto his hand. She was not letting him go.

"Now," said Katie to her father as he stood up, "can I get some of that prime rib? I'm *starving*."

Dave yelled a chuckle as he continued to hold his daughter's other hand while he wiped away the tears streaming down his face. Charlie, too, shared in their laughter. The Katie that Charlie knew and loved, the woman he thought he'd lost forever, was back.

When Dave realized that he'd trapped Julie and the nurses in the corner, he quickly released his daughter's hand and stepped back, apologizing as they returned to Katie's bedside.

"Here, Dave," said Charlie, standing back from his side of the bed to allow Dave to have some time with his daughter.

"No no, Charlie," said Dave as he stepped toward the door, his face wearing the biggest grin Charlie had ever seen him wear. "You stay there. I have some prime rib to fetch."

Charlie and Katie both laughed as they watched Dave stumble in joyful inebriation out the door, looking back and forth between them and the hallway with nothing but the greatest laughter on his face. Katie and Charlie then looked at each other, each of them smiling ear-to-ear.

"Okay, Katie sweetheart," said Julie. "I'm gonna run some blood tests and a urine test to see what's going on and make sure we're out of the woods, okay?"

Without looking at Julie, her eyes still firmly locked on the man she loved, Katie told Julie to do whatever she needed. Katie seemed to know as well as Charlie did what the tests would say.

After drawing several vials of blood and obtaining a urine sample from Katie, Julie and her nurses left Charlie and Katie alone, and Charlie climbed into bed next to his lover, wrapping his arms around her as he held her close, treasuring her like never before.

"*What!?*" Katie said softly, having noticed the world outside. Her voice was barely above a whisper. "You didn't tell me it *snowed!*" She pulled back from their embrace, looking up at Charlie with childlike glee in her face. "I *love* the snow!"

Charlie just shook his head as he laughed, kissing the top of Katie's head. "Of course you do." Knowing that she could not go out and play in the winter wonderland, Katie smiled before nestling back in Charlie's arms, her entire body melting into him as tears continued to gently trickle down Charlie's face. He could not believe that he was again holding the woman he loved in his arms.

"KAAYYY-TEEEE!" came a distant voice from outside in the hall. It was not long before the pitter-patter of small feet neared the door to Katie's room, and both Charlie and Katie laughed as they watched Grace run into the room and practically leap onto Katie's bed without any help. Grace then crawled up and collapsed into her sister's arms as she sobbed, burying her face against her sister's shoulder. "I thought I was never gonna see you again…" said Grace, her voice muffled by Katie's hospital gown.

Charlie and Katie looked to the door as a cry of joyful lament took their attention away from Grace. Angie stood in the doorway. Her eyes could not believe what she was seeing as she stepped into the room, her face overcome with tears as she stumbled in disbelief to her daughter's bedside. Charlie and Katie smiled at her as she stood there, sobbing as she ran her hands over Katie's hair.

Charlie then noticed Ellie standing in the doorway, her bottom lip quivering as she looked at her sister, sitting up in bed. Katie noticed her too, and as these two sisters stared at each other, tears began to run down Ellie's face, and with increasing speed she stumbled to Katie's bedside, joining her mother as they smiled, their faces stained with tears of joy.

"Okay," said Dave, walking with a newfound spring in his step as he carried four large bags in his hand. "I've got plenty of prime rib, and…I've got *presents!*"

No one said a word. Everyone just stared at him.

Still holding the bags with a puzzled look on his face, Dave stood by the Christmas tree unsure of what to do. He was used to his kids shouting for joy at the prospect of opening presents on Christmas.

"Don't you guys wanna open presents?" Dave asked his kids.

"We already have," said Grace, her voice muffled by Katie's hospital gown as she renewed her snuggle in Katie's arms.

Dave looked at the other members of his family with fresh tears of joy in his eyes, pausing as he stared at each of them, waiting for someone to object. When Dave's stare finally reached Charlie, Charlie just smiled.

"What she said," said Charlie, his face still dawning a full smile. He and Dave laughed as the waters of their souls splashed happily over their banks.

"Well, just the prime rib then," said Dave with an unshakeable grin as he set the bags down and pulled out six plates and several large glass tupperware containers. He then dished up their Christmas breakfast, serving Katie first before bringing plates to the other girls, then to Angie and Charlie. Together, they feasted, as their souls ebbed and flowed from tears to laughter and back again.

It was several hours later when Julie stepped into the room in a stupor of disbelief to tell them that Katie's tests showed that her cancer was gone and her kidney function had returned to normal. Charlie and the family sobbed fresh tears as they continued to celebrate the Christmas they would never forget.

Later that night, the family again dished out the prime rib with all the trimmings and sides and enjoyed another feast, laughing as they watched whatever was on TV, though no one seemed to pay much attention to the show. Instead, they dreamed together about all that they might do and see now that Katie would be with them to do it. They planned trips together, and exciting new hikes, on which Charlie insisted that they bring plenty of first aid supplies.

As the sun faded into the evening sky, firing hues of lavender, pastel red and bright orange into the sky, Katie noticed a visitor standing in the doorway.

"Ben!" said Katie gleefully. Everyone else turned their attention from the TV to the doorway to see ol' Ben leaning against the doorframe wearing his usual corduroy pants with a button-up shirt and wool sweater.

"Merry Christmas!" said Katie. Ben smiled the warmest smile Charlie had ever seen him give.

"Marry Christmas to you, Miss Katie," said Ben, tipping his head. "Ah'm glad ta see yer feelin' better," he said, turning his gaze to Charlie. As Charlie smiled at the wise old sage, Ben gave him a small wink that brought a fresh batch of tears to Charlie's eyes.

"Do you want to join us?" asked Katie.

"Oh, no no. I jus' wanted ta stop by and say helloo. Ah'm sorry Ah cooldn't make it the oother dey. Ah goat tied up with somethin'," he said, smiling at the woman he knew Charlie loved.

Charlie wondered to himself if Ben really was tied up with something the day that Katie had invited everyone to come say goodbye, or if perhaps Ben somehow knew what others could not have known. He wondered if Ben somehow knew that *this* would be how their story ended—or, rather, how it began.

Ben then turned his eyes once more to Charlie and smiled with a final wink at the young man he so loved. "Marry Christmas," said Ben with a parting nod.

"Merry Christmas, Ben," said Charlie softly.

"Merry Christmas, Ben!" said everyone else in unison. Ben gave one last smile before he turned and left.

A few minutes later, Katie's gaze snapped forward as though she'd forgotten something and turned from the TV to Dave, who was reclining in the chair next to her bed with Angie and Ellie on either side of him, wrapped in his arms.

"Dad," she said softly, "do you have Charlie's present?"

"Hmm?" said Dave, groggily lifting his head to look at his daughter. "Oh! Yeah," he said, quickly standing up from his chair and making his way over to the bags. Charlie watched with curiosity at Dave's rummaging. He had not fully heard what Katie asked her dad, but began to piece it together as he watched Dave digging through the bags that contained the presents.

"Here we go," said Dave, pulling a small package from the bag. It was wrapped in burgundy red paper and had twine tied around it in place of a bow. Dave carried the package to Charlie, whose face was filled with confusion as he stared at Dave. Dave was beaming, and after handing the package to Charlie, he turned to his daughter.

Charlie then turned to look at Katie with the same confusion he had shown Dave. Katie was not fazed by Charlie's confusion as she grinned from ear to ear, her eyes electrified with excitement.

"Open it," she dared him.

"But I," Charlie stammered, "I didn't get you anything."

"Pmph! Please," said Katie before kissing his cheek. "You *are* my present." Charlie's vision again became foggy as he stared back at the woman he loved. She smiled back at him, her eyes filled with affection as she ran her fingers through his hair.

"Well go on!" she said as her eyes darted down at the package. "Open it!"

Charlie unwrapped his arm from its place around Katie and began to open the package in his lap. Inside was a small white box, maybe four inches wide and six inches long. Charlie lifted the lid off of the box, and when he saw what was inside, his heart struggled to breathe.

"It's a first-edition signed copy of *The Voyage of the Dawn Treader*," said Katie softly.

Charlie simply looked at Katie with tears in his eyes as he smiled. "My mom used to read these to me," he whispered.

Katie smiled back at her lover, nestling into his side and wrapping her arm around him as they stared together at the book in his lap. "I know," she said softly.

Charlie was almost offended, but he'd learned by now that Katie paid much more attention than he knew. He could not hide much from her, it seemed, but his curiosity pressed on all the same.

"How did you know?" asked Charlie, turning to Katie. Katie just smiled.

"I had some help," she said, talking at the now-empty doorway. Charlie looked at the door, then back at Katie. He put his finger gently under her chin, lifting her gaze to his.

"Thank you," he said with tears in his eyes. Katie did not need to hear that Charlie was thanking her for more than just the book. Her eyes said that she knew, and as the two young lovers stared deeply into each other's souls, they slowly leaned in, gently closing their eyes as they pressed their lips together, tasting again the sparks that now burned with more passion and electricity than ever before. Something about the journey of the last two weeks had made everything seem more real to Charlie, more valuable. He treasured his world more, and he cherished Katie more than he ever thought he could.

Later that night, the entire family had fallen asleep in Katie's room. Dave reclined in the chair with Angie in his right arm and Ellie in his left. Grace stayed in her spot, snuggled into Katie's side, and Katie rested her head on Charlie's shoulder as Charlie lay next to her, his arm wrapped around her, holding her close. No one in the Monroe family was going home that night.

At half past eleven, the nurse named Cassandra walked in. When she saw that everyone but Charlie was asleep, she walked quiet as a mouse to the whiteboard, where she again stood on her tiptoes, bouncing as she struggled to write her name. But Charlie paid her no mind. He did not even turn his head as he continued to hold Katie close, gently brushing her hair behind her ear as she slept. Charlie knew what his heart wanted. The war that had once raged so fiercely in Charlie's heart was over; the better side of him had won.

When Cassandra left, closing the door behind her, Charlie looked up at the One of wonder and thought for a moment that he felt Heaven smiling down on him. His heart was filled with joy, and his lips could only whisper two, simple words: "Thank you."

An hour later, Charlie still could not sleep. Katie had rolled over in bed, positioning herself in such a way that Charlie knew he would not wake her by moving. So Charlie climbed out of bed and walked softly to his suitcase, retrieving his new journal and pen from the outside pocket before returning to bed.

He climbed back under the blanket next to Katie, sitting up as he laid his open journal in his lap. Charlie felt it necessary to document to himself the journey of the last few months, but as he lay there, pen in hand, the words did not come. He could not find a way to begin this entry in his journal that would truly capture the voyage his heart had taken with this woman.

But then, in a spark that was not his own, the words came to young Charlie Shaw, and he pressed his pen to the paper and began to write: "In the heart of Virginia, nestled snugly in the foothills of the Blue Ridge Mountains, lies a small college town called Charlottesville."

THE END

Epilogue

The next morning, when the blood cultures showed that Katie's infection was gone, Dr. Miller gave Katie the okay to go home. I still remember the joy in my heart as I walked out of that hospital room with my arm wrapped around the woman I love. I did not really think that's how our story would end. But I guess I never thought that *I* would be the one to ask for wonder.

They say that love is the greatest thing that ever happens to a man, but I disagree. Loss is the greatest thing that ever happens to him; for without loss, he can never truly know what it is to love.

For the next month I spent almost every second of every day at Katie's side. The only time we were apart is when we took our separate showers or went to the bathroom, and even then, the other was just outside the door. One would think this might have annoyed her, perhaps made her question whether she still wanted to be with me, but lucky for me, it did not scare her away. Exactly one year after that thunderstorm forced me into Jake's coffee shop, I got down on one knee in that very same spot where we first said hello and asked her if she would spend the rest of her life with me.

She said yes, and the following spring on the banks of the Rivanna River behind the Monroe home, Katie and I promised to each other before God and all of our family and friends that we weren't going anywhere, and that night—well, you can imagine how that went.

Katie still goes in for regular checkups at least once every six months; I make sure of that. But Katie has remained cancer-free since that Christmas Day almost ten years ago, and every time I come face-to-face with that truth my heart becomes heavy with the weight of glory and tears flood my eyes. What happened that day still remains an anomaly to the medical community. Julie has since traveled to some of the most prestigious medical schools in the country to present Katie's case, and the brightest doctors have yet to figure it out.

As for Katie and me, we know. We don't need test results or proof of Something for which there can be no proof. I guess that's what faith is: being comfortable with the unknown.

I know that one day in the distant future, I will have to say goodbye again to the woman I love. As much as you might think that I dread that day, I do not. Katie is living proof for me that even though she and I will one day pass on, this broken world is not the end for us, but the beginning: the beginning of our story, the beginning of an eternity spent in love, not just of each other, but of everyone to whom we've said goodbye.

Every time I look at Katie, I am reminded that there is nothing to fear in death or in loss, for one Day all death and loss will be forever undone. And until that Day, in joyful anticipation, we wait; and we love, giving grace to everyone we meet.

Speaking of Grace, it should come as no surprise to you that she has garnered quite the following as a violinist, so much so that she was just accepted to Juilliard on a full ride scholarship, where she plans to major in musical performance. Ellie, however, stayed close to home for school. Something about her goodbye to Katie on that night where all of us thought we would never see her again made Ellie and Katie into the best of friends, and Ellie chose to stay close to her older sister.

Dave and Angie still work out of their home office, and Dave's desk is messier than ever. A third desk has been added to that room, and I do my best to keep it as clean as I can, but I guess I take after Dave. I never did mail that package to New York.

As for Katie, well, after she graduated from nursing school, it wasn't long before she took the next step and applied to medical school at the University of Virginia. She was quickly accepted, and just finished her residency in oncology. At least once a year, Katie travels overseas to do humanitarian work with a number of different organizations, although she has yet to meet another girl quite like Lela.

Her travels are going to have to take a break for a season, though. Eating can be hard enough in refugee camps, especially when you have Katie's appetite, and now she's eating for two. Our first child is due sometime in May, and if it's a girl, we plan to name her Allison Joy after my mother. If it's a boy, we thought Benjamin David would be most appropriate.

It's a scary thought to some, bringing children into a world that seems to have only gotten darker since that night on which Katie and I said goodbye. But strange though it may seem, I do not worry. I've learned to see snowflakes everywhere I look, and they give me great hope that even as darkness descends, a brighter Light will shine even brighter still. That Light met me in my darkness, and I have no doubt that if we look for it, it will shine the same for

all of us, until that Day on which Darkness is vanquished once and
for all.

—Charlie

S. Wyatt Young

Stay Connected

@swyattyoung

www.swyattyoung.com